CW00862485

NAMI

Jacqueline Smith

Jacqueline Smith moved to Cornwall from London with her family, who, like Louie, found the transition hard. But the county worked its magic and gave Jacqueline the inspiration and confidence to begin writing fiction.

Namesake is her first novel for young adults, the idea triggered by discovering the significance of Cornwall before D Day and cemented seeing the graves of young Ronald and Harry. The boys died during the war, stepping on a mine on the beach, and are laid to rest beside the sea in St Winwaloe's Church, Gunwalloe, known locally as the Church of the Storms.

"John Buchan meets Malorie Blackman on the beaches of Cornwall. A fantastic romp..."

Michael Odell, journalist and author (Rock Bottom)

A Wild Goose-Media book.

First published in the UK in 2020 by Wild Goose-Media Ltd.

Copyright © Jacqueline Smith.

ISBN 978-0-9934550-2-5

Also available on Kindle.

Wild Goose-Media Ltd, Goonbell Lane Farm, 29 Goonbell, St Agnes, Cornwall, UK.

www.wildgoose-media.com

[WILDGOOSEMEDIA] ™

NAMESAKE

Jacqueline Smith

For Elsie, Millie, Thomas, Harry & Johnny

Chapter ONE

Everyone knows they will die, but only I knew I would die before I was born.

Not that I knew that then. Time hadn't started with its tricks. It was just annoying. Dragging at school but racing through weekends. I looked at the watch she'd given me. Probably slow because it was hers, but a peek at my phone said the same.

Early May, hot and sunny. Obviously. It was a school day. I sat at the back, in a polyester fest of uniform. All new and fitting like a cardboard box. Everyone else wore skirts they'd grown out of and shirts that were too tight, looking almost cool. Mum ordered mine online, before we got here – saving money and an expectation I'd keep growing motivating sizing choices.

"Eloise Shircliff, are you paying attention?" snapped Miss Probert. I loved history but hated that everyone was looking at me, hated I'd gone red and hated she called me Eloise not Louie. "We're discussing our county's contribution to the Second World War. Any thoughts?"

"D Day was a thing. Loads of troops, Falmouth got bombed – "

"A thing," she said raising her eyebrows above her glasses. "Many underestimate the part that Cornwall played. The nation was in danger of starving as all our imported food was being destroyed by U-boats," Miss Probert was warming to her favourite topic, The Southwest at War. "If it were not for the tireless efforts of women working all hours on the land – well, we might not have won the war. Many of you, I know, come from old farming families."

She had to be kidding. Most of the parents here were more familiar with hedge funds than hedgerows.

"I've a short film I found on You Tube," she said, annoyingly emphasising and separating the name. "It shows that Falmouth was indeed bombed, suffering a near disastrous hit on May 30th, 1944, just before D Day. The fuel stores were attacked, causing a firewall that travelled down the valley on the water tributaries, not only threatening Swanvale, but D Day itself. Without fuel, the troops wouldn't have been able to leave here, never mind attack the Normandy beaches. Watch carefully and see how two brave men took on and halted the terrifying progress of the huge fires."

The film was black and white, dull and soundless. Comedy quick-stepping men moving disjointedly with hoses and two guys on tractors dumping mud on the flames.

"What many visitors don't realise when they enjoy our beautiful creeks and coastline, is that Cornwall played a significant part in the biggest military manoeuvre ever attempted: the beginning of the end of World War Two. Operation Overlord, or, as Eloise said, a thing. D Day."

The class swivelled round again, and I blushed again. But I so wasn't in the mood, which was funny considering how my day panned out.

I tried not to register the beautiful scenery through the school bus windows, hearing Mum's constant proclamations of how stunning it all was, how lucky we were to be actually living there. Actually living in a place where it was okay to be called my lover, even by lecherous old men. Sure it was pretty, in an outdoorsy field, cow and sea sort of way – but could you get on a tube and check out the latest band? Emily, my younger sister, was at the front, chatting away to her new best friends. She was so shallow.

I barricaded myself with bags and untangled the earplugs from my hairbrush, scrolling through to find what I was looking for. A girl, a Zoë or a Chloe, bounced up the bus.

"Hey. What you listening to?" she said through Wotsit-breath, licking the bits off her fingers.

"Nothing."

"You just moved here?" she said offering me her mostly empty packet of processed cheese curls.

"Easter," I said, declining.

"Where from?"

"London."

"Oh my God!" she showered me in orange crumbs. "You're so well out if it – all those stabbings! Is that why you left?"

"What? Course not – my parents just wanted a change to – "

"We had to drive there to go to my Gran's funeral. It was so scary, I'm not even kidding. My dad locked all the car doors as soon as we got inside the M25. So, where you really from?" She was looking at me intently. It was all so tediously familiar.

"London."

"But…"

"Peckham Rye," I cranked up the volume of 'London's Calling' and closed my eyes against the tears I was horrified to feel prickling.

I got off a stop early, mainly to avoid walking with Emily. The boys would already be home from school making this the only time left in my day to be alone with my thoughts, not that they were great company. They clattered around in a hollow place, sharp corners catching me with memories of the fizzy mix of cultures crammed into my old London school and I thought, not for the first time, how much I'd lost and who I'd left behind.

Climbing the hill, I didn't see Higher Farm until I'd turned the corner and the cluster of barns emerged from a dip, nestling between trees and fields. The barns were not just my home but, an escape into rural life, according to the brochure. I saw a familiar head through a break in the clouds of white sheets billowing across the yard.

"Why are you doing that? I thought that was Janet's job?"

"Hello darling, nice to see you too – how was school?" said Mum.

"Is she off sick, again?"

"Give us a hand Lou, the last lot left late. Knowing my luck the next will arrive early. I'm almost done. Just need to make up the beds." I wanted to say no, I don't do domestic for tourists, but she looked tired. Throwing down my schoolbag, I took the soiled sheets from her, trying not to think what my arms were wrapping around.

"Got it. I'll shove them in the machine then help you with the clean ones."

"Thanks darling. I'll be in Granary."

I pushed open the laundry room door with my foot and dumped the toxic load. From the kitchen next door I heard the disjointed squeaks that were now a familiar part of our oh-so-shiny new life. The old woman was having a go at Dad, again. This time it was the cupboards.

"They're almost empty, Robert! You must keep stocked up – tinned ham, corned beef."

"Wheezy. It's fine. We have plenty of food – look, the freezer's stuffed." And to prove his point he opened the door from the kitchen to where the freezer was, and where I was crouching in front of the huge washing machine, hoping to have slipped back out again unnoticed.

"Louie. I didn't know you were back!" I shot Dad one of my looks.

"Is that the girl?" I knew what was coming next: "How's my watch?"

"Still going, Wheezy," I said, adding more quietly, "Just like you, more's the pity."

Ignoring Dad's pathetic attempt to look shocked, I stood up and walked towards my great grandmother. Reinforcing my assurances, I turned the watch-face to her, rather than my own. I didn't want to inhale her oldness. Every day was the same, fussing about whether we had enough food in the house and if my watch worked. The thing used to be hers for like a hundred years, and I swear she wanted it back, but she was the one who insisted I have it on my fifteenth birthday. She seemed to have forgotten why. Secretly, I loved it, It had a weighty reassuringly retro feel to it, with a big spherical winder on the side.

"Cup of tea?" Dad's answer to everything. But I was gone.

As I closed my bedroom door I heard her again, moving on to another familiar rift, "Where's my piano?" Wheezy. Insensitive pet name for a decrepit old bird, but she didn't seem to mind.

I had to admit my bedroom was quite cool: it used to be a hayloft and my bed was up a ladder on a mezzanine floor. Except, I thought, as I unpackaged myself from the hated uniform and slipped into a T-shirt and a pair of shorts, what was the point of having a cool room if there were no friends to share it with? I fumbled under the bed for my flip-flops, shunting my feet into them, loving my electric blue toenails. Unleashing my mud brown hair, it expanded on the pillow as I lay back and scanned the rafter across my ceiling. I counted the thirteen rivets, settling on mine. Second from the left. Misshapen. I didn't fit here either, where all the other rivets looked the same.

I rolled over, slid my laptop onto the bed. He wasn't online yet, but there were pictures. None of which suggested he was missing me. Before I knew it, a door in the real world burst open and an annoying little voice asked to go on the games on my laptop.

"No. I'm doing homework."

"M-u-m! Louie's on Facebook!" It was Sebastian, my nine-year old brother.

"Shut up Seb!" I said.

"M-u-m! Louie told me to shut up!"

"Louie said shut-up, Louie said shut-up, Louie said –" Ned, my five-year-old tormentor, running in.

"SHUT UP! Both of you – and get off my stuff!" They were all over my room, touching everything with fingers that had either just been up their noses, down their trousers or in somewhere else unsavoury.

"What's all the noise up there?" Mum was thudding up the stairs.

"Boys, go and sort your room out – there's Lego everywhere. How many times have I asked you not to throw it around? It's for building things," she boomed.

"We were building. We were making new-clear missiles and then we had to test them," said Sebastian.

"Very funny. Boys, c'mon. I haven't time to keep clearing up after you. Do I have to get out the charity bag?"

"No Mummy!" said Ned, frightened of losing his toys.

Then she turned her frustration on me. I'd completely forgotten about my promise to help. Did I know how hard it was for them to keep me at that school, blah; I might think changing sheets was beneath me, blah; we've all got to pull together blah, don't I want our new life to work, blah bloody blah bloody blah. That was it. A lid flipped and I didn't even try to reach for it.

"I didn't ask for any of this."

"What do you mean, this," the pitch of her voice and rise of her eyebrows should have given me fair warning.

"This," I said, waving my arms around as if it was obvious. But she said nothing, leaving the door wide open. "I was happy in London," I said, making it sound like an accusation. "I didn't ask to go to that posh poncey school and you're right, I don't want to keep house for rich Londoners, who come down here to this – a country bumpkin theme park. Pretending to live in the country, with their Chelsea tractors full of Waitrose treats. 'It's nice for a week but we couldn't do that all the time.' Why couldn't we have just done that?"

She stared back at me. I took in the grey breaking through her home hair dye, the long hanging tag that had flopped out of the jumper she'd been so pleased to buy from the Whistles sale before we left London, and the jeans she used to save for parties. For a second I wanted to step through the rubbish and say sorry, to hug her and be hugged. But as I took a step forward, she said coldly,

"I don't have time to argue with a petulant teenager. I have beds to finish for the paying guests that keep you at that posh poncey school." I winced. "The dog needs a walk – or is that too demeaning for you?" Her voice was thick. She turned and left, knowing she'd have exploded if she stayed, and that she didn't have the time.

If I had a tail, it would have been between my legs as I skulked downstairs and grabbed Reg's lead. The dopey retriever heard it clink and bounded towards me, his joy contrasting absurdly with how I felt. He was still young, not quite grown into his floppy skin, but I yanked hard on his lead, yelling Heel! Dog whispering gave way to dog shouting. Stomping through the field I ignored the call of my name as long as possible until finally spitting out,

"What?"

"Wait!" It was Emily.

"Why?"

"I want to go for a walk too."

"Mum sent you."

"What happened back there?"

"Yeah right. As if you weren't listening."

"I think the guys who own Higher Farmhouse heard you, and they're in London."

"Funny – and they're not. I saw Sheridan talking to one of his catering suppliers."

"Dad's on one as well – they're both really upset."

I felt bad then, hearing myself as Dad would have done. We walked on in silence and I let Reg go, watching him tear away, weaving in and out of the long grass catching glimpses of the top of his head, golden ears flapping. He'd whip round, so pleased with himself, his head high, taunting us in his one-sided game of tag. The sun was still fairly high and the air warm. Emily plucked at the long grass and started to chew it, until I told her dogs peed on it. She pretended not to care but I saw it drop from her mouth. It was a cheap victory that didn't make me feel any better.

We lost sight of Reg but saw the sea, looking calm for once. In the month or so we'd been here, it had been as angry as I had, churned up by high winds, thrashing waves and sometimes a weird foam that blew over everything. Mum and Dad would stand for hours, expecting us to share their reverence. Although it was peaceful today, a mist was quickly rolling in, sucking in all the shine from the sun.

"Reg. R-e-g, here boy!" Emily called out.

"He's probably cocking his leg on the gravestones."

"Lou! Are you going to say anything pleasant today?" she said, sounding irritatingly like Mum.

The church was almost on the beach, half buried in the sand and now the mist. Recently refurbished, it had escaped being sold off as a holiday home – probably due to the arrival of Rev Angela-call-me-Angel-Rev. Mum made us go as part of her campaign to show the locals we were one of them and that London had been a necessity, not a life style choice. I remembered the last time.

"Rob! We're going to be late for God's sake!" shrieked Mum.

"Best not to blaspheme darling, especially on a Sunday!"

"Where're my shoes?" said Emily

"Do we have to go to the groups?" Sebastian.

"Yes – under the sofa," said Mum.

"I hate groups," Ned.

"You love them – you always come out happy," said Dad.

"That's because they've finished." Even I had to smile at his smart answer.

"Louie's got toast – I want toast!"

"There's no time – oh for goodness sakes, give him some of yours Lou."

"What? No – anyway, it's got Marmite on."

"Emily, get a move on. We'll have to go in the car. Keys! Rob?"

Shoes got found and more toast made before we piled into the car, arguing over who wouldn't have to sit next to Wheezy, and drove the whole single mile to the church. Everyone heard us, the heavy door unforgiving, modern pew-replacing chairs scraping on flagstone floors and people shuffling to make room. Why was it always us drawing attention to ourselves? Always late. Always loud. I could never invite anyone home – they all knew exactly how to embarrass me.

"Where's my raggy?" Ned started.

"Ssh!" I said.

"Must be in the car," hissed Mum.

"I want my raggy!"

"What's the boy want? Is he hungry Robert?" said Wheezy, loudly. The boys giggled then started hitting each other.

"M-u-m," I'd said, meaning do something can't you. If she'd kept better control of the boys, maybe I'd have been braver; maybe things would have worked out sooner, rather than just as I left London.

I don't know if it was the noise that always kicked off our Sundays but, and I would never admit it, especially not to Mum, after the kids had gone to their groups I enjoyed that time of just sitting there. It gave me head and heart space to unravel some of the knots inside me, the tightest of which belonged to him. Tom. We'd tentatively circled each other, both too shy to make the first move until the week before I left. I'd waited so long, imagining how it would feel to be close to him, to be kissed. Now all I had was trying to remember how it felt.

It's funny; despite my best efforts to block out Angel Rev's sermon I remembered how she'd talked about Esther, from the Old Testament. Weird. She talked about Esther with the benefit of time and perspective. The other vicar talked about Esther, not knowing how important she became to me. But that's the thing about time. It sits outside significant events and it's only at the end that it becomes joined up. But all of that was hidden from me the day we looked for Reg in the misty churchyard. The sunlight burnt its way in, making laser-light patterns in the graveyard; Emily stood in one, reading.

"This is so sad – look Lou."

There's something morbidly fascinating about looking at gravestones, but these two went beyond that. Friends lay side-by-side, Wilfred and Roddy; both aged twelve and died in 1944. They were playing on this beach and stepped on an unmarked mine: Wilfred, was killed outright and Roddy died three days later. Emily was right, it was really sad – Roddy was an evacuee from Hornsey Rise; his parents already killed in the Blitz.

"Lou! Quick! Come and see this one – it's yours!" Away from the boys' graves was another, smaller, closer to the sea. Less protected, it hadn't fared so well against time, corrosive saltwater and gritty sand. I could just about make out most of my name:

In loving mem… of our b…loved

ELOISE SHI…LIFF

…1927 to June 5th 1944

Aged 1…years

…bravely sacrif… life … others kept theirs.

"Can't be yours – you're not hero material!" said Emily.

"So not funny Em."

"Maybe you're like, you know, a ghost but you don't know you're dead, like in that film?"

"Might as well be, for all the notice people take of me," my mouth had gone dry and my legs felt weak. Wasn't that around D Day? *Eloise Sh* something *lift*," I just kept staring at it, shuddering at the drop in temperature that had nothing to do with the clamminess of the sea mist.

"That's Reg!" said Emily as we heard the high pitch yelping of a young dog in distress.

"I'm on it," I said, running towards the sound.

"Hey! Wait!" I didn't. My heart was beating hard. Something was wrong. It wasn't just the dog. I felt panic, but I couldn't process why. I ran past floating shapes on the beach, people obscured by the mist. I heard him again.

"I think he's in the water!" I yelled over my shoulder. The sea looked as if it was hovering in a place between the earth and the heavens. I tracked my way along the shoreline. The dog loved the water, but signs where everywhere about dangerous riptides.

"Reg! Here boy!" Why would he come to my voice? We hadn't bonded in a Michael Morpurgo way; I'd been just as vile to him as I was to everyone else. Please don't drown little dog, I promise to be nicer. I looked to see if Emily had caught up, but she was nowhere. The mist had stifled all the sounds and had even shrouded those eerie shapes; there was just the shoreline with waves breaking through. Then that distressed bark again, definitely coming from the sea. I kicked off my flip-flops and waded in. Man, it was cold.

"R-e-g!" I yelled. His bark seemed to come from still further out. I started to swim. "Reg!" this time it was a gurgle as the cold engulfed me and saltwater filled my throat. I got my breathing all wrong – I was never any good at swimming – the seabed had dropped away and I was floundering.

A dog barked, but this time from behind. I changed direction but the mist was so thick it snatched away everything more than a metre from me. The sea had gone weirdly flat, which didn't help, so I couldn't tell which way the shore was. Another bark, but way off now. Then nothing. Everything fell silent. That smothering sort of silence you get when thick snow carpets a city and the whole world seems to stop. All I could hear was my own breathing quickening.

Without warning, the heavy mist suddenly crackled and shone with life. Shimmering silver slithers ticker-taped down out of the sky, bouncing and dancing in the filtered sunlight. It was so beautiful but where was it coming from? As I reached up to grab some, an intense boom reverberated and shook me to my core. It came from all around but centred itself deep within me. There was a violent screech, like nails scraping down a blackboard, followed by a flash of pale blue metal streaking out of the showering sparkles. The angry roar of an engine. A full blank second then an almighty seismic vibration radiated from the depths below.

"What the – ?" An enormous wave washed my mouth out and dragged me under, the weight of water closing above me. As I went down, I caught a glimpse of floating white. An angel? Was this when the fast film of my life plays? Would I live if I refused to look? My over-blown lungs pushed painfully against my ribs and my lips fought to stay closed. Praying was all I had; thankfully it was a slow afternoon at the celestial call-centre and I was put straight through. Something yanked then hurled me across a piece of debris. Snatching greedily at the air, I gulped, spluttered then threw up.

Heaving, I felt tentative patting on my back and through matted hair I stared into the palest blue eyes beneath dark lashes and knew everything was going to be alright. I tried to thank him, but could only hear my voice in my head. My ears were as stunned as I was by the explosion. He'd turned towards the shore, which was now clear to see through the evaporating mist. I joined in with the kicking to get us back to dry land, stealing a sideways look at my rescuer. He was wearing a heavy leather jacket with an eagle badge sewn on his chest; the eagle was holding a swastika. Great. Rescued by the most handsome fully paid up member of the BNP – my day just couldn't get any more surreal.

Chapter TWO

The shore came at us quickly and he plucked me up like a puppet, my legs dangling beneath me. As soon as the ground became solid my strings were released and I collapsed in a disjointed heap, limbs shaking. Shivering with wet and cold, I swept my arm across my forehead and saw I was still wearing her watch, before my wrist was snatched upwards.

"You are one of his?" my rescuer said, as if he couldn't believe what he was asking.

"It's stopped!" I pulled my wrist back and held it to my ear, shaking the watch. The hands were going nowhere past five o'clock.

"I have to go, he will help."

"Who? What?" But he was gone. I dropped my head and waited for the rush of concerned people, a towel even. No one came. Reg! I called out for him, listening hard for his bark.

"Em! Reg!" No one. Not a soul. I looked at Wheezy's watch and felt awful – I knew how upset she'd be. This watch meant so much to her – they'd think I did this on purpose. What a mess. Lost the dog. Broke the watch. Upset my parents. Not to mention found my own grave.

I looked accusingly out to sea but, calm and gently lapping, it was unapologetic. All evidence of what must have been a plane crashing had been swallowed up and smoothed over. The empty beach looked different; the sun had been swept away with the mist and I'd drifted much further than I thought. The church, near where I left my flip-flops, was down the shoreline but no way was I going to collect them. I'd rather walk home barefoot than see that grave again. Where were Reg, and Emily? I clambered up the dunes behind to get a better look down the beach but huge coils of barbed wire had been planted with crude signs saying, Keep Out – Danger. Too damn right, after what I just been through.

Gingerly, I made my way through and headed for higher ground. It was mad how much the temperature had dropped. I was trembling, weak with the cold and suddenly hungry. Why did he run away? What had he meant? Those eyes, but a Swastika? Hardly a fashion accessory – not even in Cornwall.

A field stretched out ahead of me; home was probably three or four more fields to the west, but after only six weeks here I wasn't really familiar with the lay of the land. There was still no sign of the dog or my sister. They must have found each other and headed home. I hoped so. Progress was slow and I regretted abandoning my flip-flops, but it give me time to think what I was going to say to Mum, and Wheezy. I wished I could love this life as much as they all seemed to but I missed the city that had been home my whole life. I was happy there. Everything was about to begin for me.

And what was the big deal about the outdoors and Ned and Sebastian? Sure boys like to play outside – what's wrong with London park-life? Worked for me. Even I had to admit though, Mum and Dad seemed happier, together even, which was a first since after Ned had been born.

My ears were still ringing from the sea drama, which is why I didn't register the sound in the sky until it was almost overhead. An old-fashioned well-preserved plane, probably practising for one of those air displays that Dad and the boys loved, was bearing down on me. It looked cool in a kitsch way although the pilot, all kitted out, was taking the role-play way too seriously. As he swooped past he tilted upwards, showing off black outlined crosses on the underside of the wings and a swastika on its tail. What was this? A convention? Swinging around again, he flew directly towards me, except this time I heard a different sound, even through cotton wool ears, and saw the ground spiking up ahead in vicious darts of dust. He was firing at me!

I ran faster than I'd ever run in my life: up the field's edge; dry crop slicing into my feet; machine gun snapping at my heels. I dived. Heart pounding, chest sore. The ditch was a minefield of razor-sharp rocks and stones. I crouched low and kept running in the gulley between two fields. The plane climbed then swooped again. Gunfire ricocheted along the line of the ditch, sounding nothing like when the boys pretended to shoot each other. My only defence was the trunk of a tree; I lunged for it. The engine roared overhead. Bullets blistered into foliage.

I stayed very still. Curled into the tightest ball, I played dead. He circled again without firing. What if he landed and came for me on foot? I had never been so scared. What was happening to me? Listening for every sound, I didn't uncurl until I was sure I couldn't hear the engine and only the sound of birdsong filled the sky. The light was fading. I wanted so much to be home.

Then, Emily – oh God, no, Emily! What if he'd found her? The dippy dope would have waved at him, making a perfect target.

I clambered up the steep bank and scanned the dimming skies one more time before running as fast as I could in the direction of where I thought home was. It started to rain. All that was missing was thunder and a random bolt of lightning. Finally I was on the lane leading up to Higher Farm, although by now only the moon's batteries seemed to be working. The sun had deserted me, the stars shied away and I guessed there must have been a power-cut as there wasn't a light switched on anywhere. As the hill dipped, I saw the shadow of the familiar gates and limped towards them.

"Emily! Mum – Dad!" I tried to yell, but it was like that dream when you can't make your voice loud enough to be heard. The dream was a nightmare. I let out a scream but it was caught in the palm of my hand, clasped to my mouth. All the adrenaline that had been pumping round my body evaporated and I felt dizzy and faint. The scene whipped around me, like a spinning park roundabout. How could this be my home? It had been totally destroyed.

The barns had been ravaged by something – fire? A bomb? But not today, or anytime recently. Moonlight showed grass and weeds growing through where the kitchen should be and where the new group of holidaymakers should be installed. I ran back to the gates. Maybe I'd made a mistake and this wasn't our farm. Except, on the gatepost, although the lettering was different, the words spelled the same. "Higher Farm." It was impossible.

I staggered back to the broken barns, terrified of what else I would find. But there were no signs of life, only pungent cow slop that squelched and smacked around my sore bare feet. Rain ran down my face but didn't wake me up or help me make sense of anything that had happened since I left this exact spot barely five hours ago. Creepy mists, crashing planes, a sadistic machine-gunning joy rider and now, this. Whatever this was.

My grip on everything was slight – I saw the lowest of lights from Higher Farmhouse. I didn't know the guys who lived there that well, they were mostly in London, using this as a base for their catering business. But I was desperate for some answers.

I banged on the door and almost fell in as it opened immediately. A middleweight, middle-aged ruddy-faced fierce looking woman stood astride, balancing a toddler on one hip and a large protective hand over two Ned-sized children clinging to her skirt.

"Good. You're here then," she barked.

"Sorry?" I said.

"We was thinking you got lost. Where's your things – and your clothes? What you dressed like that for? You wasn't on the bus and they said you'd walked. Damn fool thing to do – just 'cos you're an evacuee don't mean this is no holiday – "

I didn't hear the rest of what she said as what little light there was went out and I fainted on her doorstep.

15

Chapter THREE

Morning broke heavily and crashed around me. I couldn't stick it back together. A drum banged or a door slammed inside my tin head. Fractured sounds of something tuneless. It was cold. No soft warm duvet, something scratchy instead. I kept my eyes shut tight and strained to hear the familiar: the drone of Mum's Radio Four, boys' squealing over whose Weetabix bridge would collapse first under the dam busting milk. Even great granny Wheezy carping about tinned provisions and pianos would have done.

But the sounds jarred, arranging themselves into a picture I didn't want: cows, chickens, scraping of chairs and unknown voices, sparring but trying not to. A door shut heavily. Heavier feet on wooden stairs headed my way. I pulled the rough blankets tighter and turned away from where I guessed the doorway was.

The floor creaked. Someone large came up to me. Laboured breathing. Pause. Hesitation? A shake of my shoulder. I pretended to be asleep. If I tried hard enough maybe I would be and wake up properly in my own bedroom, the one with the laptop on the desk that Dad had made for me. He would be tip-toeing in with a cup of tea telling me apologetically it was time to get up for school. I squeezed my eyes really tightly trying to imagine myself where I should be. A hand shook me again and I heard the voice from my nightmare.

"Come on Missy, time you was awake, day's going to be over. Feelin' any better?"

The Cornish voice was not unkind, but neither was it warm. I turned over in the dim light to face what I had no choice to avoid and began to sit up. My clothes had been taken off and I was in a nightgown. I flushed at the thought of someone else undressing me. Mum had always joked about wearing your best knickers in case of an accident – I definitely wasn't wearing mine.

"Had to get you out of them wet things, you was catching your death. Done none of us no good. What sort of clothes is them anyway – that the fashion in London, or wherever it is your kind comes from? And blue toenails? That's not neither right nor proper."

I pulled my legs up under my chin, gripping my toes, watching her. "Not the way it's done here my girl, best you think on that. Not decent to show so much of your legs – and a vest was it? Lose your blouse did you? What happened to you girl?"

Endless words. I stared back, weighed down by my fear, unable to move. "You getting out that bed or what?" Her noise was relentless. "Where's your things and that?" It became a rope that I tried to pull myself up on. "Hasn't been nothing sent from the station, not even a gas mask." With each word, I hoisted myself into the scene, into an inter-active movie. I said my lines.

"I lost my stuff – when I was shot at – by a plane." My voice sounded weird and my words ridiculous.

"Shot at you say? Careless getting in the way of one of them. Best you keep an eye out, if you're going to be any good to us." Not what I expected. "Put Cassie's old clothes on, over there on the chair. She won't be needing them no more."

"Cassie?"

"Sister-in-law," she said flatly. "Fancied herself as a nurse and got herself posted further than she wanted to go, leaving us to look after this lot." She had been sat with her sausage shaped arms leaning heavily into her knees and now eased herself up in two stages to make for the door. She paused just long enough to say, "Little 'uns'll want feeding so get a move on. If you want water, standpipe's in the yard. You can fill up that jug, but that's it mind for today."

"What? I need a shower – where's the bathroom?"

"Take ash with you when you go," she said over her shoulder, half way out the door.

"There's spare in the bucket next to the range. Privy's out back." She had to be joking. My body clamped down in a protective shell. I'd wait until I got home. As the door closed, I shot out of bed but I'd forgotten about my sore feet and limped to the little window. Pulling back the black sheeting that stood in place for curtains, tape criss-crossed the unbroken glass and peering through the crude diamonds, I tried to make sense of what I'd seen last night.

The barns were battered, broken. Like decaying teeth, their edges confusingly softened by time. The layout looked different from this viewpoint but then I'd only ever been in this house once when we first arrived, when I was secretly slugging Mum's gin and tonic, so my perspective wasn't reliable. Granary was still next to the naff Badger's Lookout, but cows were doing the looking out. The fields looked different, smaller, with more hedgerows and colour, and were being sketched in as I watched by the figures working in them. All very lovely, but all very wrong.

I turned away, slid down the wall and hugged my knees tightly. What had happened? Where was everyone? Why was this odious woman here instead? Huge waves of panic crashed against me, making full breaths impossible. Nothing made sense. I started to rock gently backwards and forwards, had I gone crazy? The room was blurred through my tears but the irony of it wasn't lost on me. It was the look Mum strived for: muted, sparse with uncluttered lines broken only by the creepy cast offs draped over a battered wooden chair. It wouldn't look out of place in an interiors magazine. But this was no holiday cottage.

I pulled myself up and hobbled to the clothes. They smelled worse than Wheezy. Was this the best she could do? If I put them on I'd be complicit in whatever was going on, but my clothes had gone. Man, I needed a shower. I picked through the stiff shirt, dungarees and – were those huge things pants? A pair of worn boots was too big for me, but some thick coarse socks filled them and helped to cushion my sore feet. I pulled down a small mirror from the chest of drawers, angling it to see myself. Yep. My bum looked big in the dungarees.

The boots clacked clumsily on the stairs. I paused at the bottom. The scene from the kitchen to my left was playing out like in any other large household: children squabbling, the mother trying to keep the peace and the seductive smell of bacon wrapping it all up in an acceptable package. I wasn't buying it. The front door was straight ahead. I marched forwards and tried to open it, but it was locked. I tried again and again, shaking the handle and finally beating against it.

"What you making that racket for?" It was the woman.

"Let me go!" I shouted. "I want to go home!" She took a step closer and cornered me in the hallway. "KEEP AWAY FROM ME!" I screamed in a voice I hardly recognised as my own, "Where are my parents? What have you done with them? LET ME OUT!"

"S'alright. You want to go outside, s'no problem – you could use the back door, we don't never use this one." She was talking to me as if pacifying a lunatic, which I probably was. Slowly, she opened a drawer in a side table and carefully pulled out a key, which she showed me, before putting it gently on the table then backed away. I quickly snatched it up.

"That's the way, you're free to go wherever you want," she said, too calmly. Barely taking my eyes off her I put the key in and felt a reassuring crick as it released the lock. Turning the handle, I pushed the door open and was dazzled by the sunlight after the darkness of the house – but I was free.

I hobbled to the barns, not sure what I was looking for until I got there: the hayloft where my bedroom should be, the mezzanine-floor where I slept – except only bats and mice had made their beds here – and the rafter. Second from the left I found it, my rivet. Betraying bastard thing! How could this be? How could this be my home?

"W-what's happening?" I stammered to the woman who'd followed me in.

"You mean the barns? Lazy Jerries. Too much of an 'urry to get home. 'Stead of taking their bombs to Plymouth, was easier to drop 'em on our little farm."

"Was – was anyone…?" I hardly dared ask, and what did she mean, Jerries?

"Susan – and Polly."

"Oh – I'm sorry", I lied, relieved she hadn't said the Shircliffs from London.

"Best damn milkers we had." Cows. The stupid woman was talking about cows. "Why don't you come back to the house and have some breakfast?"

"But where are they?" I said.

"Who, my lover?"

"Mum, Dad, the boys – Emily?" She shook her head and looked genuinely sad.

"I know you've had it rough and they said to expect something like this but I can't have you going all hysterical. I've got the younger evacuees to think about – you'll scare 'em witless."

"I don't understand – please – just tell me where my mum is – " I wanted to cry. She went on, her voice now unbearably soft and kind.

"P'raps it was a mistake taking you in – maybe you should think about what they said, that you should spend some time in the asylum. I know it sounds like something to be afraid of but I hear they do great things. They use electrical things and that, I heard, to help people like you – what's lost a lot."

It was a sobering slap: I didn't understand what she was talking about, but I did understand the word asylum and knew it didn't mean spa retreat. I looked at the woman and wondered what the game was – my head was hurting and I didn't want to play. I wanted to go home. But getting shut away wouldn't make that happen.

"Look, come and have something to eat, then we can have a chat." Food. Suddenly I was overwhelmingly hungry – I hadn't eaten since the school canteen a lifetime ago.

"OK. I'm sorry, it's all so – I'm just…Ok," meaning, I'll come quietly. I had to keep a cool head. Besides, where would I go? I couldn't explain anything, not rationally, but the answers were here. I could feel the pull of them.

The noise of the kitchen had had been turned down to a cautious simmer. A large table hemmed with a mismatched row of children dominated the room. Had she meant refugees instead of evacuees? Did that make these children asylum seekers, rather than asylum avoiders, like me. Maybe the woman was a bit simple and had got herself involved in something she didn't understand – probably getting money from the council to house them all. Maybe this was a human trafficking scam, this was the halfway house and I was another product to be sold on. But the children looked too settled, too at ease with each other and their surroundings. The room was brown: crockery, tables, walls, dim sepia tones from taped up windows and half drawn heavy curtains. It had the same art directed quality I'd felt upstairs.

Their clothes looked vintage rather than second hand, stylish almost, with a hand-finished quality and total absence of polyester and logos. And their hairstyles - severe and pudding basin-like. Maybe this was some sort of sect. Cornwall's answer to the Amish?

"Hey," I said to nobody in particular, while eyeing the crusts left on the table.

"They was hungry, couldn't wait no more. Doreen – take them fingers out of the jam. Bread's all but gone 'cept for that bit. Here. There's jam but no butter – go easy mind, that's all that's left 'til I make some more." I nodded gratefully, but disappointed not to be offered the bacon I could still smell.

I sat down at the large table before putting a knife into the pot of jam that had been pulled away from the child called Doreen and, looking at her fingernails, tried to take some furthest away from where she'd been delving. I dragged the jam across the thick crust and bit into it hungrily. With my mouth full, I tried a smile on the several pairs of small eyes trained on me, but they flicked away in unison at the sound of a door clicking open behind me.

A large man walked in, sitting down wearily at the head of the table. A cup of something hot and what looked suspiciously like a bacon sandwich was placed in front of him. A small child disengaged from the others and climbed up into the man's lap, curling himself up into the crook of his arm where he contentedly sucked two fingers.

"How do," he said without looking at me. "So, you're the one we've been waiting on, that right Mother?" Was he addressing me, or the woman who surely wasn't his mother? "Like to make an entrance do you? Almost called the doc, you was out so long. We're not good with hysterics round here," he bit into his sandwich and grease ran down the side of his mouth. "How're you with pigs?"

"She's not here for you, George, she's here to help me with these blessed children and the washing and all the chores I can't get done on my own. Anyways, I'm not sure she's staying." The look she gave him would have stopped a lesser man dead in his tracks. But he was fearless.

"Mother! I'm at full stretch what with Clive gone and the new lot from the hostel having to be trained up. I need more than I've got, for a while least ways."

"She's too young, and too soft by the looks of her, to be a land girl – "

"Touch of the tar brush an' all, I reckon," he said looking at me for the first time. "How many years you got then?"

"Fifteen – I'm doing my GCSEs next year at school," I bristled.

"School is it?" he said. "Well, what you don't know by now won't be no good to you – is it the washing you want or farm work?" I didn't want to do any of it. I just wanted to go home. They both glared, daring me to choose between them.

"Do you have a radio?" I needed an anchor, a connection to the outside.

"What sort of answer's that?" said the man.

"I thought I heard…when I was upstairs, I,"

"You mean the Accumulator? We don't bother charging it no more. Nothing but bad news comes out o' that thing – that right Mother?"

"I'm not talking to you George."

"Finish up and we'll set to on them pigs."

"George!"

"Mother. There's more important things than your washing, and I thought you weren't talking to me!" 'Mother' ignored his teasing and turned to me instead.

"Keep a steady head; like he said, there's no place for hysterics here, but I knows a place where there is."

The bread stuck in my throat, but the grating of my chair on the stone floor obscured my choking sounds, as I stood hastily to follow the man called George heading towards the door. Slugging down his tea, he wedged the rest of the sandwich in his mouth and plopped the child to the lap of another child, not much bigger than the first. They both started to cry.

"Here boy," a nimble Collie rushed to his master's side. "We'll see how you go – if you're not up to it, you can get back in the kitchen," he was looking at the dog, but I guessed he was talking to me.

Chapter FOUR

The farmer man called George marched and I stumbled behind in my too big boots and sore feet. We passed again what used to be my home and stopped where Dad planned to put a swimming pool if the business took off. Instead there was a low range of curved shelters and the cloying smell of pig crap cut with cigarettes.

Three girls leaned against the pens, wearing dungarees and what looked like matching 'Pets at Home' bottle green jumpers with patterned cotton scarves wrapped around their heads. They reminded me of an 80's band Mum used to like. All were smoking, flicking away their cigarettes as we approached.

"Hey," I said. No introductions were offered, and it occurred to me that none had been since I'd pitched up at Higher Farmhouse.

"Louie," I said. "My name is Louie," more to reassure myself than anyone else.

"How do you do," said the smallest one, stepping forward to extend her hand to shake mine. "Ellie," she said.

"Shirley," said the prettiest of the three who wore her clothes in a way that made them look less institutionalised. "Have you lost your curlers or are they still in there somewhere?" I put a hand to my hair.

"Blanche" the last said with a nod, no smile but a quick look to my matted mop.

"No time for gassin'. Come on. Watch this carefully as you lot'll be doing the rest o' the boars." George had crouched down and was holding a squealing piglet upside down by its hind legs. From his back pocket he whipped out a pointed knife and with its tip quickly sliced two little cuts into the piglet's belly. There was a high-pitched yelp that came from me and not the creature. Was he butchering the thing in front of us – what sort of brutal parallel world had I stumbled into?

"George – I'm awfully sorry, but I really am going to have to pass on this." It was Ellie.

"Eh? Oh, right you are – 'course," agreed George to my surprise. He was still holding the piglet upside down, ignoring its screeches, and the blood oozing from the slashing. He went on calmly: "You got to take your thumb and slide it down gentle, but firm like 'til you can feel its little balls, there, pull firmly and slice your knife on these stringy bits, see? And – out they pop." Before the bloodied little things had hit the ground, the dog was there, greedily gobbling them up. "Keep holding the boy up like this 'til all his fluid runs out. There. Now. Louie is it? Here you go," and he handed me the knife.

I stood there incredulously with the cold blade in my hand, feeling faint in the collision of horrors – the pungent smell of animal excrement and fear, the piercing pitch of the piglets, and the whole wrongness of where I was. It was too vivid to be a dream: "Why?" was all I could muster.

"Got to be done, or meat'll taste bad." What was happening to me? Was I an unsuspecting victim in a truly unfunny episode of 'I'm a teenager get me out of here?' I crouched down in the filth, my knees centimetres from pig detritus. An enormously fat sow eyed me warily from one corner with her young boys scampering in innocent ignorance in another, and one poor little soul cowering in mutilated bewilderment.

I looked up at George and saw no trace of him having a laugh. The other girls dared me to bottle out. I was back at school, the new girl primed and ready to fall. Well, not this time: I picked up a piglet by his scruff, flipped him upside down and grasped his back legs tightly.

"Here?" George nodded and as quickly as I could I nicked his belly. Over its screams I said,

"What am I looking for?" George leaned in and took the knife, then grasped the base of my fingers making them stroke the soft underside downwards so that I could feel two tiny little lumps.

"Pop 'em out." I tried to imagine I was just shelling peas from their pod; as they came out, I pulled gently, the balls soft and wet between my fingers, and George whipped them off. The dog wasn't slow to claim his second snack. I stood up and felt weirdly triumphant.

I handed the knife to the one called Shirley and stood at the back of the pen, nearest to the open air. I took in huge gulps and steadied myself against the makeshift shack before looking back in as the barbaric ritual was repeated. I was gratified to hear George berating her for her clumsiness, but sorry for the piglet. I went to stand next to Blanche, thinking she might be able to throw some light on what was going on, why I was here and why we were violating pigs' privates.

"Man, that was rough. Are you training to be farmers? Is this, like, some sort of an apprenticeship scheme?" I said.

"What? I'm a land girl," she said

"Land girl – right."

"You just arrived?" she said, as if that explained everything. I nodded but would have loved to know where I'd arrived to.

"You're from London?" I said.

"Yeah. Clapham. You're not from 'round here, nor nowhere close by the looks of you."

"Peckham Rye."

"Ooh-er – there's posh!"

"You're kidding, compared to yummy mummy's Clapham?"

"Yummy's what?" Bad call. I tried another tack: "Did you move down with your family?"

"What's left of 'em. No. Ed's posted somewhere up north, he's my brother, and Dad's putting out fires."

"In the fire brigade."

"Ain't heard it called that. He's in the AFS – the Auxiliaries? I'm here on me tod and I don't mind it, mostly, 'cept I could do without cutting up bleedin' pigs!"

"I know, gross!" As soon as they were out, I knew the words were wrong and the pale-faced girl's expression confirmed it.

"Right. Well. I'm next up – see if I can do as good as what you done." She ducked back into the pen and I headed back to the yard.

I smelled it before I saw it, but I was desperate. Inside the privy was a wooden bench with a hole in it, a bucket full of ash and bits of newspaper pierced together by a hook that hung precariously next to where I sat down. The stench was as bad as at any music festival, but I did what was necessary then reached for the crude loo paper. The print was old fashioned and in the top corner of one, above the partial headline "Our Boys Press On…" was the date. May 5th, 1944. For the second time that day, shock pulled down a trapdoor that I fell through.

Staggering outside I found the standpipe. Pulling down the heavy lever, ignoring how scarce water allegedly was, I filled a tin bowl before throwing it over my head. I gasped then shook myself dry like a dog, hoping the water droplets would be like scales falling from my eyes and I would see clearly. See that I was really in a convincing wartime theme park, one of those living history museums, or else the unwitting victim of an elaborate TV game show. The newspaper proved nothing – it was probably a fake, knocked up on a Mac.

But looking up, my foothold slipped again. There was nothing phoney in the scenery – it just looked younger. Before, the trees were bigger, more deeply rooted and weathered; now they stood fresh-faced with lean limbed branches and fine leaves. All except for a statesman like oak holding court in the field behind the farm. That hadn't been there when I had marched through, yanking on Reg's lead. The skyline had been emptied of electrical pylons, telegraph poles and the wind farm that had stood on the far hill. Surely no TV company had a budget big enough to change a landscape so effectively, and so quickly.

So, what was the alternative? I'd somehow shifted the gear stick of time, taken a wrong turn and crash landed on the shores of 1944? Show me the wardrobe. The wibbly wobbly portal suspended in the temporal whatnot. The idea was ridiculous.

"I say! You look like you've got the collywobbles – you're as white as a sheet!" It was the smallest of the Pets-at-Home crew, Ellie. I watched her prattle on. "The privy can do that to you if it's ready to be emptied." She was so play-acting, no doubt in on the scam. "Thankfully that's a POWs job rather than us land girls."

She'd sat on the ground next to me. I was on a bank of green, clutching my knees and looking at the pastoral scene laid out incorrectly before me. Blissfully unaware of its impact, it looked peaceful, until I thought of the flying toy baron slashing through the canvas. Was he a sadistic joy rider, an actor, or a Luftwaffe pilot on a mission to kill?

I rattled through the tinderbox of theories; scared I might ignite one. Maybe I hadn't survived the ordeal at sea, I was dead and this was Heaven… or I was actually in the process of drowning but someone played the wrong film and instead of my life flashing before me I was watching a re-run of someone else's? Or maybe I was in a coma? Maybe nothing was real, and I was lying on a hospital bed somewhere and if I tried hard enough I'd hear the reassuring beep bleep of monitors and doctors fussing over me. That would mean all of this was a product of my drugged-up imagination. Except, surely, I could have come up with a fantasy world more exciting – being a farmer was never on my wish list.

"I say. Are you sure everything is okay? I've lost you again." Ellie was whittling through her Enid Blyton-like script.

"Sorry. I'm having trouble adjusting to all this," I said throwing my arm in a vague sweep before grasping and tugging hard on a clump of my hair to see if it hurt. It did. I had hoped to sound contemptuous but a wobble in my voice gave me away.

"It can be frightfully bewildering when you first start – certainly was for me – undeniably bucolic but still a bit of a shock after East Finchley. Got all your uniform yet?"

"Uniform? I, no," I looked at my dungarees understanding the connection the Famous-Fiver was making. "I'm not a land girl – is that what you are?" Or a weird, subliminal figment of my comatose imagination? Or an actress over-doing it a touch?

"The girls said you were jolly decent back there with those horrid little pigs – I just assumed."

28

"I think I'm supposed to be an evacuee, from London," I said trying to sound bored with the charade, while surreptitiously checking her for sound mikes.

"Technically, I'm an evacuee too. I'm not really old enough to be in the Land Army, but my parents sort of fudged it for me. They work hellishly long hours at the hospitals – both medics of a sort – and I was just hanging around. I wanted to do something useful so they agreed I could sign up."

Good recovery I thought, she's good. I played along: "You swapped London for this? Don't you miss it – or your family?"

"No – not the bombing, but I do miss Mummy and Daddy although I'd rather got used to them not being around. And Ruben and Jacob have both been called up, of course – they're in the RAF, posted somewhere awfully top secret. My biggest worry is for Grandma and Aunty Ruth, Isaac and the children. They were in Germany when war was declared and we've barely heard from them."

I registered the girl's aquiline nose, dark eyes and passing on the pig game. "I'm sure they're fine," I offered uncomfortably.

"We've been hearing some ghastly stories, but I told Mummy that's just part of the propaganda. Women and children will be properly looked after, won't they?" She looked at me, searching my face for reassurance. This was sick. Was a TV producer playing for laughs with the grotesque tragedy of the Jews? Or was this the surfacing of a suppressed previously unrealised fascination for the macabre? But, again, why? If I were imagining all of this, why would I place myself here?

I was way, way out of my depth. What if the unthinkable had happened and she was for real? I felt the ash from the privy up my nose and, as a hot wind blew across me, I thought of the fires from Hitler's concentration camps and the stench from the gas chambers of the Holocaust. What if it was going on right now?

"Oy! Lazy daisy! I'm not doing these piggin' pigs on me own!" It was Blanche. Piglet savagery was a walk in the park compared to the grim world Ellie had taken me to.

Chapter FIVE

No one mentioned lunch and I was too afraid of the 'Mother' to go in search of some. If she had called in the men with strait jackets I might have been tempted to go quietly. Given the limited grasp I had on unfolding events, less far-fetched was the idea that I'd gone mad.

I spent the afternoon bent over beets, which had nothing to do with beetroot. I thought of running, but it wasn't just the hedgerows in my way. Truth was, I was scared. I was hanging on in there with the blurriness and the 'what if?'s But a definitive answer? I had barely enough resources to paddle in the shallows. I didn't have enough to dig deeper and deal with whatever, wherever or, especially, whenever I was. Not yet, anyway.

So, I played along, relieved to find myself working away from the so-called land girls and the toxic combination of Ellie's shrill enthusiasm and provocation of holocaust imagery.

By suppertime George herded me in with the cows and I was sitting once again at the big kitchen table. No little eyes bothered to look at me this time; the children were hungry and noisily slurped a watery stew. Some potato floated in my plate with whatever gristle George's hearty portion hadn't scooped up. My hunger dissipated as quickly as the steam that rose from it, but later as I lay in bed I wished I hadn't been so picky. It would have at least eased one of the pains that tormented me.

I was badly hung-over from the cocktails of revelation, fear and exhaustion with side orders of hunger served up throughout the day. I had no power to prioritise or deal with any of the demands that were screaming at each other from one side of my head to the other. My limbs felt like weights that wished they were dead and my back like it would never again experience the joy of being upright. I prayed for sleep, the oblivion it would bring and the hope I'd wake restored. As well as where and when I should be. But it was slow to come, even as I lay there, totally spent in the darkness.

Every window, every opening to the outside world was blocked by black sheeting, intensifying the closeness and inescapable feeling I was trapped. I finally drifted off and dreamed of an untended gravestone in a churchyard in the cove, my name barely visible.

Wispy threads of an out of tune radio were just out of reach; the persistent bark of a dog blocking the way. I shot up and gasped for air. "Mum!" I cried, then sobbed as I realised where I wasn't. Laying back down on the hard bed my eyes adjusted to the restrained morning light. The room was uncompromising: less twenty first century trying to be retro, more twentieth century-so-deal-with-it. I re-tuned to the dog that had barked its way out of my sleep and into the yard below.

Rolling over I saw great granny's watch sitting on a stool next to the bed. It was the only thing I had from home, and it wasn't even mine, not really. But it felt solid, familiar – and old. How old, I wondered. Old enough to be around in 1944? Was Wheezy around then? She must have been, she was pushing ninety at least. A hot prickle of shame caught me as I thought of her. The random ramblings I'd never bothered to follow, zoning out of them just like I did when the boys squabbled. White noise. An irritant managed by ignoring it.

A scroll through my memories failed to locate a section marked 'Helpful Memories of Wheezy', apart from the odd fragmented recollection. She'd recently been given a medal and a letter. Signed by the Prime Minister, she'd said. As if, I'd thought, not bothering to look at it. The only time I'd seen her get cross was when she caught Ned pinning the medal to Sebastian's chest next to a Simpson's badge, before saluting then shooting him. I'm sure it was for something like the Land Army – was she a land girl too?

How could I possibly accept that I had gone back in time? The game-show theory was worth clinging to; if this was a game then games had rules.

What were the stakes? How did it end? I had a horrible feeling that I knew how it was supposed to end, picturing that grave, my name and date of death now newly etched. When was it? June, the something, 1944. Getting home before that date had to be the way to win, but – when was it? June, just before D Day Emily had said – but when was that? Come on Louie – I was supposed to be good at history. June 6th. It was meant to be the day before but bad weather had delayed it.

Pain radiated from my hand; I'd clenched Wheezy's watch so tightly the winder had imprinted on my palm. I thought of what my mystery rescuer had said when he'd seen the watch – what did he mean, was I one of his? I paused for a moment to think of him, it felt like we'd made a connection. Or maybe I just wanted to make a connection – man, with those eyes, who wouldn't?

Turning the watch over, I thought how this linked me to the future, or present, or whatever the technical term was for the time in the future that should be your present, but may not be. My head hurt. I thought again of home, and Wheezy. I just couldn't deal with her on top of everything else: leaving my beloved London, my friends, Tom, or at least the promise of him, and for what? To live in Dullsville; wasn't that bad enough without the batty old bird that came with the package? I wasn't convincing anybody, especially not myself. I'd been a biatch, as Emily would have said.

I tried to focus on my great grandmother and what I did know. She never married, but I hadn't bothered to find out why, and had a child, Grandpa Joshua. The implications of that only occurred to me then. The hardship and prejudice she'd have faced bringing up a child like Joshua, on her own, in post war Britain. I thought of Joshua's father and realised Wheezy must have been quite an independent spirit in her time.

Dad had said she came to Cornwall in the war and stayed here, which was why they chose this area. Grandpa Joshua had died the summer before of prostate cancer, a year exactly after he'd lost Granny Helen, and Dad had wanted to do the right thing and look after Wheezy. Except, she barely seemed to notice. No one really knew if she had accepted that her son had died. For Wheezy, Dad and Granddad were interchangeable and it seemed too cruel, even for me, to point out otherwise.

The business at Higher Farm came up for sale just as Dad's redundancy came through and so the cosy rosy-tinted plan was sealed. We left a life I loved and headed hundreds of miles west to take over the holiday business in the back of beyond – the back of beyond that this will become. My head hurt again but I had to stay focused. Wheezy moved in. She knew the farm. She knew the farm…why? I was so wrapped up in feeling sorry for myself I had made it my mission to show everyone, including a bewildered old lady, just how unhappy I was. I hadn't bothered to show her the slightest bit of interest, a decision I now bitterly regretted. If I was in the past, or something was recreating a game show of my probable past, then it would make sense to try and find the key players, and Wheezy suddenly seemed like a key player.

Chapter SIX

The morning was spent with the land girls on a field west of the farmhouse trailing behind a noisy contraption doing something called harrowing, which seemed appropriate. Doubled over, some of us poked seeds into the mud for kale that I was told would be used to feed the cows in winter; those same cows that provided the stinking manure that other girls were shovelling over the top. None of the land girls liked the jobs any more than I did, but no one moaned, except Blanche.

"Piggin' cows, piggin' war…" She suited her name: pale-faced with small pointy features and eyes ringed by dark shadows. She made short angry stabs with a pitchfork into the putrid slop, tossing it blindly behind her.

"Watch where you're firing that!" A fork-full had narrowly missed a much larger land girl with cheeks rosier than Mum's after drinking red wine.

"Sorry Queenie – hey, how's corporal-what's-is-face?"

"I assume you are referring to Sergeant Hal Johnson the Third?" she puffed up as she said his name.

"Looked like you was gettin' to know each other pretty well on Saturday night!" said Blanche, missing off the nudge-nudge, wink-wink. I half expected a cheeky roar from a hidden pantomime audience.

Queenie answered with an attempt at an impish smile through plump, well-risen cheeks, before catching sight of me. "What you gawping at?" she snapped, in time with me snapping shut my open mouth.

It all felt so false, I felt false. And tired. Weird, and self-conscious. Making small talk with girls who were either playacting for cameras I couldn't see or, worse, were old or dead in my own timeline, was just wrong. And creepy.

I kept thinking, hoping, if I turned around quickly, I'd catch them off guard, off character, checking a script or talking to a hidden director.

But, no matter what I felt, or what theories were more probable, the focus had to be on winning these girls' trust and finding Wheezy. Whether or not as part of a game, it made sense to find a link between yesterday and today. Or, today and tomorrow, depending on your perspective. It was hard; what did I have in common with them? We had no shared experiences. We couldn't talk about our recent binge TV favourite, the music we liked or suss out each other's fashion sense. Although, when I began to relax a little, I realised that's exactly what they were doing. It was a bit like school, except the hot list of sixth-formers was replaced with a hotter list of corporals, sergeants and lieutenants.

Then, almost without warning, the sky darkened, and a deep ominous drone of aircraft filled the sky.

"Run!" I screamed, abandoning my seeds to the air and sprinting to the ditch. There must have been at least ten of them and they'd have no trouble mowing us down. I leapt, crouched, buried my head in my knees then waited. The noise was tremendous, coarse and guttural and I braced myself for the machine gunfire. But it didn't come. Instead, the rumble intensified as it passed over then moved away. I lifted my head from my knees and saw that I was alone. Peeping over the top of the ditch, the land girls were just where they had been. How was I supposed to know the planes were on our side?

As I tried to limp back nonchalantly, the same silver shower that had rained down in the sea trickled down again. I looked to the heavens. Was it a sign? A supernatural portal intended only for me? Did this mean I was going home? But the bits landed on the ground, crumpled, limp and unexciting. I bent down and picked up a handful. Bit thicker than Mum's kitchen foil – nothing mystical, magical or in any way related to time travel. Deflated, I stuffed some in my pocket, before spotting 'Mother' talking agitatedly to George.

She must have seen my loonish leap into the hedge; I'd be packed off to the funny farm for sure. George took off his hat and scratched his head before looking for me in the gaggle of land girls. I wasn't quick enough, he knew I'd seen him, signalling for me to come over. I looked directly at him, avoiding contact with his wife. "Mother needs a hand in the kitchen with lunch and that, so go make yourself useful – she'll show you what's what." That didn't sound too shabby, especially as it involved food. I was starving. Having been picky over what small rations there were yesterday and breakfast being hours earlier, I was feeling weak and light-headed. How did people here manage on so little?

The kitchen offered cool relief and was filled with the swoon-making smell of freshly made bread. A big cheese, homemade chutney and a regal looking ham sat on the side. Yesterday's piglets squealed momentarily in my head but were silenced by the anticipation of tearing off a hunk and satisfying my hunger. 'Mother' scored a line in the ham but barely a thumbnail width from the end, telling me to slice only to that point. The rest she said was for some club.

"Pig Club – we can't have a whole pig to ourselves. We agreed to share it with the hamlet."

"What about those pigs we were, you know, tending to?"

"Same – gotta share 'em. The War Ag will have us if we keep too many – don't suppose you had to deal with stuff like that where you came from?"

"No." Supermarkets and Sunday roasts were the extent of my relationship with pigs. I was instructed to share the meagre portion between several open doorstep sandwiches on the waiting tray. I sneaked a slice to my mouth and thought maybe mutilating piglets was worth it if they'd taste this good when old enough to be fully butchered. "Is this for the land girls?" I asked.

"You think this is a charity? They brings their own, but we'll take some milk if they wants to buy some. This is for the POWs – got to feed 'em decent or there'll be hell to pay. It's the law." My first thought was I wouldn't mind being fed 'decent' and second, POWs – Prisoners of War?

"How many d'you have?"

"Eight today: five I-ties, three Hun, including a new boy."

"Is it safe – I mean, are they chained up?"

"String 'em up I would! But protected aren't they? Geneva Conflaberation business: world's gone mad."

"So they can roam around then?" I was listening but far more diverting was the cheese. The stolen morsels of ham hadn't satisfied but ignited my hunger.

"No, my lover, there's a guard with them – just in case."

"Shall I start on the cheese?" I'd never been so anxious to be near food before and felt weak at the thought of the Cheddar and how it would feel in my mouth, creamy but spiky with its salty, crystallized after-taste. A good Cheddar bites you back, Dad always said. Where are you? I thought. Was he worrying about me? A memory popped up of him teasing me about a boot-camp he'd read about; gritty hard work, eating road-kill and insects being the new life lessons for wayward teens. Was that what this was about? I felt empty in every sense, cut adrift, isolated and hungry.

"Well? You going to cut that or just stare at it?"

"Sorry – here?" I asked hopefully positioning the knife well into the cheese.

"No. No more than the ham, that's got to last 'till you make some more, my girl." I quite liked that idea, although I didn't plan on being around long enough to make cheese. I secretly scoffed as much as I could until I felt a tug on my dungarees and looked down to see two big eyes in a tiny face looking up at me.

"Give us some. " I pointed to the Cheddar and raised my eyebrows as if to say, what this? I looked warily at Mother who'd shuffled away with an irri-table grumble about evacuees. It was Doreen, the one who'd had her fingers rammed in the jam on the first morning. If I gave her a piece she'll go away, I thought, but as I bent down, she backed off. Maybe it was my breath after all that cheese and no toothpaste.

"You do know that's the child's entire weekly ration?" we both froze and looked at Mother's back. How could she have seen? "Go on," she said, without turning round. "But give her some bread, or she'll be sick on all that richness." I smiled at the little girl and although she snatched the cheese, she didn't smile back, looking at me instead as if I couldn't be trusted.

"Are you an evacuee?" I asked, handing her some bread.

"Me mam said I'd be here 'til Christmas," she said in a soft Yorkshire accent, not quite between mouthfuls. Mother had turned around and I clocked her expression, which softened unexpectedly. She was no doubt complicit in the lie repeated all over the country as mothers gave up the care of their babies to people they'd never met, hundreds of miles away, in the hope of keeping them safe. It just didn't seem plausible that this little girl was play-acting.

I looked closely at the tiny child. She was wary and uncertain, having to trust that the grown-ups would make it all better for her. I thought of the boys' graves I'd seen, trying not to think that they were near the one marked with my name. I thought of the boy called Roddy; he wasn't going home to his parents, they were dead already, the Blitz had seen to that. I felt an unexpected lump in my throat and hoped things would be different for this one.

"What's your name?" I asked.

"D'reen." She whispered and something gave way as I thought of Ned and Sebastian and wished I'd been kinder.

"Well, D'reen. My name's Louie, and I'm very happy to meet you." And I was.

"I've a friend called Louis at home, she's a boy."

"Come on, look sharp," said Mother. "Doreen, bring the milk but be careful mind." We made our way out of the back and into the fields. I took the milk from the child, who was juggling it with her cheese and bread, and gripped the tray tightly. I'd never met an enemy before.

Clusters of people were scattered on the grass, either stretched out in the sun or huddled in small circles under the shade of the trees, cigarette smoke drifting above them. They wore mismatched uniforms, most just in shirtsleeves, heavy trousers and black boots. Some had kept their uniform jackets on, despite the heat. Mother laid her tray on an already positioned trestle table and I followed trying to keep my eyes down, but curious to see the POWs close-up. Doreen had skipped off when she had spied a little boy pretending to shoot his friend who was making daisy chains in another field.

"Signora! You're so beautiful – marry me!"

"No – marry me. He's married already!"

"Pipe down lads," it was the English guard, reassuringly armed, but looking pretty relaxed with a group of very young, very handsome Italians. I kept close to Mother who was pouring out the milk.

"Here," she said – take this down to the girls in the bottom field. Ha'penny a cup. Don't take no jip." As I left, I walked past another group. They were German, judging by the their uniforms, but they could have been extras from a movie taking time out between scenes.

"You've dried out then?" I jumped and almost dropped the milk. Could it be him? He was lazily looking up at me from lying down on the grass, shielding those glorious eyes from the sun. The recognition and shock to my insides came from a much deeper place than just a few days ago.

"Hey," I said. "You cut and ran," which sounds as if I was chilled about seeing the guy who'd saved me from drowning, but my breathing had gone all weird.

"I did not get far," he said tilting his head to one side, smiling.

"If you'd wanted to work here you could have just asked – no need to have crashed your plane." My nervous smile and attempts at banter froze as I met the ice-cold stare of a short, stocky guy to his left.

"Missy! That milk'll curdle!" Mother was shooing me off so I headed down the hill. I'd started to think I'd imagined my rescuer. Seeing him lifted everything. For just a moment, I loosened my grip on all that I'd been gripping since I'd got here.

There were more familiar faces in the next field, but none that made me feel like he just had.

"Hello again," said Ellie.

"Hi – want some milk?"

"Only if it's free," said Shirley. How did she manage to make dungarees glamorous?

"Sorry, 'Mother' said it's a ha'penny – what is her real name?"

"Tight-Fisted Trout," said Blanche.

"Olive. Olive Dorcas, and she's really not as frightful as she seems," said Ellie with an encouraging smile.

"She's got a cheek," said Blanche. "I milked the bleedin' cow this morning. At Trenogar Farm, Lady what-ser-face lets the girls have as much milk as they like."

"And gin gimlets too! Barbara from my hostel was telling me – I want to get transferred there," said Shirley.

"Your hostel's full of dunderheads – they don't even have milk at Trenogar. The War Ag made her swap her cows for chickens," said Ellie.

"The war what?" I asked.

"Ministry of Agriculture. Blimey, don't you know nothing?" asked Blanche.

"They didn't have many cows in my part of London," I snapped back.

"Here. I'll buy some," said Ellie. "Anything to take away the taste of these nasty Bovril sandwiches. The double summertime means we've got a long afternoon ahead of us – sadly without any gin gimlets to help us on our way."

"Double summer time's wretched," said Shirley

"Should bleedin' give us double money," said Blanche.

"Who's on beets this afternoon?' asked Ellie. "Blanche? Shirley you're thinning turnips – "

"Again? The mud stains my fingernails. Looks ghastly when I play the piano."

"It's that or onions old girl – "

"Turnip tops," Shirley sighed, her petulance reminding me of Emily when Mum asked for help. Even though they seemed grown up, with their uniforms and BBC way of speaking, they weren't that much older than my sister and me. And the tiny Ellie, who seemed team leader, or forewoman, was probably my age.

"Louie – you can buddy up with me," she said, but I'd stopped listening. "We ought to cut back those boundary hedges – should have done it weeks ago." A thought was tapping away. It was important. But, watching the land girls leave, it disappeared with them.

Ellie was handing me a weapon. "Sickle," she said as if it should mean something. She'd also said boundary and we were now at the edge of the farm. I felt nervous about what might be out there, but a mass of brambles and blackthorns were barring the way. Ellie set to work attacking the hedge like a pocket-sized demon. I was driven by a random memory of an old Ladybird book where princes in tights hacked their way through the brambles to get to the sleeping princess. I was no princess and the theory that I may be sleeping was up for debate, but the need to hack my way out of here and find a way home was irrefutable.

It wasn't long before I was fantasising about power tools, protective clothing and a proper loo. I paused to take in what my hard work had uncovered. Which was nothing. Beyond the hedge there were no signs of twenty-first century life, not a cat's eye, road marking or signpost – not even a brown tourist one for pseudo farm-like attractions. Just hills, trees and patchworked fields tightly sewn together with more hedgerows. I sighed and asked instead about the tin foil that had fallen from the sky. Ellie laughed gently at me. She'd heard about my ditch dive.

"It's called 'window,' planes drop it to obscure their signal on Jerry's radar. You'll get used to it – why were you so jumpy? You must have seen oodles of planes over London."

"It's so full of air traffic, you stop noticing," besides, budget airlines made a poor comparison to warplanes, friendly or otherwise. I explained about the plane that had used me for target practice.

"It happens," she said cheerily. "You were luckier than that poor chap in Coverack. Strafed ploughing. Both him and the horse," she drew a line across her throat, not that I needed a visual aid.

We lapsed into merciful silence and I plugged into the sounds around me, especially those from the sky. As the afternoon wore on the need to pee became urgent. A squat in the hedge was the only solution. The relief was immense but short-lived. I screamed at the point of a knife, then a gun, then a grin.

"Mighty fine toosh, ma'am!" It came from the blackened face of a soldier slithering on his belly, clinging to a gun fixed with a bayonet while I frantically scrambled to pull up my dungarees. More rustling, tittering and an entire pod of the seal like soldiers squirmed out of the undergrowth on their bellies. Ellie came running over, briefly touched my arm and gave me a sympathetic smile before crouching down.

"Ma'am," said the same soldier, touching the tip of his tin hat with his free hand.

"Are you on training manoeuvres? Is it awfully hush-hush?" My mortification at peeing inches from their faces made it hard for me to get into the chitchat.

"Gum?" GIs. The cast was getting bigger.

"Rather!" said Ellie before more rustling, frantic hand signals and a shuffling back through the hedge and out of view.

"What fun!" said Ellie. Not so fun if, or when, they do it for real.

That night I so needed a hot shower. Instead I had to make do with tepid water in a tin bath in the middle of the kitchen that I had to fill from a kettle. It was a farce trying to keep everyone out. The little boys in the house thought it was great fun to try to spy on the big girl with boobs. Doreen stepped up as my protector and stood guard, but by the time I'd cleaned out the bath and filled it, I was too tired and self-conscious to enjoy it. Especially when Mother marched in.

"You're milking tomorrow," she said. "Then out on the rounds."

"Ok," I said shooting up in the water to fold myself over my knees to protect what little dignity I had.

"What day is it tomorrow?"

"Dunno," she said, "Mind you don't slop all that water on the floor – you can bath the little ones in it after."

"Great." Just what I felt like doing. "Have you got a calendar?"

"What I want one of them things for? Got a sun and moon to tell me all I need."

"So, what's the date then?"

"Dunno. Doreen, pass her ladyship the towel and call the others in."

Later, after scrubbing five filthy children and needing, but obviously not getting, another bath myself, I slumped on my bed before picking up the watch. I should have asked him about it, him with the incredible eyes and wonky smile. It seemed to mean something to him. But more pressing was the disappointment that I hadn't made any progress with Wheezy. I turned the watch over and over, looking for something I may have missed. Holding it tightly I made a wish. The next thing I knew the dog and cockerel were competing for the dawn chorus. My wish hadn't been granted

Chapter SEVEN

Despite the watch's lack of quantum leaping powers and being trapped in Cornwall At War, the game show or otherwise, and being another day closer to the date on my grave, I woke with a sense of purpose rather than panic. It was just beginning to get light with the promise of a beautiful day, but as I approached the milking shed my resolve wavered. Illuminated with lamps, the scene looked like an old oil painting that hadn't been restored. And it stank. The land girls were sat at little stools with their faces pressed into the hot flanks of the huge black steaming cows. I wanted to run, but George had seen me.

"You sitting down or what?" he said from behind a bovine backside, nodding towards a stool dwarfed by the humongous beasts, as Ned would have said.

I felt a longing for my brothers; they would have loved to be here, so close to the action, except I would have said something cutting. It had annoyed me how easily everyone else had made the move to Cornwall, but I yearned for my family now and bit down hard on the inside of my mouth to stop myself from crying. What in the name of Dr Who and all things time-travel was I doing here, and would I ever see them again?

I sat in front of an enormous set of dangling udders. "Stroke and pat her here so she relaxes and lets down her milk," said George, leaning in to show me how. "There, there girl…good girl. Then you got to take your whole hand – clean is it?" Was he having a laugh? What did it matter compared to the state of the shed, the smells, the total absence of anything related to health and safety?

"With your thumb and first finger squeeze tight right at the top of her teat so the milk don't go back up, and then with the rest of your fingers squeeze and pull, drawing down on the teat to coax the milk into a flow. It might take a minute or two but, there, see?" Watery stuff was squirting into a bucket underneath. "Now, keep it going until the proper milk comes in – there. Right. Over to you."

Grappling with elongated nipples wasn't going to help me get home, but I wasn't a quitter. Maybe it was the whole game show thing – what if I really was being watched? Although, in my heart I no longer felt that to be true; tugging on teats was easier to get my head around. I grasped them with both hands and pulled. She mooed, kicked out and I fell off my stool.

"Whoa!" said George. "You're not ringing bells!" He put his hands over mine, pulling them down to simulate the action, trapping me between the cow's backside and his morning breath. Soon though, milk started to spurt into the bucket.

"She'll kick out again if you come at her too quickly," he said. "Don't want that bucket knocked over." I was more concerned about my head. I eventually got the hang of it but, looking down, I didn't see the pure white milk I was expecting. Instead it was topped off with black hairy floaters and crud that must have fallen off the cow. But George didn't seem bothered when he came back to check on me; he laid a muslin cloth over an empty bucket and strained the contaminated milk through it. All good until he scrunched up the muslin and wrung it out into the clean milk. I would never, ever drink milk again.

The sun was fully up when we finally left the shed and I was feeling dizzy with hunger. We heard a truck pull up before we saw it. "Bleedin' marvellous, innit?" said Blanche. "They starts after us, gets chauffeured while we has to cycle, is better fed and better paid for less work. Bleedin' cushy war they're having." She was talking about the POWs who were getting out of the truck.

"You oughtn't to think like that, I'm not sure it's entirely fair," said Ellie.

"Oh, oughtn't I?" said Blanche mimicking Ellie's clipped tones.

"Look old girl, most of them are just boys and are probably more at home on a farm than behind a gun– I doubt they want to be in this war any more than we do."

"Oh, how remiss of me not to take account of their hurt feelings," said Blanche. "Let me tell you, Miss Prissy Pants: it's bastards like them what killed my mum, and half my sodding street!" Ellie was mortified, Shirley and Queenie said nothing and I, shamefully, wanted my breakfast. I was feeling hot and faint with a mouth that could barely contain my bone-dry tongue.

The POWs herded the cows past and I searched for him. The bulky flying jacket, dark hair and the light, liquid blue eyes. He saw me too. He smiled and something amazing released inside me

Chapter EIGHT

Leaving Higher Farm was a huge moment – I'd accepted a crowd wasn't waiting to cheer my success in completing the trials in the Big Brother War. But was I ready to experience a Cornwall ravaged by bombs and over-run with military and downtrodden civilians? I didn't need to be, as it turned out. For a while at least, the countryside looked pretty much as it always had done, except now I was scouring the fields hoping to catch a glimpse of him again.

Blanche had jumped in the cabin at the last minute, saying she had chores to run for Mother. It seemed everyone, even her husband, knew her as Mother. She'd been kind that morning, slipping a rasher of bacon onto my plate and soaking the bread in dripping. I was beginning to think she wasn't as grim as she liked people to think. Ellie told me that the Ministry of Agriculture put her and George under huge pressure: everything had to be properly accounted for, milk, pigs, fuel for the truck, how much they were producing on the farm. They did spot checks and if the books didn't balance the farm could be downgraded and they could lose it, or at least some of the land and livestock. That was why she was so tight when it came to doling out the food. Also, if she was as mean spirited as she seemed, why take in all the evacuees?

I thought about the evacuee I'd replaced; they were expecting someone but surely not me. What happened to her? Had she walked from the bus and been less lucky with the joyless rider? Was she lying dead or, worse, dying in a ditch somewhere?

"Penny for 'em?" It was Blanche.

"I was just thinking how I got to be here. What about you – I'm sorry about what you were saying, your mum and that," I said.

"Yeah. 'Effing bastards. Smoke?" I shook my head. "It was really hard at first," she said dragging deeply. "I came down here to get away – but bleedin' Jerry's everywhere."

"What happened?"

She exhaled thick white smoke from the side of her mouth. "Air raid. We'd always dodged the bombs by sheltering under the railway arches at the end of our garden – all the neighbours did. Bastards dropped one right on the house and the blast got trapped in the arches where we was standing. Least that's what they said – we'd have been better standing in the middle of Clapham bleedin' Common. Mum protected me, but there weren't no one to protect her – she had no chance."

"I'm so sorry," what else could I say?

"You must have seen action, where you was?" said Blanche looking at me now.

"Yeah, course," I lied, looking away, "but losing your mum…"

"The worst was Dad, when he came back from his shift. He blamed himself for telling us we'd be alright in the arch and not being with us." She dragged on her cigarette again, before flicking it out of the truck. "I felt like it should have been me instead of her, and I think Dad was thinking that too. Having me around just made him worse, so I left as soon as I could. I signed up for the land army the day I turned seventeen and got posted here at the beginning of the year." Wherever I was in the past, the grief on Blanche's face was painfully present.

We'd pulled up at Trenogar Farm, the one without cows but chickens, gin and Lady-what's-her-face. And I guessed it was her who floated out to greet us as like guests for a weekend of country pursuits.

"Darlings. You must be parched. Come in, come in, Primrose will fix us a drink," she sang accompanied by a wink.

"How are you with neat gin this time of the morning?" whispered Blanche. Having spent the morning with lactating cows and in much need of a shower, a mid- morning slug of gin wasn't top of my wish list.

"A fresh one! Oh darling!" said the Lady.

"May I introduce Louie, Lady H," said Ellie.

"How do you do? What a fabulously exotic complexion!" she said.

"Thank you," I said, unsure if I should add m'lady.

"Ah! Drinks! Thank you, Primrose," she said as a much older lady tee-tered across the hall with tray of rattling glasses. She smiled so that her pen-cilled-on eyebrows crinkled and red lipstick showed on her teeth, and I in-stantly warmed to her.

"Thanks awfully," said Ellie as she was handed a glass. I held mine awk-wardly, watching the other girls to know when I should take a sip. I wanted to refuse, but knew it would be rude.

"We'd like just one jug of milk today, please," said Primrose.

"Absolutely and would you like your butter ration too?" asked Ellie.

"How kind," said Lady H, as if she'd been offered an unexpected present. "Drink up! Chin-chin!" She said, raising her glass to me. I smiled and took a tentative sip; it was watery but unexpectedly sweet and perfumed. Elder-flower! It wasn't gin at all. Blanche turned away and I could see her shoulders shaking with laughter.

"When you come on Saturday with the cream, time your visit for late afternoon, say six o'clock? And wear frocks rather than those ghastly uni-forms. I have a delivery of gentlemen from the American encampments for the evening."

Primrose's eyes lit up, "They bring such lovely gifts!" she said.

"Primrose is rather taken with the stockings, but where would we be without the essentials? Like gin and sugar?" said Lady H, raising her glass. "I thought we might have a bit of a sing-song, if your friend will play for us again?"

"Shirley will be honoured, Lady H," said Ellie.

"Excellent. So far from home; I think we can show them Cornwall has more to offer than pasties."

"We'll do our best, and cheers for the drinks!" said Blanche. We head-ed back to the truck and I was glad we'd only drunk elderflower as Ellie had enough trouble driving sober. She crunched her way loudly through the gears and I did something I hadn't done for an age. I laughed and it felt brilliant.

Further confirmation that the laws of time and space had been defied and I'd slid back to 1944 came on the journey into town. It was one thing to transform a farm, but no way could a city be re-built. Acknowledging the supreme weirdness of it all, it was also hard not to be intrigued. The smell came first; I thought the truck was bucking against Ellie's driving and spewed a leak, but the closer we got to town, the more acrid the stench of diesel. "Can't you smell that?" I asked through my hands.

"The mighty war engine, cranking up for the invasion," said Blanche.

"You can't say that!" said Ellie.

"Come off it – we all know it's going to happen, else what's the point of them all?" said Blanche, looking out the window. Crammed onto what should have been the golf course were military vehicles and hundreds of bell-tents, except this was no festival. Instead, it looked like a well-organised refugee camp in a sea of mud green, brown and khaki.

Then there was the collision of noise from the military traffic and kit loading onto or off trucks. The activity and sense of high alert made it hard not to believe the war machine was cranking up for action. If that newspaper-cutting I found in the privy was genuine, then that action would be D Day.

We pulled up to a sentry post and were greeted by two soldiers fully armed and fully intimidating. "Hello there!" said Ellie, undeterred.

"Ma'am," replied one in a heavy Texan drawl. "It's you, Miss Ellie, Miss Blanche and?"

"Miss Louie," I said, wishing I hadn't. He touched his cap in a salute.

"I hope you got fresh supplies, I've a heap of empty churns cluttering up my post and hundreds of grown men crying like babies for their milk!"

"When have we ever let you down?" said Ellie playfully. She and Blanche began exchanging empty churns for full ones. I tried to pitch in but the churn was so heavy I staggered and it thudded noisily on the ground.

"Hey little lady, let me help you with that," said the Texan. I looked up gratefully only to see him taking a churn from Ellie. I decided rolling them was the way to go.

"Sort yourself out, they don't want bleedin' butter!" said Blanche on her third churn. A jeep pulled up.

"I'd recognise that toosh anywhere!" My bum was in the air and as I looked behind it, I saw the grinning face of the GI that I'd nearly peed on. He swept up my churn, balanced it on his shoulder and with his free hand extended it towards me. "I don't think I properly introduced myself last time we met. Ira," he said. "Corporal Ira Charleston, from Illinois."

"Louie, very embarrassed from London." I shook his hand, warm and strong around mine. It was a long time since I'd felt physical contact, which is why I held on longer than I should.

"Hey Ira," said Blanche, quickly stepping in, "will we see you at Trenogar? Lady H's throwin' one of her specials."

"Try stopping me Blanche – you going, Louie-very-embarrassed-from-London?"

"You know each other?" I said.

"I make it my business to know all the pretty girls in Corn-Wall." He winked, Blanche blushed, and I laughed at the cheesy line.

"Corporal!" barked a voice from another jeep that had pulled up. "You keeping these ladies from their war work?" Ira snapped to attention, which was impressive given the milk churn over his shoulder.

"No Sir, Sergeant Sir!" A short stout serviceman with a crew cut as square as his jaw line marched towards us, and the atmosphere changed. In a sudden frenzy the work was done and we were driving away from the camp.

"He wasn't much of a laugh, was he?" I said.

"Queenie's Hal, she's rather taken with him I'm afraid," said Ellie.

"There's water!" I shouted. We'd stopped on the quay and I was so excited to see that it was a quay.

"You what?" said Blanche.

"Water! I've never seen it like this." In my day the quay will be concreted over, shopping mall-ed with the tidal river banished to one end and forced to flow underneath, hidden and unloved.

"It's just a skanky river, mostly bleedin' mud when the tide goes out," she said.

"It's amazing!" I could feel them exchanging glances, but it changed the whole feel of the place, opening up possibilities to the wider world. I cursed the town planners of my century. Everything seemed lighter, more open. Beautiful even. Little fishing boats bobbed between the huge military hardware, linking the Cornwall of the past to this present and my future.

"Each to their own" said Blanche as she climbed out. Looking beyond her, up the hill, I saw my school. The gothic building peered down imperiously but more graciously, the chapel being framed by green fields instead of the modern languages block and new gym. Ellie jolted me out of my historical exploration by mangling the gears to pull away. "Sorry," she said, trying to find the gear that wouldn't make the truck jump, and everyone look at us.

"When d'you pass your test?" She looked at me quizzically. "Driving test?"

"There's a war on old girl, haven't you heard? George showed me the basics on the tractor then moved me on to the truck. A few more things to think about on this, but I'm getting the hang of it," she said as we lurched forward again. "Want to try?"

"No, no. You're doing great," I lied.

Traffic stopped us outside a dress shop. A notice in its window listed the coupons needed for each bit of clothing:

Dress, gown or frock, woollen: eleven coupons;
Dress, gown or frock, other material: seven coupons;
Undergarments: three coupons.

I got not being able to afford to buy stuff, but not being allowed to, even if you could afford it? I thought about my drawers back home, so stuffed I could hardly close them – how many coupons-worth were in there?

As we moved off, we passed queues of people with small children, baskets and coupons in their hands. I remembered an incident with Wheezy. We'd come here early one morning and I was in a strop, obviously. We bickered and lost Wheezy, eventually finding her waiting patiently in a queue outside a bank, closed for customer care training.

"Wheezy! What are you doing? This isn't even your bank!" Dad had said trying not to be cross.

"If you see a queue Robert, you must join it," she'd said lowering her voice conspiratorially. "They might have oranges!"

Poor Wheezy. What a muddled world she was in; I could have made it so much easier for her. I scrutinised the faces of people queuing for the butcher, baker and candlestick maker – not that I saw one of those – trying to picture how Wheezy might look now. I gripped her watch in my pocket, willing it to be a divining rod to guide me to her. It didn't. But as we passed a watch-maker's near to the cathedral, I looked down at the broken timepiece. What had it meant to the mysterious POW who made my heart race every time I thought of him? To Wheezy? And what could it mean to me?

It was late in the afternoon when we finished the milk round, having visited every house, smallholding and habited establishment within a three-mile radius of Higher Farm. Delivering milk was only half of what was expected. "What d'you think then?" asked one lady, holding out a blue and white striped jug in one hand and two small children in the other.

"About what? To the top, Mrs Barnicoat?" asked Ellie.

"Please. Give the lady our coupon," said Mrs Barnicoat to her daughter. Ellie poured the milk and I would register who had what, taking the right coloured coupons. "About the invasion – when's it happening?"

"I think when your Frank gets back he'll be able to tell you," deflected Ellie.

"If he comes back," she whispered above her children's heads.

"Mrs Pascoe's boys came back," said Ellie, rubbing the lady's shoulder kindly. "Didn't they Mrs P?

"That's right, dear love 'em," said a lady in a headscarf. "Just half please. Last weekend, both turned up on my doorstep."

"I'll take two," said a lady in curlers. "Got any butter?"

"Absolutely," said Ellie gesticulating for me to pass it to her. "Mrs Jago's expecting so she can have two pints of milk a day."

"Not the only one, from what I hear," said Mrs Jago. "Dolly Moyle's got herself caught with one of them coloureds."

"They're everywhere – camped in the park they is," said Mrs Barnicoat.

"Golf course's what I heard," said Mrs Pascoe.

"What's her Jared going to say?" sniped Mrs Jago. "Don't fancy her chances when he comes home to find a little coloured bastard!" She handed me her coupon, took a brisk look and said, "That what happened to your mum?"

The world stopped for a second as my mouth fell open.

"I wouldn't stand in the heat too long Mrs Jago," said Ellie. "Your milk's turning sour."

"I don't mind them my lover," said Mrs Pascoe quickly, helping to fill the space with words I couldn't form. "Much more polite than them white GIs. Got any cheese?"

The next few days saw many more jugs of milk poured, patties of butter doled out and small portions of cheese exchanged for coupons, gossip and some, but thankfully not much, prejudice. Most people just wanted to share their theories on why there were so many GIs, when the invasion would happen and why the creeks were out of bounds. No one seemed to take notice of the posters tacked up everywhere, warning about careless talk. I used the deliveries to try to find out about Wheezy; she hadn't married and the line going back to her was male, so I guessed we'd both be Shircliff.

"I knows of a Tunicliff, over at St Agnes, but he's passed on," was one unhelpful offering.

"That's not a Cornish name – where you from then?" was another, sizing me up like Mrs Jago, making it clear it couldn't be from any place she'd like to go.

One of our stops was a tiny school full of children racing around the playground; the boys playing war games and the girls pretending to be nurses, tending to their wounded soldiers. I tuned in to their voices, hoping to hear the names of Roddy or Wilfred, the two boys whose graves I'd seen on that mad day. If I were in 1944, and it seemed churlish to deny it, then maybe I could save them, stop them playing on the beach and getting blown up. If I saved the boys, maybe I could save myself… I blanked out the dire small print that was shouting warnings about space-time-continuum from the corner of my brain marked 'all things time-travel'.

I kept up the internal rationalising as we pulled into a British camp so well camouflaged I didn't know it was there. Neither of us spoke as we passed through a chilling collection of war contraptions. Covered in netting and leaves, I thought of iron monsters playing dress-up in flimsy fishnets. But there was nothing comical about where they were headed and the job they had to do. How much would be blown up before it reached the French shores? And how many men would die trying to get it there?

Through the trees, soldiers worked beside the creek, laying down long stretches of concrete matting that I knew to be 'biscuit.' Dad always pointed out odd bits when we were out with Reg; it was chocolate bar shaped with bits in. Here the 'biscuit' was newly baked, ready to transport the military hardware onto the mammoth vessels waiting to take them on their epic journey. They drew brutal broken lines on these gentle shores I'd only ever seen softened with trees and dog walkers.

We came to a halt outside a shed that passed for a canteen and began the backbreaking churn exchange. Ellie was different, on the alert. Then deflated as we drove away.

"You OK?" I asked.

"Tickety-boo!" she said in between wrestling the much-tortured gear stick. "I'm fine. It's just…there's this chap."

"At the camp?"

"Jake. He's based here. I know him from my group," she said. "We meet with a Rabbi who comes down every six weeks or so."

"At a synagogue?"

"There isn't one my friend," I liked the way she called me friend. "So he travels around, administering pastoral care," she said, mastering the gear change as we got on to the open road.

"But he wasn't here today."

"No. Thought he'd be back," she said. "Slapton Sands; some training mission. Queenie let slip some disaster – she heard from Hal but it's all hush-

hush, you know how it is."

An alarm bell rang. A holiday. Ned and Sebastian clambering over a tank dredged from the sea. Me bored. A plaque: a tragedy, huge secret, suppressed for forty years. Practice for D Day, Operation Tiger? Something about wrong radio signal and American ships sitting ducks – ships carrying tanks. Hence tank on beach. German E boats get lucky; picks them off. There was something else, one of Miss Probert's D Day link-ups. Something about each body had to be recovered and searched. That was it. She'd said they had to make sure the handful of men that knew the secret D Day details were all dead and not captured. I remembered. And I felt sick.

The war was all around me. It was like that smell of diesel. I could forget it for a minute and then it would be back, in the pit of my stomach, nauseating and all consuming. I feared for Ellie, for her friend Jake and her Jewish family, stuck somewhere in Germany.

Chapter NINE

I hadn't seen my mysterious POW since milking the cows, but I couldn't get him out of my head. I caught myself recreating each meeting, well, the two, very brief ones. Admittedly he had saved my life in one of them, but nevertheless – he was a German. The first thing we're taught in school about Germans is that we were at war with them – not their art, music, culture. I was haunted by images of concentration camps and cold, robotic Nazis rewriting the rules on degradation, depravity and cruelty. And yet I couldn't stop the delicious warmth that rose up within me whenever I recalled those eyes and the sense of arrival I felt when I saw him.

"They're billeted in a farm towards Falmouth," said Ellie when I'd asked her earlier about them as we unloaded the truck. "The nearest POW camp is in Columb Minor I think, and there's one at St Erth. Fuel rationing makes it cheaper to billet them where they're needed."

I was watching him now, from my bedroom window, climbing with the armed escort into the truck that would take him and the other POWs to their billet. I willed him to look up. He didn't but his scary friend did and I backed away from the window. How could I get to know him? Hang around in the yard and hope he'd turn up? Offer to carry his spade?

I'd been given the blessing of an early night; even Mother could see I was done in. I was permanently tired, hungry and dirty. I'd been here a week at least, had no luck tracking down any connection to Wheezy and, having given up all hope of being rescued by a TV crew, I was facing the prospect that every day bought me a day closer to the date on that grave. I wasn't ready to face what that meant – that I would die, be killed, cease to exist. Instead I focused on strategies, trying to keep positive that if I tried hard enough, I'd find a way home and dodge my fate – after all, if I could swim into the last century, anything was be possible, wasn't it? I held Wheezy's watch, trying for the umpteenth time to prise open the back to reveal the secret magical compartment with a time travelling formula. I rubbed it like a genie's lamp, pressed it to my heart, prayed over it and finally threw it on the bed. It wasn't even working. And that was the most sensible observation I'd made since I got there. Finally, I had a plan.

It was pitch black when I heard a tiny knocking at the door. I was disorientated thinking I was back in my old home in London and my friends were at the front door to walk with me to school. "Come in!" I said, out loud or in my dream I wasn't sure. The door pushed open and a little head with a pageboy haircut peeped shyly round. Doreen.

"Hey – you okay?" I said, trying to sound more awake than I felt.

"I wet me bed and Mrs Mother's going to be awful cross with me." I could see she'd been crying and her nightdress was soggy. I could have cried too, seeing the tragedy of this little girl, so far from her mummy on a farm where everyone had to work so hard there was no time to try to make her world softer.

"Come here," I said, "let's see what we can do." I wasn't exactly sure what 'we' could do, as there was no hot shower I could put her under or bubble bath to soak her in. I took off her nightdress, wrapped her in a thin towel I'd been given, then the scratchy blanket as I sat her on my bed. "Right. I'll be one sec."

I went downstairs and dragged the tin bath in front of the range, much to Mother's annoyance. "It's not for me. It's an emergency but I'm sorting it out and I'd be very grateful, Mother, if you just let me get on with it. I've worked all week without any complaints and now I'd like to have a little time off to help someone who needs me. OK?" She was so surprised, I think, to hear me assert myself in a sentence that managed to string more than a few words together, that she simply raised her eyebrows and said nothing.

I got on with filling the bath with hot water from the stove, mixed with cold water I fetched from the standpipe. "Do you have any soap?" She indicated towards the kitchen sink – nasty smelly stuff. I saw instead some tired wildflowers and lavender on the table and grabbed them, picking off the petals and throwing them like confetti into the water. "There." I was satisfied.

I skipped back upstairs to find my little bundle huddled on the bed; she hadn't moved. I scooped her up and carried her downstairs. She tensed in my arms when she saw the bath but I was insistent and gently lay her in the warm water among the petals. She looked at Mother in anticipation of being scolded, but she surprised us both by smiling and saying she'd put the kettle back on for more water if we needed it.

It felt good to care for Doreen. I washed her hair, primped and pampered her, pretending we were in a beauty salon, asking her if she wanted her nails done and where was she going on holiday – except I found that more funny than she did. After I lifted her out and dried her, Mother gave us some clean sheets and we went to the room she shared with the other children to change her bedding and sort out some clothes for her. I brushed her hair and swept away the heavy fringe to one side, tying it in a piece of ribbon. She looked beautiful and gave me a hug. It felt wonderful to have such close contact and I thought of my two young brothers, somewhere, very many years from now, wondering if they were missing me like I was missing them.

After that, Doreen was ever present. She came with me when I worked in the fields, tended to the pigs, shifted silage from one place to another, everything except milk the cows and deliver it. I would have found it impossible to be trailed by my younger brothers, but it was different with Doreen. She didn't want much, just company and reassurance. She would sit closely and make dollies out of whatever crop I was grappling with; it was on one of those days that Doreen made the introduction I'd been hoping for. "It's Horse, look Louie!" she squealed when I was bent double, head down in the mud with sweat pouring through my matted hair.

"Hello liebling!" The sun was in my eyes, but I saw him crouching down to greet her.

"Horse!" she squealed. "This is Louie, he's my friend," she said in her sing-song Yorkshire accent, holding his hand and pulling him towards me.

"She, Doreen – I'm a girl," I whispered, using my sleeve to wipe away the mud that must be smeared all over my face.

"A very intriguing girl, I think," he said. He was tall close up. Skinny. His smile was still wonky, wide and embracing. His hair stuck up at odd angles making him look boyish. I was finding it hard to breath.

"Horse?" surely not.

"Horst," he said, roughing Doreen's hair. All the signals were friendly, he'd saved my life and I'd been fantasising about him since I'd first met him – but he was a German. He was the enemy and he was meant to be a prisoner of war – where was his guard?

"You're allowed to wander around?" I said nervously.

"Albert has me in his sights – he's my English guard – and he's an excellent shot," he said, watching me scour the field, looking for reassurance. There were odd little groups of POWs, including one with the short scary guy who now clocked me looking at him. "He stays close to my comrade, Heinrich – he has to," I didn't doubt it.

"So, thank you, for, you know, saving me that day," I said, sounding so lame.

"I am sorry that I had to rush off," he said doing that lopsided grin thing, making him look everything opposite to threatening.

"Well – you had all this pressing farming stuff to tend to," I was trying to flirt, badly, with a German called Horst. I liked his name – at least, I liked it better than Horse.

"I had flown all this way so I was keen to get started," his eyes were playful, holding mine.

"Is it hard? To be stuck here, I mean." I was determined not to break eye contact, but hoping I didn't look weird and intense.

"There are compensations and surprises – I did not expect to meet you in the water," he said it as if he had expected to meet me somewhere else. I was flustered and had to look away then.

"I knew if I treaded water long enough someone would fall out of the sky," I tried to sound light-hearted.

"Are you still treading water?"

"Kind of, like you, I guess. Hoping to find the way home."

"You cannot return?" he asked.

"I'm working on it," I said.

"As also am I," he said, lowering his voice. "But with Cornwall over-run with allies we must wait, yes?" I tried to look noncommittal, not sure if I should be doing war talk with the enemy.

"Your accent – you hardly sound like a German," I said, wishing he wasn't.

"Ich studierte hier," he made it sound cool, whatever it was he said.

"My German's worse than my French, and that's pretty rubbish."

"I studied here, before the war, and my mother is English. I dreamt of being an artist," he said. "But the Fuhrer does not value Yeats."

"Tread softly because you tread on my dreams, we did it in English. Hitler's more a jack-boot and nightmares man," I said. He laughed, but this time it didn't reach his eyes – was that because I was disrespecting Hitler or because he agreed with me?

"And what do you dream of Louie?" I loved how he made my name sound.

"Me? I used to dream of going home, when that meant going back to London, where I grew up, where my friends are, where I thought my life was about to begin. Now home is more simple, but it's everything. It's being with my family." I felt a lump in my throat, saying it out loud. He held my gaze again and neither of us said anything until Doreen tugged on his shirt.

"Can you make her a friend?" She meant the corn dolly she was holding up, not me. They sat down together on the grass and Doreen leaned into him. I envied their closeness as I stood awkwardly.

"Sit. Please sit with us," he said.

"I should go – George. He's probably looking for me," I lied.

"Rest a minute – I will leave soon. Albert's indulgence stretches only as far as he can see me," he said, shielding his eyes against the sun trying to locate his guard. I sat down and tugged at some long grass for the dolly's playmate.

"She is so much like my sister, Gisella. So full of life," he said ruffling Doreen's hair again so that her ribbon slipped.

"Here," I leant in to tie it back for her but squealed as a man with a rifle emerged from the long grass. It was Albert, the guard. He nodded to Horst, who was standing up, but shot me a look that made me feel I'd done something wrong.

"See you again?" said Horst. I tried to give a shrug that said yes please to Horst, but as if to Albert. Instead I looked as if I had a tummy ache. The grass swished behind them as they left, and I tried to conjure up all the reasons why I shouldn't be feeling the way I was.

Next morning, my waking thoughts were not on how to get home, or dodge death, or even Lady H's party that night, but Horst. I replayed the way he looked at me. His smile. How it made me feel. Guilty thoughts of Tom popped into my head, but this was different. It wasn't awkward; despite the wrongness of everything, it felt right to be with Horst. With Tom I'd felt excited but intimidated and almost relieved we moved away. I'd been scared to let the relationship develop but it was way easier to blame Mum and Dad for making it end before it had even started, than admit I'd felt uncomfortable about it in the first place – which was kind of bonkers because he wasn't even a Nazi. How could I have all these feelings for Horst? But that excitement wouldn't stay down, it kept bubbling up and I loved how it felt.

While I was thinking of Horst, everyone else was thinking about the party. Last night, the land girls talked about nothing else on the milking shift. I'd been watching Shirley. It was hard not to, she was so beautiful: willowy with a natural grace that meant even mundane farming tasks looked feminine and considered in her delicate hands. Where I would grab something, she would clasp it. I'd thought she was a bit distant, vague and probably not that much fun, but as I listened to her, stressing about what company had been invited to the Lady H's party, I discovered there was more to her than curly hair.

"I don't know who's been invited old thing," said Ellie in reply to Shirley. "Just the people Lady H likes – why?"

"I was thinking of asking Mallory and his friends, from the 531st Engineers," it meant nothing to me, just numbers and letters.

"The coloureds?" said Queenie. That meant something. "They won't get in."

"What? Why?" I asked.

"Segregation, ain't it?" said Blanche.

"You're kidding!" I said.

"The party's for military – they're not even proper soldiers," said Queenie. "My Hal says their brains is slow, only good for fixing and cleaning stuff. Says they smells different," she said, screwing up her nose and looking at me.

"Mallory's corps' been commended," snapped Shirley.

"Changing tyres don't make them heroes," said Queenie.

"Your Hal wouldn't be able to shift his jeep out of first gear, not even see a frontline, if it wasn't for them," said Shirley.

"Okay ladies, back to work," said Ellie.

"Mallory's Shirley's bloke," Blanche whispered. "He's bloody lovely."

"I can't believe they're segregated," I hissed back. "What happens when they go to war?"

"They don't," said Ellie who'd overheard. "The coloureds mainly do maintenance – a highly valuable and skilled service," she added looking at Shirley.

"But they do fight," my voice had gone weirdly high. "There's this black pilot, in the Red Arrows, no Red Tails." I was trying to remember. "Benjamin Davis. He was treated like sh- rubbbish, but ended up leading a squadron…I learnt it in Black History week."

"Black what?" scoffed Queenie. "Don't matter what week it is, no coloureds is allowed out tomorrow night."

"It's a private party," said Shirley. There's nothing to stop Mallory coming – Lady H likes him."

"So, blacks and whites go out on different nights?

"It's the colour bar, the yanks set it up – they have it in London, don't they?" asked Shirley.

"I – well. I didn't see much nightlife – what with the bombing and that," I hated lying.

"Most people here love them," said Ellie, looking at Queenie. "In the paper it said everyone in Cornwall liked the Americans, but not the whites they brought with them – the white GIs arrived after the blacks. Don't they mind being called black?"

"Mallory calls himself black but when I'm with him it doesn't matter what colour his skin is." said Shirley.

"You'd best keep that quiet if you wants a chance with a proper GI," said Queenie. "They won't touch you if they knows you's been with a coloured." I really didn't like her.

"When your Hal grows a bit taller you can talk to me about proper GIs," said Shirley.

"So you and this chap...?" began Ellie.

"Friends – he sings me the blues."

"The bleedin' whats?"

"Blues," I said. "I woke up one morning and my dog was dead – that sort of thing."

"Well, I prefer Glenn Miller," said Ellie. "And these cows won't milk themselves."

Lying in bed, I looked at my hands. Without sunscreen and an overdose of outdoors, they were getting darker; I looked in the tiny mirror. My hair was as big and wild as ever, my eyes had lost that scared saucer stare, but my face was darker. My colouring had never been an issue for me; obviously I was aware of my heritage, in that Grandpa Joshua was mixed race, but Dad was practically white, and Mum was white and the four of us kids were just another dilution away. I had half-heartedly tried to get more engaged with black issues, mainly at the insistence of Grandpa Josh, but I didn't think they affected me. Living in a multicultural place like London, it wasn't such a big deal as everyone was a different shade of something. It was only when we had moved to Cornwall that I began to feel different. But being here was a revelation. I couldn't believe I'd been so callous and disinterested in Wheezy.

How hard must it have been for her to bring up a mixed-race baby in post war Britain? I felt properly ashamed of my apathy.

Downstairs, Mother was washing sheets in the large kitchen sink. "Doreen again?" I asked.

"No, she seems much better since she took to you," she said. "This is what happens when three mucky boys shares a bed!" I rolled up my sleeves to help, but washing was hard work in 1944: scrubbing, wringing, rinsing and feeding heavy sodden sheets through a mangle.

"Right, my lover," said Mother as we mangled the last sheet. "As it's Saturday, and you done a lot better than I thought you would, you can have the day off," I wasn't expecting that. "You'll be wanting to go with the girls to Trenogar this evening?"

I'd decided I wasn't even going to bother asking. "Just don't be late back and don't have none of that gin she's famous for – those Yankies sees she has it on tap! You can take a bicycle, but make sure you keep them lights mostly taped up – don't want you getting shot at again."

I could have kissed her. Plunging my hands into the deep dungaree pockets, I felt the watch there and knew exactly what I was going to do with my day.

I found George in the yard, sorting out the bike for me making sure I understood that the lights must be taped over, leaving just a small slit.

"What's the point? I may as well just not turn them on."

"First off, how will you find your way home? There's no moon tonight. Second, how you going to pay for the fine when the policeman stops you?"

"The police have better things to do than catch cyclists with no lights!"

"Tell that to the lad what got fined a shilling last week in Probus. Keep 'em on."

"Yes, sir!" I saluted and George tried not to smirk.

In my room, Mother showed she was a step ahead of me. She'd left some dresses and cardigans draped over a chair and a pair of worn, but not awful, shoes on the floor beside them. I resisted smelling them and tried them on, settling on a pretty dress with small dark and light blue flowers. I felt strange not to be in dungarees, almost naked, as the cloth was so light. I chose the dark blue cardigan – I couldn't do peach, not even in wartime – and gave a little twirl in the room. My hair was less of a disaster as I twisted the long fringe to one side, weaved it into a loose ponytail at the back and tied it all up with a belt I took from another dress. I tried to angle the small mirror but seeing myself through Doreen's eyes told me I looked more than passable.

Inelegantly and uncomfortably, as the bicycle was heavy enough to be made of brick, I waved goodbye. Checking the skies for airplanes and tinsel, I saw only birds and white fluffy clouds. I felt happy. Finally, I had a plan that meant doing something practical.

Chapter TEN

The town was busy. I pushed the bicycle through the unfamiliar familiar streets. It was the weekend so there were more children, making the queues more playful. Games of tag were underway, hopscotch and that clapping thing that young girls do together, while mothers knitted and chatted above their heads.

I headed straight for the cathedral and found the watchmakers' I'd seen the other day. The window display was sparse but, stepping inside through the tinkling doorbell, I was overwhelmed by the number of clocks crammed into the tiny shop. Timepieces of every size and shape filled the walls, competing with each other in an orchestrated din of time passing.

"Yes?" said a voice. From a small door, behind the counter that divided the shop, came a grey man, his colour sucked out like juice from a lolly on a hot day. Sallow and gaunt with hollow cheeks, he had wild grey eyebrows that framed dull, disinterested eyes. The creases on his face sagged downwards, following the droop in his shoulders that didn't fill his jacket. Deflated, empty and weary, I couldn't decide if he was pitiful or scary.

"How come there's so many watches and clocks?" I said peering into the glass counter-top that was set out like an old fashioned sweet shop, with descending rows of wristwatches and fob watches.

"There is a war on, yes? There is rationing also." He spoke in quick staccato. "People can no longer afford the luxury of time. I buy their time; they buy their food. You want to buy or sell?"

"Why's your window's so bare then?"

"It is depressing for people to walk past the things they have had to sell."

"That's very thoughtful."

"It is just good business – who would want to visit a store that profits from misery? I select a few good pieces, not set out a jumble sale. Again. Are you buying, selling or just taking free commerce advice."

"Oh," he spoke so fast it took a moment to catch up with his sarcasm. "Neither. I have a watch. But it's broken. D'you do repairs?"

He allowed himself a brief sigh and I could tell he was about to say no until he saw my watch. He rammed a magnifying glass his eye socket, which was so bony it looked painful. It was strange handing it over, seeing it in his hands.

"Where did you get this?" He looked at me through the eyeglass, so he looked like a cartoon, but I didn't feel like laughing.

"It was my great grandmother's."

"That is not possible," the disjointed ticking of the clocks hurried him along.

"I'm sorry?"

"This watch. It is a new model, and yet it is undeniably old. How can this be?"

"Oh. It was new to my great grandmother, she, just didn't like it so she gave it to me,' I hadn't thought this through. "I'm a bit heavy handed."

"But it is worn, very worn and – full of sea water?"

"Yes, well. I wish I –"

"I have never seen anything like this," he interrupted. "This type, yes, this I am very familiar with, but the condition. Who sent you?"

"Who…? No-one. I – saw your shop. Maybe I should go somewhere else," I reached out for my watch.

"No. No. I am the only one who deals in these. Curious."

"Can you get it going again?"

"This is not a motorcar. It will take time – you have money?"

An excellent question to which I lied, "Of course."

Stepping back onto the street, it was a relief to close the door on the sounds of time ticking away. But I was bereft. I'd let go of the only tangible thing that linked me to my own timeline. I looked at the receipt: Wolenski and Sons. I didn't see any sons and was that a German name? He certainly sounded German.

Military traffic roared past, the cobbled streets amplifying their noise. Back on the brick-bike, I followed the line of trucks and wobbled my way out of town. Technically, it was a city not a town as it had a cathedral, but compared to London, the city I knew and loved, this place was a village. Even in my day it was small and parochial, but that was a good thing, given that we were at war, its timidity making it an unlikely target.

Traffic lessened, roads narrowed, and the countryside grew. Bluebells were everywhere, great blankets of them dusted by little yellow flowers that looked like dandelions but weren't. Ferns were unfurling and fresh leaves filling trees with life and newness. Spring continued, oblivious to the war machine – that was about to slam right into me! An American jeep had thundered out of nowhere, giving me a split second to choose which body part would be least mashed if I swerved left or right. I can't remember how I chose but I do remember I closed my eyes. When I opened them again the jeep was behind me and I shouted a blisteringly ineffective "road hog!" The driver made a hand gesture that had none of the hallmarks of charm for which the Americans were famed.

My heartrate slowed and I came to a junction, but a convoy stopped me from going any further. I had to wait at least five minutes while hundreds of jeeps and lorries, cram packed with military personnel and paraphernalia, barrelled past. Unsure if I should be saluting or waving, I did the British thing and ignored them.

As I approached the smallholding, she was picking wildflowers from between the rows of vegetables growing in front of the house. "Such a bore not to be able to grow real flowers in this dreary war. Flowers do so lift ones' spirits, don't you think?"

"They do, Lady H," I felt awkward saying her name. "But wildflowers have a softer beauty that can be just as cheerful as more formal arrangements," I sounded like a Jane Austen character.

"You can't possibly believe that?" She said, but with a smile. "Do you know, my second cousin Hattie, over on the Roseland, grows the most marvellous Marigolds in between the vegetables we all have to grow. If anyone asks, she says they keep off the aphids. She smuggles them to Mayfair in a coffin! Isn't that marvellous? So much more fun than a potato, don't you think?"

She was a striking woman, shining conspicuously in the middle of rural Cornwall. The dress she wore was exquisite, with every shade of blue swimming lightly around her so that she always seemed to be moving. I felt intimidated but knew I had to keep going and asked if I could have a word. But I ended up using too many, too quickly and too loudly.

"I'm not a land girl, I'm not old enough, so I don't earn a wage and it's as much as the Dorcas' can do to feed me given all the other evacuees and their own children," I took a breath. "Please don't think me impertinent, but I couldn't help noticing it's only you and Primrose and I was wondering if you might need a little help, like with the party tonight. I'm great at washing up, cleaning, cooking even…"

"You want to char for me?"

"Well – I," I hadn't thought of it like that.

"Splendid! Between us, Primrose ankles swell terribly and those bunions, well, they don't help – would half a crown suffice?" I had no idea how much that was, but it was a start. I was on my way.

"Well, carpe diem, or whatever that ghastly Latin phrase is. Primrose will be in the pantry." The house suited Lady H. It was Georgian with high ceilings, huge sash windows and would have been grand in its day. It was still an elegant, calm place that felt self-assured but not imposing. It didn't seem to mind that its paint was flaking, paper fading or ornate cornicing crumbling in places. In a different time, walls will be pulled back to pencil sharp lines, floors levelled and doors will close properly, but something will be lost. Now its worn limestone entrance hall at the foot of a sweeping staircase would greet Lady H's guests, making them feel special just because they were there.

Primrose welcomed me into her domain and, over the next hours, revealed the stockpiled treasures of her pantry. As I was to discover, it was a fair exchange. Lady H flattered, entertained, and in many cases, put back together broken soldiers. In return the regiments, American, British and otherwise, brought gifts that enabled Lady H to be such an abundant host. Primrose showed me how to make the cocktails, including the Gin Gimlets the girls had talked about. It was Rose's Lime Cordial, which, Primrose said, was naval issue for preventing scurvy, mixed with gin. But her favourite tipple was Black Velvet, Champagne and Guinness. Champagne was a stretch, even for Lady H, so Primrose was substituting it with something homemade, fizzy and potent. In between musings over the correct quantities to achieve optimum velvetiness, Primrose began to fill me in on the lady of the house.

Lady H's family, the Hempsteads, had lost their money in the depression and had to move from their elegant country house in Hampshire to this smallholding in Cornwall. She had two sons who were away at war; her husband had been killed in the First World War. She knew little about farming, and Primrose even less, but, somehow, they had managed to scrabble together a small business supplying eggs and chickens. The economics of the venture had something to do with keeping clever books and the Ministry of Agriculture.

Unfortunately, Primrose was sampling all her attempts to make the perfect Black Velvet, so she was making less and less sense. It was a bit like having a conversation with someone whose' mobile kept going out of range, so I missed about one in every five words. I was grateful to escape when I heard Ellie, Shirley and Blanche in the hallway and went through to take their coats, and cream.

"Swapping your boots and dungarees for the good life and a pinny?" said Blanche.

"I'm just helping out, so I can earn a bit of cash."

"Good for you," said Shirley, "now where're the drinks?"

"Make mine a pale ale," said Blanche.

The guests arrived all at once. Young men self-consciously smart in new military uniforms, older men comfortable in their well-worn ones and elderly men in their tweed countryside uniforms, hankering after the military uniforms of their past. Transcending the ranks were the girls in frocks.

"Shall I help with the nibbly bits?" asked Ellie and I gratefully thrust a tray of unappetising dry biscuits spread with grey meat paste in her hands. The GIs came laden with their gifts and one, very young with shiny hair, offered me an orange.

I was in the process of waving it away, preferring easy-peelers, when Ellie stepped in and caught his crest before it fell, "Ooh an orange! May I? How clever of you to find it!"

Queenie was proudly parading Hal, who, with his red and over-scrubbed face, looked as unappealing as when he'd bawled out Ira. She was holding a canapé as if eating was an inconsequential activity that she rarely took part in. Blanche was head to head with Ira, sharing an intimate joke. I wished Horst were there. Ira caught me watching them and patted his backside; I think that joke had run its course.

Ripples became gales of laughter as drinks flowed and stories of daring do were passed round, like the RAF officers with dogfight tales of how they chased Jerry down. Then the wind dropped, the tenor changed, and haunting music rose gently throughout the house. In the drawing room, Shirley was sat at a grand piano, playing Clare de Lune. Everyone stopped to listen to the beautiful young woman lost in Debussy's magical waves. I'd heard the tune on a hundred soundtracks, but never felt it in the way I did then. Shirley was spinning a whispery web of enchantment, throwing it further out in ever more mesmerising patterns, so that we didn't know we'd been pushed to the edge.

My tricky friend time held everyone in the moment and I saw what they did, peering over the edge: fear, loss, destruction and degradation; the noise of bullets, explosions; friends falling, dying or dead in the water, on the beaches, the horror of having to keep moving past their bodies. And my heart felt weak from the pain it carried for them all. The faces that had filled the house with vitality now betrayed a longing for home and a life different to the one ahead.

Shirley wasn't looking down at the piano keys, but up to a tall soldier who had his back to the party. There was a look of pure joy on her face as she met the kiss he bent down to give her. Someone applauded, a glass tinkled, the moment was broken.

"What the hell?" It was Queenie's Hal.

Shirley's soldier drew himself to his full height and turned to look down at the apoplectic Hal. It must be Mallory. As Blanche said, he was bleedin' lovely. He had a softness about him that was instantly appealing, his eyes shone like coal and his skin was a rich chocolate that ran smoothly over the strong, elegant contours of his face.

"How did you get in?" the piano stool scraped as Shirley stood up and linked her arm through Mallory's.

"I'm a guest here, same as you, and I would be grateful for the opportunity – "

"You are NOT the same as me. Get the hell out of here. That's an order, soldier."

"I'm awfully sorry to interrupt old man," said one of the elderly tweed-ed-brigade. "This a private party on British soil, not an adjunct to your military base," he was leaning on a stick but doing his best to raise himself and stand shoulder to shoulder with Shirley's friend. The pair of them easily outclassed Hal. "We are all guests of our generous host Lady Hempstead and you will find, sergeant, that there is no colour bar in operation here. If you are unhappy with the company in which you find yourself, Lady Hempstead would not mind if you made your excuses and left, quietly."

"Quite so," said yet another tall but much younger man in a British military uniform. "This is most off," except he didn't say 'off' but 'orf.' He turned to the old man and extended his hand. "Hello sir, still keeping us all in line then?"

"Hayward? My word, a lieutenant. I never doubted it!"

"Ha! Oh yes you did! So, you're still heading up the old place, sir?"

"I was about to retire, but this blasted war – school needed a safe pair of hands."

"Well, none safer sir," they shook hands again as Lady H came over.

"Thank you, Cornelius," she said to what I guessed was a school headmaster, taking his hand and patting it gently. He lifted hers to his lips and kissed it gently.

73

"Would be a damn shame to break up such a wonderful party, Kitty," he replied.

"Louie. My guests need drinks," she said sweeping her eyes across the group gathered around the piano.

"Thank you, Lady H," said Shirley. "You remember Mallory, from the 531st Engineers?"

"Of course, hello again Mallory," she said extending her hand to his. "I do hope my old friend Dickie is treating you well during your sojourn on his golf course."

"Sir Richard is a generous host, ma'am," he said smiling. "We're always sure to return his golf balls when we find them in between all the tents and tyre tracks."

Hal, a boiling kettle of a man with a dodgy off switch, ignored the offer of a drink and hooked his arm through Queenie's to march his woman away. She gave me a backwards glare that told me I was to blame, before colliding with some of Mallory's friends walking in with trumpets, saxophones and great dance music.

Everyone took to the floor: girls, skirts, stockings and big knickers flew through the air, over the heads of the GIs then in between their legs. How freeing it must feel, tossing aside the restraints of past social etiquette and, for some girls, enjoying the first thrill of being physically close to a man.

The evening slipped into karaoke, circa 1944. I hid in the kitchen; there was no dishwasher, just me, a sink and hundreds of glasses, so I had an excuse. Primrose had passed out long ago. I gave up at just before midnight and sat at the back of the drawing room to listen. Lady H was doing a Vera Lynn but saw me as she finished and beckoned me over. "Louie, this is Louie everybody!" She was introducing me as if I was the next act, and the guests were applauding in anticipation – of what?

I'd been tossed back in time, crashed into, shot at, taken for a crazy – how much worse was it to have all those tipsy faces looking at me, with the expectation that I would be able to sing. Horst, who had never been far from my thoughts, and his reference to WB Yeats came to mind so I recited the poem we'd learnt at school:

Had I the heavens' embroidered cloths,
Enwrought with golden and silver light,
The blue and the dim and the dark cloths
Of night and light and the half light,
I would spread the cloths under your feet:
But I, being poor, have only my dreams;
I have spread my dreams under your feet;
Tread softly because you tread on my dreams.

I was applauded enthusiastically, no doubt because everyone was wasted, and made a hasty exit to the kitchen, the back door and the sanctity of the night sky and my bicycle.

Double summertime might have pushed the clocks and stretched the daylight by two hours, but the sun had long since taken its hat off and gone to bed. The slim slit of brightness from the bicycle lamp did little to lighten the velvety darkness, but the stars... Man, they were amazing. Without a hint of light pollution, the panorama was epic, crystal clear and truly magnificent in all its sparkling glory as it stretched effortlessly across the heavens. Every star had a purpose making the one next to it more beautiful just by being there. I prayed, asking God what my purpose was, desperate for a sign or, better still, a doorway to take me home. But the silence that swept across the skies was empty and unsatisfying.

Chapter ELEVEN

Sunday. Early. Light peeped unapologetically over windowsill. Black outs. Forgot to pull across. Sunday. Shouldn't find its way to me until I let it. Or until Mum yells, "We're going to church, you're coming." Love to hear her yell now. No voices from the space between waking and sleeping. Sunday. Church. Meeting place. Opportunity.

There was no choice about going to church, options weren't discussed or even considered. It was the one on the cove where I'd seen my own grave a lifetime ago and, despite telling myself I wouldn't, I couldn't but help look at the plot where I would be buried. I gripped Doreen's hand tighter and concentrated on the land girls instead, surprised to see so many of them. "Wow, they look smart!" I said.

"I'm going to be one when I grow up," said Doreen. They wore sandy jodhpurs with long socks pulled up to their knees and boys' shoes; bottle green sweaters with a green felt armband worn on the left sleeve with red WLA lettering and a crown; buttoned up shirts, green stripy tie and a brown trilby hat. Dressed in their official uniforms they looked official, validated and valued, except Blanche had told me a story that suggested that wasn't necessarily the case.

She'd been travelling back from visiting her dad in London. "I'd been on eight or nine bleedin' trains and I was parched. I'd stopped at Exeter to change again and the only railway canteen open said 'servicemen or women only,' that's okay, I thought, I had my kit on, even the stupid bleedin' hat. But the dozy cow behind the counter said she weren't allowed to serve me "on account of me not being a WREN or a WAAF."

"But you're in the Women's Land Army," I'd said.

"Tried that one, but she was having none of it. I know her type, thinks she's something special. Cooks with herbs, as my mum would have said."

I tried not to smile, "What did you do?"

"I was just about to throw out a choice swear word I'd heard down the underground in the air-raids, when this soldier geezer behind me goes: 'Give her a cuppa cha and throw in a bath bun. My shout.' He was bleedin' lovely, and came on the train with me, at least until Plymouth. Hope he's survived the bombing they've had."

I'd have given Blanche a cup of tea. These weren't teenagers on a gap year; this was proper war work, as the annoying Miss Probert had said on that day back in the classroom. They worked hard, doing heavy manual farm jobs that men usually did; Ellie explained that some land girls were in the Timber Corp which meant tree felling, land clearance and rat catching. I suddenly felt angry that Wheezy had had to wait over sixty years after the end of the war to get her medal of recognition, and she was one of the lucky ones. Many of the land girls didn't survive that long. I shrank again from my callousness to the lonely old lady that had come to stay with us.

The church entrance was unchanged; I froze for a moment. Maybe it was a portal, linking both time zones. I braced myself on the threshold and closed my eyes. "Hurry up dozy mare!" It wasn't. I took an offered hymn-book, surprised to see who was further down the welcoming line.

"Hi, Mr Wolenski," he looked puzzled. "You have my watch? The old, new one?"

"Ah."

"How's it going? The repair?"

"Please. Pursue your enquiry at my shop, where I can be found every day, except today."

I scurried red-faced to an empty seat. A POW walked past, and I turned quickly to see Horst walking in; his hair was sticking up again and I could tell by the sweet smiles the old ladies gave him, he had flashed those baby blues and crooked grin at them. He made his way to Wolenski.

It was done so deftly I wasn't sure I'd really seen it. The watchmaker handed Horst a book from the bottom of his pile, no eye contact, flash of recognition or even a smile. He walked past and sat down across the aisle with the rest of the POWs and I checked out his profile, for reconnaissance purposes, watching how he handled the hymnbook, half expecting a hollow, cartoon gun-shaped cut away. But I saw nothing suspicious, just his comrade, Heinrich, whispering incessantly.

The first hymn started, accompanied by an organist who I knew to be Shirley just by the back of her elegant frame and curly hair. The tweeded headmaster stood up to give the Bible reading. I wondered if he was the current-past-headmaster of my future school, thinking how convoluted terminology was for time-slippers, which meant I didn't immediately notice that he was reading from Esther, the same passage that Angel Rev had preached on.

The vicar, austere in his dark robes, thanked the headmaster and made his way to the pulpit. I suppressed a sigh in anticipation of the boredom that would surely follow. Doreen must have felt it too as she rested her head on my shoulder and settled down for a nap. He looked over the heads of everyone, making a poor comparison to Angel Rev. Her robes were never dull; she always wore a stole that children must have scribbled on and someone clever had embroidered over. She'd smile, draw the congregation in, soften and relax them, then fire her darts. They'd be pointed and hard hitting, usually about intolerance, judging others or exclusivity, but done so lovingly the sting was rarely immediate.

This vicar was disengaged and dry, but he didn't need any darts. His words were like a sledgehammer to me. Unlike Angel Rev, he didn't have the benefit of hindsight; he didn't know that Haman, Esther's antagonist, was a forerunner to Hitler.

Haman wanted to slaughter all the Jews: 'to destroy, to kill, and to cause to perish, all Jews, both young and old, little children and women, in one day…' Esther was faithful to God and accepted that she was born for such a time as this, that she shouldn't just keep quiet. Her bravery meant she outwitted Haman, saved all the Jews and got him killed on the gallows he'd had built for her uncle, Mordecai. He repeated part of the reading:

"For if you remain completely silent at this time, relief and deliverance will arise for the Jews from another place, but you and your father's house will perish. Yet who knows whether you have come to the kingdom for such a time as this?"

It felt like he was talking just to me.

There would be no deliverance for the Jews! I wanted to shout. I'm not keeping silent, but what can I do? It's happening now, but I can't stop it. I can't. It's not fair that you expect me too! I clasped my mouth, kept my head down and shuffled my way out of the pew. I wanted to run, get away from this place, where a week ago all I had to worry about was stopping my dog peeing on its headstones, until I'd found my own grave.

"I say, you alright?" It was the guy from last night – Hayley or Hayworth. I hastily wiped the snot from my nose.

"No. Yes. I don't know. Sorry."

"Here," and he handed me a huge handkerchief. I blew my nose, loudly – I'd never mastered doing it quietly – and hesitated before offering it back to him.

"No, really, it's all yours," he smiled, and I could see that he was very good looking: blond hair, green eyes and the chiselled features of posh English actors.

"Thanks. I, " I didn't know what to say. Do you know that millions of Jews are being murdered now, on this sunny Sunday afternoon? You wear a uniform, what can you do about it? What can I do about it? How can we make it stop and re-write history? Instead I just looked at him and sobbed again.

"Hey, it's alright, really," he said softly, sitting down on the grass next to me. "Nothing can be that bad."

"D'you think?" I snapped, not caring about when I was. I blew my nose again, even louder and I think he flinched. "It's just, right now – terrible things are happening, horrific, worst ever – never before, or after – so many children, innocent people, weak, old, so much loss, unimaginable cruelty and pain. Right now." I could barely speak through my tears. "So hard to know it… and not be able to stop it…" I took a moment to try to compose myself and looked at him directly, "Are you a good soldier?"

"They tell me I am." He was taken aback, either by the question or my incoherent ranting, but was obviously too well brought up to show it. "I'm not sure if shooting down young German pilots makes me a good man, but it makes me a good soldier, if that helps."

"It helps," although I felt guilty when I thought of Horst; was he shot down by someone like this guy? "But. What would you do if you had a really big secret, too big to hold in, and the information, if it was believed, may help to save millions of people, but if it was revealed it would change the course of history with possibly catastrophic effects that would be dangerous, dangerous for everyone, not just now but forever after. What would you do?"

"I'd share it with a friend, I think."

"Ha! Phone a friend" I shook my head in my lap.

"That would be good, and win a million too." I knew I wasn't making sense but I didn't care. "I'm sorry – I'm sure you are a good soldier, or airman – is that the right title?"

"Friend would do. My name is Johnny." Johnny Hayworth, it sounded a good name.

"Louie," I said.

"Louie!" It was Ellie. "Gosh – you alright?"

"She's a bit overwrought," said Johnny.

"Over-tired from the party," she said.

"I am here, y'know!" I said getting to my feet.

People were trickling out of the church: some desperate to make a hasty retreat, others lingering in the doorway, hoping to shake the vicar's hand and have their attendance noted in the register they thought he kept in his head. Doreen saw me and ran over; I stuffed the hanky and sense of helplessness in my pocket and forced my face into a smile. She slipped her little hand in mine as Mother and the rest of the Dorcas tribe congregated around us.

"Didn't take no heed of what I said 'bout Misses' gin then," said Mother.

"I did, it's not that – I,"

"Mother Dorcas, how splendid to see you, and George," said Johnny.

"Johnny? Look George, it's little Johnny all smart in his RAF uniform. How's your mum?"

"She's quite well Mother, and I'm sure would send her best wishes if she knew I'd seen you," it seemed good old Johnny was everyone's friend. Doreen was tugging at my arm. She had seen Horst and was frantically waving at him. He rewarded her with a glittering smile that he tried to share with me, but I couldn't return it. He was Hitler's or Haman's; he couldn't be mine.

"Are you really alright, old thing?" whispered Ellie.

"Not really – I didn't expect to see you here."

"I'm on safe ground – I don't think Reverend Merryweather's much of a one for the New Testament!"

"Didn't it bother you though – all that about killing Jews and that."

"It's an allegory – from a very long time ago."

"But –"

"I come to be still, trying to connect with God however I can, even using a different doorway."

"But – your family, Ellie, the ones in Germany."

"Aunty Ruth? I spoke to Daddy, he's sure they're fine. Ruthie's very cautious, probably keeping her head down until it blows over." That hellish wind wasn't going to blow over, not until everything had been torched.

"Ellie, there's something you should know."

"It's bleedin' hot in this get-up," Blanche, on cue. "Gawd – look at you. What was it, permanent wave that went wrong? Why ain't you in uniform?"

"I'm not a land girl," I said, trying to flatten down my hair. "Too young. I'm an evacuee, staying with the Dorcas."

"Really? I thought you were just waiting for your kit to arrive," said Shirley. "Queenie's not here is she?" she said looking around anxiously.

"Nah. Squirreled away with that ugly little git of hers. What a piece of…"

"And how's Ira?" asked Ellie quickly.

"Ira…well, he gave me something to think about instead of – Hey! Check out blondie from last night. The old trout's flirtin' with him!" She was looking across at Mother, who was smiling and laughing with Johnny, totally transforming her face.

"Those things destroy your lungs," I said as Shirley lit up. "Clog your arteries. Make it hard to get pregnant…"

"Pass 'em round then!" said Blanche with a look to Shirley that said dancing wasn't all they were trying out last night.

"You're careful, aren't you? I mean, you know, using protection?"

"Gawd love us, hark at her!" said Blanche. I was beginning to understand how Mum had felt when she tried to have exactly the same conversation with me.

"Just be careful – these guys, I mean, they're leaving soon. Any day. Off to – goodness knows where. And what happens to you?" I was bright red.

"Louie. It's terribly kind of you to be so concerned," said Ellie. "No one is doing anything daft. Everyone needs to have a bit of fun, there's precious little of that around here." I looked towards my plot in the graveyard – maybe they were right. None of us knew how long, or how short, that life might be.

Chapter TWELVE

The sky was that perfect blue that made everything look unreal. Mother said it was going to rain, but there wasn't a hint of it as I stood at the edge of a field, next to one of those tall pieces of ragged granite.

"It is strange, yes?" It was the good-looking Italian POW who had wanted me as his wife.

"Probably signifies a stage of the summer solstice," I said. "A focal point for worship."

"No, my lover. T'is a scratchin' post for cows," said George. I was working with him and the Italian POWs, determined to keep away from Horst who was at the far end of the field. George kept us all hard it, making no concession to age or gender even when, like Mother predicted, the weather broke. She either had that farmers' sixth sense, smelling rain out of a clear blue sky, or had heard a weather forecast. I copied the others and grabbed a sack from the back of the tractor, ignoring the stink of animal feed as I threw it over my head.

Only when the thunder roared, lightning crackled and rain cascaded so that we couldn't see in front of us, did George relent. He ushered all the crews under the semi shelter of a large oak tree that was furniture and firewood in my timeline. The lightning spooked some of the Italians as it ripped across the sky, but I knew it wasn't looking for me; I was safe, at least for a few more weeks.

"We seem to be thrown together with water," said a voice close to my ear, instantly diluting my determination to despise him. I didn't turn around but was fully conscious of Horst's presence. The air was heavy with smells from the rain, the ground, tree, feed-sacks and maleness. It was new to me; it wasn't the smell of boys in the gym. "It would be good to be this close when the sun is shining," he said, lowering his voice and dropping his head so that I could feel his breath in my ear.

He moved closer and an electrical current that had nothing to do with atmospheric conditions shot through me. The rain bucketed down, eased then stopped as quickly as it had started so we emerged from our huddle, our wet cottons and woollens weighing us down. George took one look at his sorry crew and gave up, letting us make our way down the hill for a break at least. The rain allowed informality to the bedraggled group.

"In a different time, I'd take you out, we'd see a film, walk in the sunshine – or rain," said Horst. His hair was flattened and water was dripping down his nose. I so wanted to wipe it away.

"But you're a Nazi."

"I have to wear the badge. It doesn't mean I share the ideology."

"But you do their work. I know what's going on over there."

"It is war."

"It's carnage!"

"I don't under-"

"No." I checked myself. "Maybe you don't. But I do. In the camps. To the Jews."

"Louie, war is –"

"But – "

"Let me finish. War is complex: for some it is noble, bright. Courageous. For others it's dark, malevolent. A perfect foil to feed evil, vile fantasies that become real –"

"What's it for you?"

"It's a deadly game I have to play, in the shadows, without rules."

"In the dark then."

"War is always a shade of darkness – there is light, but my job is to hide it."

"Hide or extinguish?"

"If I had a choice," he sighed. "I wouldn't be at war. I'd be here, studying art, reflecting on how beautiful you look with your wild hair and eyes so full of compassion and concern, wondering how I could capture the intoxicating essence of you." I blushed, but he was avoiding the issue.

"There's always a choice."

"That is surprisingly naive," he looked directly at me, fixing me with those eyes. "The Fuhrer. He offers no choices, not when you have family, people relying on you – you must know that. If you don't do as you're told," he ran his hand through his hair in exasperation, "the consequences are swift, brutal." I did know, but only because history had shown me. I didn't know because I had experienced it, my family had never been in danger.

"I'm sorry," I said.

"Can't we use this precious time to talk about something else?" So, we tried to shift to safer ground – art. I'd loved Henry Moore's sketches of people sleeping on the Underground platforms during air-raids, but didn't know if he'd even drawn them yet. Besides, I didn't know if I should tell a Luftwaffe pilot that that was where Londoners took shelter. He wanted to talk about Kandinsky and Pollock. "A Russian and an American – controversial," I teased. "And, of course, you know what Hitler says about artists like them?"

"Yes, Louie I do," he sighed. "Anyone caught paintings skies green and fields blue will be sterilized. He calls it Entartete Kunst, or Degenerate Art that corrupts young people like me, giving us dangerously free-thinking ideas. It is heart-breaking how many artists are in hiding, fearing for their lives, and how many masterpieces have been destroyed. They say that art transcends politics and war, but we both know, in these dark times, that is a lie."

"I'm sorry – I didn't mean to be flippant." I'd read about the drunken burning parties where stolen precious artworks were thrown on mass pyres. "I promise not to go to go off on one again," I said.

"I'm not sure I understand off on one!" I laughed and tried to explain but we were half-way down the hill and had reached the upper entrance to Higher Farm.

"Right my girl, get yourself indoors and dried off," said George.

Long after watching the POWs being driven away, I'd pulled across the blackouts and was shivering in bed. I hadn't felt cold at all when I was with

85

Horst but, without a hot shower and being too tired to tackle the bath drama, dampness had seeped into my bones and I couldn't get warm. I pulled the covers up tight, closed my eyes and waited. Before long the tiniest of bubbles began to rise and pop, releasing a burst of warmth that came from recalling being with him.

Even though I knew I shouldn't, I let more bubbles surface and surrendered to their warmth, wondering, as they fulfilled such a need within me, what had filled that space before? What was there before this excitement and longing? It wasn't Tom – what I felt now seemed childish by comparison. I realised I hadn't come alive, I'd been waiting for something to happen and now it was happening, but in a time outside of my own. What was the point? There was no way forward. Getting home meant leaving him behind to get old, like Wheezy, or even killed. Not getting home meant me filling that hole in the ground in a few short weeks. Even if it were possible to put all of that to one side, he 'wore the badge' for the most infamous personification of evil, ever.

Sleep was slow to come. One moment I picked up memories of the day like seashells from the beach, the next I was drowning. How was I going to die? Would it hurt? How could I just be no more…I stared into the complete darkness of my room, the blackouts doing their job, feeling very scared and very alone. Was that how it would be?

I wasn't with Ellie on the rounds the next day, but Shirley. I was tired from lack of sleep and irritable. I wanted to get through it quickly, but it was like cycling uphill with a chain that kept coming off. Shirley had her own agenda and way of doing things. We went a different route, but the same people met us to demand their milk and gossip.

Yes, Mrs Dorcas is fine, she says, and don't worry she says, she won't forget to remind her about the whist drive on Thursday. Betty Grable on at the Regent? Mustn't miss that, she says, thought it was on at the Plaza, which is a shame as the Regent is so much nicer, she says. What she didn't say was who gives a damn? Which is what I wanted to say. I wanted to line up all the jugs then fill them like shots on a bar. But I didn't. I dutifully trudged back and forth with milk, butter and fake smiles until finally we were on our way back. Except we weren't.

Shirley had turned off at the golf course that was now a camp, the one that wasn't a festival full of bell tents. Today they looked like colourless, miniature big top circus tents, except they were filled with black GIs, not performers. Who needed circus clowns with Shirley next to me? She was singing a terrible song:

"Maizy doats and dozy doats and liddle lamzy divey!"/ A kiddley divey too. Wouldn't you? Yes!" Mercifully, she brought the song and the truck to a halt as a black man in a white helmet asked us both for ID.

"Sure. Louie. My card, I threw it under the dashboard." I rummaged around in the wide shelf below the dials, finding the unassuming little folded card, briefly glancing at it. I froze. "Come on. Pass it to me," it was so weird. "Louie!" I stared at the woman next to me in the truck. She was saying my name again, something about the guard then reached towards me and snatched the card from my hand.

"And yours ma'am?"

"Sorry?" I said.

"Your ID, you great 'nana," said Shirley.

"My ID," I said, snapping back to where I should be, patting the empty pockets of my dungarees. "Must have left it behind," I lied.

"Well, ma'am, by rights I should not be letting let you pass. All these here camps, and in fact the whole goddamn area down by the creeks and waterlines are now in the restricted zone."

"I can't lug those churns by myself! Come on Frank, you know me – please?" Frank was having difficulty resisting a pretty face, but not as much difficulty as I was having with that same face. He must have succumbed because we were on the move again. I was pretty sure my jaw was in my lap.

"Yes? Why are you staring? A simple thank you would suffice," Shirley said pulling up outside a large wooden hut.

"Why didn't it say Shirley on your ID?

"Why didn't you have yours?"

"I lost it, when I got shot on my first day here," I improvised. "I thought your name was Shirley."

"Oh for goodness sakes," she said and grasped a handful of her pretty curly long hair, holding it towards me as if it should mean something. I stared back blankly.

"You really are a 'nana aren't you?"

"I don't get it."

"I'm Shirley Temple," she was singing again, "the girl with curly hair…!" Either she'd lost it, or I had. "There were two Eloise's in my class, and as I had curly hair and my surname is Shircliff, my teacher called me Shirley and it stuck."

"Wheezy?" I said, trying to find something of her reflected in the beautiful face.

"Sorry?"

I coughed and smacked my chest, embarrassed.

"Wheezy," I said. "Bit congested." How was this possible? How could I reconcile this stunning young woman, with the shuffling, slipper-wearing old lady from my future world? Shame wrapped itself around me once more, heavy, hot and suffocating. I vaguely knew I was my great grandmother's namesake, but distanced myself, preferring to think of her as Wheezy, an unimaginative nickname for an old lady who couldn't get her breath quickly enough. Now I could see it was a cute derivative of Eloise. Wheeze… Wheezy: a name given to her by someone in the family way more affectionate than me.

I looked at Shirley, or my great grandmother, and was overwhelmed. Her poise, delicate English rose beauty and gift for music – none of which I'd inherited. I didn't even know Wheezy played the piano. But I realised she still wanted to; we'd all ignored her pleas for a piano as inane ramblings. A surge of emotion welled up inside.

I'm so sorry, I said silently, making a promise to do everything I could to make it up to her, if I ever got back. Instantly, she became someone I wanted to please; I wanted her to like me but, having felt slightly intimidated, now I just felt awkward. It like she was famous, not that I knew anyone famous, but how I imagined it would feel. Everything I did and said felt fake, as if I was trying too hard, which of course I was.

We unloaded the milk churns, the weight of them less of a shock now and besides, I had enough adrenaline pumping through me to lift two at a time. An evocative smell wafted out of the hut. It was food, but not the 1940s meat and two veg variety. I was walking through Brixton Market on a steamy summer's day: heat over-ripening the smelly food stalls; exotic pop-up restaurants, uncollected rubbish, smoking, traffic jams. My empty tummy cried out; it was like smelling someone else's takeaway when you were really hungry. Then we both saw him, and all thoughts of hunger banished. Tall and glorious, taking a few long happy strides to meet us, Mallory shared the widest smile that was really just for Shirley. Was this my great grandfather?

I hung back. Some large jugs sat on the table; should I start filling them, or leave the churns and look around for the empties? I made the wrong choice; the churn was way too heavy to lift, balance and pour with any accuracy into the jug. It buckled under the weight, clattering to the floor unmusically, milk pouring from the lip of the churn that had slammed onto the edge of the table.

"You clumsy clot!" shouted Shirley. "There's milk everywhere!"

"I'm so sorry – don't worry, I'm on it," I lied, up-righting the churn and looking for a cloth. I tried to appear calm and in control, but it didn't help that it looked as if I'd wet myself.

"I think this may be helpful," it was Mallory, swinging a bucket and mop. He was still smiling.

"Thanks," I said, "leave it to me. You guys, you just carry on." But I'd broken their spell and Shirley was furious. The three of us worked to clear up my mess, organise the milk, store the churns and take away the empty ones.

"Beats me why you'd want to pour milk into the water jugs," said Mallory.

"Oh! Are they not – I just – I thought, like, on the rounds," I felt an idiot, but Mallory seemed more amused than irritated, unlike Shirley. I mouthed an exaggerated sorry, but she was unimpressed.

"So, you're Mallory," I said as we finished up.

"Sure am – didn't I see you at the party?" He had such an open, kind face.

89

"I was pouring drinks."

"You were kept real busy!"

"This is Louie – she works with us, sort of," said Shirley, unhappy how her rendezvous was panning out.

"Good to meet you Miss Louie," he said with another broad grin, extending his huge hand to mine and shaking it firmly. "Hey, you know a jazz man called Louis Armstrong?"

"Satchmo? Sure do." Sure do? I never say 'sure do.' Shirley eyebrows shot skywards.

"D'you play?" asked Mallory.

"The trumpet? No – well, I used to, I did grade four – but, no, not anymore," No, would have done.

"Great – join us for one of our sessions, hey Shirley?"

"That would be 'swell'," said my great grandmother with the sort of smile that said it absolutely would not be.

"Well… this is cleared up," I began, "I'll go wait in the truck. Take your time; I've got some notes to write – letters, that is, not musical notes – " Shut up! I backed away, trying discreetly to pick up the last two empty milk churns, but still managed to bump them noisily together and then against the table as I left.

Outside, I tried to piece together what just happened. If Shirley was my great grandmother, Mallory was surely my great grandfather. But that would mean he wouldn't come back from D Day. Shirley would be pregnant, unmarried and alone. Left to bring up a mixed-race illegitimate child through the forties and fifties, an era not noted for its tolerance. No wonder she retreated to the land of make believe in her dotage.

Meeting them both was weird but quite cool. For the first time I felt the thrill of time travel; how many people get to meet their great grandparents when they're young? I'd only ever thought of Wheezy as shrivelled and deflated – I never pictured her flying. I longed to get back to be with her, hoping there would be time to make amends. I was her namesake. I felt a rush – we both shared the same name. Did that mean we were both in a game of musical gravestones? Which one of us would be in that hole when the music stopped?

Chapter THIRTEEN

The truck was quiet, apart from,

"Mallory seems nice," and

"Yes."

I was scared to say anything else. My heart wanted to befriend this beautiful woman, make her like me and try in some way to make up for the shabby way I'll treat her when she's old. My head said keep quiet and slip into her background; just by being here I was running the risk of changing outcomes. Who knows, the scene I'd just made could have distracted the lovers from progressing their relationship to a vital stage.

And that grave: was my purpose here to be heroic and get myself killed so Shirley wouldn't be? If I found a way home before June 5th, would that mean she'd die? The grave was there, I'd seen it, it was a real and physical thing that had been in the graveyard for almost eighty years, and it had my name on it – most of it, anyway. It could be for either one of us. Except if it was Shirley's I wouldn't be here, not in the future or now, in the past. Dad wouldn't be born, or Emily, Ned or Sebastian. Our existence erased, like a mistake in a schoolbook.

That night I dreamt of two boys running on a beach. I was shouting at the top of my voice to make them stop, not to run towards the water, but like me they ignored the warnings. I woke to screaming, but it wasn't my own; it was outside. Three or four planes were piercing the night skies, hurling themselves at each other in a dogfight. It was thrilling but terrifying, a deadly version of the Red Arrows – except those pilots train for years; these guys were lucky if they'd trained for a few days.

"Is it the Messerschmitt or Focke-Wulfe?"

"Doreen! How on earth?"

"I can hear it's our Spitfire and I think the other two are Fockes," she snuck under my arm and together we watched them.

"How d'you get to know so much about planes?"

"Me dad's mad on 'em. They kept bombing us docks and we'd watch 'til Mam fetched us to go down shelter. Dad said no Jerry'd chase him from his bed." Bet he'd change his mind when the Doodlebugs start; Hitler's revenge for D Day. "We always knock 'em for six, me dad said."

"How can you tell who's who or what?"

"The Spitfire's the nippy one," she said. "She's dead clever, you'll see." I pulled her closer as the little plane zipped across the sky, out manoeuvring and out witting the other two. Chaser-fire spat across in lethal lines and arcs, beautiful but vicious as one found its target and an explosion lit up the night sky. A whine, a dive and a crash into the water; I hoped the pilot managed to escape like Horst. Game over, the dots separated, one out to sea, the other up the coast.

"Come on. Let's get you back to your bed."

"Can't I stay with you? What if a Junkers comes and drops his bombs on us?"

"Doreen – how? Don't worry, it won't," I said with more certainty than I felt. What protection did we have at the top of the house? The smashed-up barns outside the window a constant reminder of what could happen. "Come on then," I held up the bedcovers. "Shove up." I wasn't sure who was comforting who; a Focker-whats-it, Misher-thing or Spitfire – how would I know the difference until it started shooting at me?

In the morning I made a beeline for Mother, finding her scrubbing away at the laundry; the dogfight might have thrilled Doreen, but it terrified the other children, which meant wet beds. Joining in with the cycle of scrubbing, dunking and wringing, I asked about last night and what to do in an attack. "Used to be, hear church bells – hide in the fields, as we was being invaded. But them what's in charge's decided we can't do without our bells," she said, in between dunking a sheet in and out of the water. "Now everyone's ringing 'em, even them coloured's is at it."

"That a problem?" I bristled.

"Not a bit of it, but they needs more practice – you heard the racket they made on Sunday!"

"So – what do we do now if there's an air raid?"

"They got sirens in towns now, same as London. But out here, when you hear trouble, best you jump in the coalbunker, or under that kitchen table. My old grandpa made that.' she said proudly, helping me to squeeze a sheet through the wringer. "If you're in the fields mind, make sure the cows and pigs is safe first – what you do last time?"

"Dived in a ditch," I said, uncertain if she was joking about the pecking order.

"You know they found a young girl in a ditch, over by the Cove. Shot at, like you was, but..."

"You mean killed?" Ellie's collywobbles came back.

"Outright they reckoned– not much older 'an you. No one knows who she is – not from round here."

"That's terrible," I said quietly, knowing I'd stepped into the dead girl's shoes. "Mrs Dorcas," I said, not able to call her Mother to her face. "When I was assigned as your evacuee, did you choose me in any way – I – I can't quite remember the process."

"No, my lover, your orphanage, in Whitechapel?" She said as if to trigger my memory, using the soft voice she kept for livestock. "They was getting so full they asked us country folk to do their bit and take in more evacuees – stop you poor buggers from getting bombed on. Amazing how any of you survived the Blitz from what I hear. We weren't fussed who we had, but I'm glad we got you."

The compliment was so unexpected tears fell from my eyes, huge ones that sloshed onto the washing. Mother caught the change in my breathing and put one of her big sausage arms around me and I leaned into it, comforted by the cool softness of her fleshy limb. I let the tears fall for myself, the dead orphan, my parents who must by now think they'd lost me, Shirley and what she'd suffer on the journey to becoming Wheezy, for all the soldiers who were just weeks away from being slaughtered and now Doreen who was walking through the scullery door to find me. She'd worry if she saw me weeping so I blew my nose, loudly, which made her laugh, before leading her away to find the coalbunker, just in case.

Chapter FOURTEEN

"Room for a helping hand?" I shouted through the open window. I'd heard the truck trying to resist the tortures of Ellie's gear change and had run to meet her. George had earmarked me for the fields, but the story of Esther had been messing with my head, so I was trying to avoid bumping into Horst – although bumping into him was very much what my heart wanted to do.

I looked sideways at Ellie who turned and smiled, and I longed to talk to her. About Horst, me, everything. If she knew what I knew, would she try to warn me? It was no longer a past event sympathetically explained in a museum or textbook. It was real, present and terrifying – people, children, Ellie's family maybe, being slaughtered right at that moment. The camps wouldn't be discovered until later, after D Day.

I'd watched a TV interview once with an old major, first in line to liberate Belsen, his voice breaking "…Impossible to tell the living from the dead, propped and stacked up, like broken deck-chairs…" The camera had zoomed in on his face: skin paper-thin, pulled taut over grim memories.

I let my thoughts roll with the countryside. The same sun shone, the same creeks meandered, and the same hills lolled into the water, just as beautifully as they would in my time. Except now their beauty was compromised by the stench of diesel and cradling of war contraptions. We pulled over to let a convoy of American soldiers thunder past, whistling and waving as if on a school trip. How did they see the landscape? How many of them knew it was the last bit of heaven they'd see before the fast approaching hell of the French beaches. How many knew, like me, that they would be dead in a matter of weeks.

Oh God, I said, silently but not randomly.

"Ellie, I know your father said not to worry about your family in Germany, but," another jolt and gear shift, "I have heard things."

"Propaganda old thing."

"You know what? It isn't. If there's any way to get them out – can your dad help?"

"That's awfully sweet of you to be concerned but, truly, Aunt Ruthie and the others will be fine. They're children for heaven's sake – who would want to hurt a child?"

"Hitler. Children, old people, disabled people. He doesn't care. He wants a pure Aryan race – which would be funny if it wasn't so grotesque, considering he's short, dumpy and Austrian. He's set out to wipe out anyone he thinks is unclean, thinks differently. Doesn't fit the model. That includes homosexuals, Gypsies – but most especially Jews."

"How could you possibly know such things?" she took her eyes off the road to look at me, which was a bad idea. We swerved, narrowly missing an oncoming jeep, so Ellie pulled over, just inside a small hamlet. With the engine still ticking over, her arm over the steering wheel she turned to me, "Why us, especially?"

"That's huge," how could I answer without sounding trite? "At school, we learnt he blamed Jews for everything from Germany's failed economy to the Russian Revolution, even losing the last war. But, Ellie," I said, trying to choose my words carefully, "This hatred has poisoned a nation. It drives him. Made him immensely powerful, feeding off people's prejudices, inadequacies and fear. I know many things I wish I didn't, and many things I wish I could stop, but I can't."

"But how do you know – and what devilish sort of school did you go to?" she persisted, turning off the ignition.

"It doesn't matter – what matters is getting your family out."

"Ruthie is well respected, has heaps of German friends. It's not like you think."

"It so is. Very few Germans in Hitler's domain are friends to the Jews.

They'll be betrayed, if they haven't been already, sent off to concentration camps."

"What d'you mean – what camps?"

"Hellish places. Millions of Jews. Herded up, packed onto trains like cattle. Sent to these camps. They're gassed. Starved. Tortured, experimented on. It's horrific and few survive. But some will, and they'll tell others so that the men, women and children Ellie, who die in these vile, evil places will not be forgotten. I've been listening, and I'm telling you. Get them out!"

"Louie, stop! You're scaring me," she was deathly pale.

"I'm so sorry," I whispered. "But it's all true. You have to trust –" we both jumped as something hard rapped on the window. A lady with an enamel jug had spotted us and wanted some milk.

"Mrs Simmons!" said Ellie, snapping back to life and turning on me. "Your stories are beastly. I don't know what you mean by them, but I certainly can't scare Daddy, just because an evacuee from Peckham tells me to." She practically ran from the truck, slamming the door behind her.

Soon there was a small gathering and I set up my stall a little way away from Ellie. Children whizzed past on bicycles and one of them shouted out a name; I almost spilled milk over a woman in a housecoat pondering over the best use of powdered eggs. "Did he say Wilfred?"

"That's my son – what's he done now? Has he been messing around on your farm?" She asked wearily. "WILFRED– get yourself here!"

"No, no," I tried to reassure her but it was too late. The boy skidded his bike up to his mother's side and she grabbed him by his ear. Another smaller boy skidded alongside and sniggered.

"This milk lady says you've been running around on her farm – what you got to say?"

"It was Roddy what done it!"

"No I never!" said the other boy.

"I don't care who done it – say sorry," said the woman.

"Sorry missus," he smirked. She let go of him but not before delivering a light wallop around the ear still red from being pulled.

"Little monkey – he'll be the death of me. Just can't get through to him since his dad left." She sighed then and softened as he straddled his getaway vehicle. "Still, he's not a bad lad really – it's this damn war." I was flummoxed. The boys had whizzed off on their bicycles leaving dust and distant giggles. I'd barely registered what they looked like, except young, cheeky and full of life.

"I'm sure he's a good lad – we won't worry about the farm," obviously, as nothing happened. "But," I took my chance. "Keep him away from the beach. D'you understand? We – we've had reports of boys going down there but it's dangerous, very dangerous. There are mines, explosives. All sorts." I was trying out Ellie's posh BBC voice. "So, keep a tight rein on them." It wasn't breaking, just bending, the golden don't meddle rule of time travel. I'd read the stories, watched the films – was even wearing the T-shirt. Interfering with the space-time continuum was never a good thing as the results were rarely encouraging, but these were just boys.

Chapter FIFTEEN

"Shirley's cried off with some sort of tummy bug. Didn't look too clever, George says you're with me," said Ellie, giving me a thin smile as I joined her in the truck again. There was a definite distance now; not the whole time travelling from two different centuries sort of distance, more a fear of being subjected to more rants about her family being doomed sort of distance. It was getting to be pretty lonely in 1944. I hadn't seen Horst for ages, or Shirley since discovering she was great granny Wheezy. When I had I'd been in awe and awkward.

We'd come to a standstill at the British camp's sentry post, queuing for ID to be checked. When it came to our turn, I knew there'd be trouble. Brown, flimsy and inconsequential looking, they were a long way from chip and pin.

"You're going no further without it," he was clad head to toe in a coarse itchy looking uniform with shiny buttons, boots and buckles, and loving every minute of his power. "This area's officially locked down. No ID, no entry." I started the patting dungarees routine, hoping Ellie would say something clever and rescue me. "Step out of the vehicle please," he said. I looked at him with what I hoped was an enchanting plea. He wasn't having any of it. "Miss – get out of the truck."

And then I remembered. "There! That's me. Eloise Shircliff!" I handed over the ID Shirley had thrown back under the dashboard the day I'd discovered she was Wheezy. He eyed both me, and the card, suspiciously.

"Trouble private?" It was the voice of a boy dressed in his dad's uniform. Instead of sending him home to his mummy the shiny private snapped to attention.

"Just sorting out ID, sir. What with this being an exclusion zone."

"Jake!" said Ellie. " You're back!"

"It's OK private, I'll take it from here," said the boy called Jake, grabbing Shirley's ID and jumping into the truck next to me as we drove on.

"It's so good to see you," began Ellie. "I thought – "

"I know," he said. I felt sandwiched and unnecessary and was glad when we stopped. He jumped out of the truck first and skipped around to Ellie's side.

"It's OK," I said, scrapping the milk churn on the concrete. "I've got this."

"Don't be daft, we'll all pitch in," said Ellie except after one churn the couple were too engrossed in each other to come back for more. I tried to make less noise than when Mallory and Shirley had their moment, and so heard snatches of their conversation in between churns.

"I've missed you – you've been away – how..? "

"Did you? It wasn't like the Devon I remembered." Of course, Ellie had said he'd been to Slapton Sands. He'd been on that mission that went wrong.

"Was it awful?" asked Ellie tenderly.

Splodges of red had broken out on the smooth young face barely touched by a razor as he struggled to contain his thoughts. "Grisly, barbaric – they had no chance," his voice snagged and I knew why.

"Exercise Tiger." Damn. I'd said that out loud.

"What?" He said. "What did you say?"

"Easy rider," I offered. "This churn's an easier rider than the others..." Damn, again.

"No. No you didn't – you said Exercise Tiger," he dropped his voice and came over to me.

"How the – how could you know?" He took on a deep shade of panic, firing a look at Ellie, mentally checking if he'd let anything slip. She stared back, opening her face and eyes wide to show she'd no idea what I was talking about. I picked up the churn for want of something to do, then felt foolish with it hanging heavily and pointlessly between the three of us.

"Some things I just know," I said lamely, not looking at Ellie but hoping she'd get the message. Why didn't I stop there? I wasn't in Miss Probert's Southwest at War history lesson, trying to prove how much I'd remembered; I was living at a time when security and secrecy were everything. But I couldn't help myself, "I heard over five hundred were lost?"

"I wouldn't know, and I couldn't say. I'm sorry, but who are you?" At which point he drew out Shirley's ID that he'd pocketed earlier.

"Sorry Jake, this is Louie – joined us from London. Well, not officially, she's an evacuee but you'd hardly tell as she's such a jolly good sport with all the beastly jobs we have to do," she said at top speed. "I'll get the butter?"

"What? Butter…Louie? It says Eloise Shircliff here."

"Yes – my full name's Eloise," I put down the churn finally. "After my great grandmother. Let me do the butter," I was desperate to get away. Exercise Tiger – I'm so clever and know all these secret things. Prat, I said to myself as I made my way back down the corridor. I slapped the blasted butter into its tray; maybe I could just slip it back, unseen.

"It was horrific Ellie," Jake's husky, hushed voice slowed my steps. "So many bodies, popping up out of the water…hideous waterlogged dolls. Eyes open, staring – at nothing. Burnt, arms, legs – just not there. All of them – dead," he paused.

Ellie was saying nothing, just letting him talk. "So heavy, dragging them onto the boat, reading their tags, checking names against the list." His speech was broken, empty spaces where I guessed he was trying not to cry. He shouldn't have been telling her anything; I knew that. There'd been a news blackout prohibiting anyone from talking about it – in fact the story didn't emerge for over forty years. But I didn't blame him. How could you not talk?

I hid behind the open door and, thanks to Miss Probert's passion for local history and a seaside holiday near Slapton Sands, I could fill in the blanks.

The American flotilla practicing to storm a Normandy beach; a problem with radio signals; Nazi E boats pitching up in the middle of it and getting lucky. It took just seven minutes to sink almost the entire flotilla and torch or drown over five hundred men. Boys mostly. It was no longer an obscure history lesson, or plaque read when bored on holiday. It was real: I pictured them; lined up on the recovery boats. Broken dolls, Jake had said, except they weren't. Each one was someone's son, brother, boyfriend, husband or father even. He must have been involved in the operation to retrieve the bodies and check to see if any of them were Bigots. Miss Probert had proudly told us, as if she'd been one of them, that these were a select group of men who were involved in the planning of D Day. Jake wouldn't have known why they had to retrieve every body, searching each one, no matter how disfigured. He wouldn't have known that if he, and his fellow soldiers, hadn't been so diligent, the men at the top would never have been sure that a Bigot hadn't been captured and tortured. D Day would have been aborted. Poor Jake. I looked at him now, and tried to see the man that he was becoming, but I couldn't. He looked even younger to me now and I found myself trying not to cry.

My flippant words must have cut deeply and painfully. But if I was really honest, part of me enjoyed letting slip the fact that I knew something. It made me feel important, special. Now I just felt cheap and crass. I'd also proved myself a threat to national security at an extremely sensitive time in our history and, never mind the lack of an ID card, I'd seriously increased my chances of getting locked up. I turned away from my hiding place in panic. What a jerk! What a stupid, stupid –

"Hello!"

I swung round smacking into a soldier way more at home in his uniform than young Jake. "Is that really all for me?" he asked, looking at the butter smeared across his jacket. It was Johnny.

"I'm so sorry," I fumbled, looking around for something to try to wipe it off with.

"Here – let me," and he calmly took out a knife from somewhere in the folds of his uniform and scraped off the butter, slapping it back into the tray pausing only to flick a small amount with his finger into his mouth. "A little fibrous perhaps, but not bad." I grimaced apologetically and he smiled back boyishly.

"Hello again," he said.

"Hi," I replied. "And I'm sorry – you'll have to clean that, or you'll smell of vomit."

"An extra deterrent for when we're in combat – we will fight them with rancid butter. Louie, isn't it? So, you're new to the team and from up country?" he said in the rubbish sort of fake accent I over-used when we told people we were moving to Cornwall.

"London," or at least I will be. "You're so not Cornish," it was hard to relax knowing any minute now Jake would shop me, but Johnny had a very calming presence.

"Actually I am. I went to that school on the hill, then Oxford, then off to fight for King and country. I'm back for the briefest sojourn."

"Not for a holiday, I'm guessing – I thought you were a pilot. How come you're at an army base?"

"I'm here to liaise."

"How very forward thinking."

"It's also an excuse to remind myself how beautiful my home county is."

"Even with all the troops, camps and stinky smell of diesel?"

"Even with all that – the incomers are not entirely without merit," he said with another smile that this time wasn't at all boyish and made my cheeks go as blotchy as Jake's. "So, missing London?"

"I miss my friends," the ones that aren't born yet.

"It takes time but I'm glad to see you're faring better than the last time we met," that would be when I sobbed in the graveyard and blew my nose loudly into his pristine hanky.

"I seem to have a habit of soiling your clothes," that didn't come out right.

"Sadly, I do have duties to attend. Perhaps I could show you some of my Cornwall. You're at the hostel."

"No – no, I'm not." I didn't want him to know I wasn't a land girl. "I'm staying at Higher Farm – with the Dorcas?"

"With Mother!" he pretended to look afraid.

"She has a soft underside," I said.

"Ah, she obviously likes you if you've spotted that. Well, I know where to find you." He gave me a lazy salute, turned on his well-polished heels and was gone.

Walking back towards the young couple, I could see their intense huddle had relaxed. Relieved, I left the butter on a table and slipped away but remembered Jake still had Shirley's ID. Did I risk reminding him I was a threat to national security, or leave my great grandmother in the lurch? I decided to go back but stopped when I heard hushed voices coming from a side room; maybe I was being reported. I peaked in, but it was the watchmaker, Wolenski, talking agitatedly to someone. It looked like a furtive exchange similar to those I'd seen many times on the streets back in London. I felt like I was looking at something I shouldn't. I slipped away unseen, abandoning the ID retrieval plan.

Chapter SIXTEEN

Ellie came back to the truck flushed. She'd asked Jake if he'd take her to the Plaza when he next had a weekend pass, "I had to do something – he was in such a spin after your wretched talk of tigers."

"The Plaza?" I latched on to the diversion.

"Watch the Rhine with Bette Davis will be showing; I do so admire her. Do you think I'm awfully brazen?"

"No way. Go girl!"

"Of course," and she started the engine.

"No, no I meant…never mind." I tried again, "He's probably wondering if you're a sweet or salty kind of girl!"

"Is that London-speak for the wrong type of girl?"

"NO! Sweet or salty popcorn?"

"Pop what?" Small talk was hard over the bumpy roads, military convoys and a whole century.

"Popcorn," I shouted. "Maybe you don't have it in Cornwall – it's all the rage in London. An American invention – they won't watch a film without it."

"How uncouth." I smiled; Wheezy had a thing about people eating in public. We'd stopped outside the hamlet where I'd met the two boys.

"Poor Jake, he was so dreadfully upset. There's been some awful cock-up. A training mission went wrong; he was part of the crew that had to retrieve the bodies before they were even sure the fighting had stopped. Terrifying, simply ghastly. Hundreds, he said…so many drowned because they put their life belts on wrong, round their waists instead of under their arms. Their kit became sodden and they were dragged down. What were they all doing out there and how the devil do you know so much?"

"I'm sorry Ellie – I shouldn't have blurted it out like that – I was – I was – I am. Aghh! I so want to tell you!" I so did. "This stuff I know, I don't want to know it." She stared straight ahead. "It's doing my head in. I don't know why I'm here, how I'll get home. Or – or what the point of any of it is. Except, I do know I could help your family – if you'll – "

"No," she snapped, turning on me. "I tried to telephone Daddy after your last terrifying rant, but all the telephone boxes have been sealed up. He's so busy working in the hospital – which was bombed at the weekend by the way – I simply won't add to his or Mummy's burden. Now, I need to stop off here – maybe you should wait in the truck before you upset someone else!"

I watched Ellie walk over to meet the farmer. Ignoring her advice, I got out and wandered off, longing for my phone. I missed all the ways it connected me and how I'd used it to make things better – a quick text to say sorry, that came out wrong.

"Hello," Horst!

"Hey! How come?" I was spluttering and probably spat on him. "You're here."

"Yes. We are billeted here – the food's better, but the company's not so good." He was smiling that smile.

"The food! You're much better fed than the land girls," I said, trying to regulate my heartbeat. I thought I'd decided he was bad news.

"The land girls – they will win you the war. More so than all these GIs."

"Ha! It just seems like lots because Cornwall's small and they all look the same – you probably keep seeing the same ones in different places," my heart was showing no signs of slowing.

"Louie, I am not trying to get you betray any secrets!" He laughed gently and took my hand, stopping my heart just long enough to release something warming and delicious that melted all my resolve to distance myself from him.

"I told you about my sister Gisella – she's a bit younger than Doreen," those eyes – so many blues, such long eyelashes. "I have exercised my privilege as a newly captured POW and sent back my twenty-five words on your Red Cross form." He lifted his elbow to lean on a fence, bringing his face close to mine. It was intoxicating. I fought down an urge to smooth a frown that was creasing across his eyebrows. "So few words will not reassure one so young," he was hesitating. "I have written her a letter. It is a lot to ask, I know, but could you post it, via my aunt in Switzerland?"

What? He was pulling a letter out of his pocket. "I'm not sure," I said, suddenly feeling ten years old and dared to nick sweets from the Spar by the alpha girl at primary school.

"I have written in English." I didn't know what to do. I wanted to be that person for him, but was that right? "I have not sealed it so you can read what I have written."

That seemed reasonable; I didn't have to post it, even if I took it. If I did this for him, maybe he could answer some of my questions. I snatched it before I changed my mind and stuffed it into my pocket, but as I looked back up, his lips found mine. It was fleeting, unexpected, but his touch was soft and tantalising, making me alive to every millimetre that was mine.

"Thank you," he said. I'd never been thanked like that before and was keen to be thanked again. I could barely breath. He lifted my chin to his face. This was new, Tom hadn't kissed me like this, and I certainly hadn't felt what I was feeling at that moment. I didn't want it to stop, but I had to.

"My watch," I said, reluctantly pulling away. "That day. You said he would help me with it. Who did you mean? The German watchmaker, the guy who handed you the hymn book?" He looked taken aback.

"In church?" I wasn't very good at this; on TV they always seem to say the right thing to catch out the other person. I was telling him everything I knew – not the other way around.

"You are not wearing it," he said, examining my wrist with one hand, but pulling me closer with the other so that our bodies almost touched.

"No – he has it – the watchmaker guy," it was very hard to concentrate.

"The one who handed me a secret message in church?" My eyes widened but I knew in an instant that he was laughing at me. "No one handed me a secret message, Louie, just a hymnbook and I don't even remember who. All I remember was seeing you, upset, running out." I liked that he'd noticed me.

"But you said, he will help me – who did you mean?"

"Did I? I was disorientated – I thought maybe," he stopped and ran his hand through his hair in a way that was becoming familiar. "I'd just crashed my plane and found you half dead in the sea. I'm not sure what I said." I think he did. "But I do remember your watch – that is something I can help you with it."

"How?" this was interesting.

"Patience Louie," he planted the lightest kiss on my lips again. "All in good time."

That night, rain pounded against the window as I sat alone. I missed Emily. I missed Mum. I wanted to talk to someone. An oil lamp glowed in one corner. I still disliked the smell and hiss of it, but its' warm yellow light was a comfort. I reached under the mattress and pulled out Horst's letter. Holding it I felt anxious but not because of what it represented, or the ominous legacy I'd inherited from Esther or even the grim fate that ended with my name on the gravestone. It came from kissing Horst. And it wasn't even guilt. It was panic. Had my mouth been too open? I blew into my cupped hand to smell my breath. Toothpaste was different here – no breath freshening stripe. It came in a tin, a hard block of gunk that softened with a bit of water and brush scrubbing – Doreen had shown me how – but the whole household dipped their brushes in, so I wasn't that keen, relying on apples instead. It was just a kiss – but what if Ellie had seen us? What was I doing? Scaring her witless at lunchtime about demonic Nazis, then snogging one by teatime. It wasn't going to happen again. Except, I so hoped it would.

I propped the letter on the chest of drawers with the cast-offs from Mother's sister-in-law, making a mental note to ask her about my mysterious clothing benefactor. She'd made some cryptic remark about being posted further than she wanted to go – did that mean she'd died, or just gone to Swindon?

Was Switzerland open for letters from Britain? They were meant to be neutral but Grandpa Josh had always moaned about them, saying they banked all the Nazi stash. But that didn't make it illegal to send a letter there, did it? From a POW? What if Horst's sister was having nightmares about her big brother being shot down? What about my young brothers, Ned and Sebastian – would they be missing me? I went to tuck the letter back under the mattress. I'd sleep on it, literally. Mum always said things seem clearer in the morning. Unlikely in this instance, so I opened it.

May 10th, 1944
My dearest Gisella,

I hope all is well with you. You must not worry about me. I may be a prisoner of war, but compared to what you must be going through it is like being on a holiday camp.

I miss you terribly but know your safety is assured and that you are looking after Mother and Father – give them lots of extra cookies from me with their afternoon tea.

I love you and will be thinking of you next month – I can hardly believe you will be five, my darling. I will think happy thoughts of the croissants on the beach we had to celebrate your last birthday; it seems the shortest time ago and remains a memory very close to my heart.

All my love,
Horst x

I'd intruded on something private: a sweet simple note to reassure a little girl that her big brother was not in the scary place she imagined. It turned a rubbish situation into something good by telling her that she was in charge now. When I babysat for my own brothers, Dad would whisper to Ned that he was in charge, just to make him feel in on a grown-up secret and better about being left behind.

Reading it renewed my ache to get home; I had a different sort of ache when I thought of leaving Horst.

Chapter SEVENTEEN

The morning sun was already burning off the overnight rain left on the ground. "How do you mean, creepy?" I was trying to persuade Ellie to make a detour so I could check up on my watch and the watchmaker. "Sort of queer?"

"No!" I smiled at the way she made the word sound even though she'd had been curt with me all morning, and who could blame her. "Just a bit dodgy, you know?" although I knew she didn't.

"We can slip into town before going to Trenogar," she sighed. "Have you got that letter you said you wanted to post?" I nodded, feeling it burning a hole in my dungarees. "I'll have to log it, or George will get into a row."

"Why?" Why log a letter? Did she know? Had she seen me with Horst?

"His records – he has to show the fuel he's allocated is used strictly for farm business or he could be seen as profiting unfairly, but I'm sure it's okay, it's not much out of our way." I tried to look as if I wasn't relieved but felt guilty nonetheless.

The town was stuffed with military, which it would be with D Day only a few weeks away, the massing of troops becoming harder to camouflage. Posters were everywhere. They didn't pull any punches, showing soldiers parachuting into battle zones, or forlorn orphaned children: His needs come first: lend don't spend, Dig for Victory, Save Fuel for Battle, Make do and Mend. Another showed a glamorous Lady H character, reclining, surrounded by eager military men at a cocktail party saying, Keep mum, she's not so dumb! Careless talk costs lives! She must know way more than she should.

Ellie dropped me off while she waited in the truck. The sign said 'Closed' but I tried the door anyway. It opened. "Hello?" No answer. The shop was just as dark and eerie with the hundreds of clocks ticking loudly around me. "Hi?" I tried again, moving towards the counter. I leaned over and looked towards the back but couldn't see anything except a workbench through a small doorway. On it, small parcels were wrapped up in brown paper packaging and tied up with string – a few of my favourite things? It was just one I wanted. I scuttled under the counter-top at the side, my heart pounding.

"He-l-l-o?" I called out again. A tiny workroom was through the doorway; boxes piled floor to ceiling. I picked up a parcel from the bench – it had a Swiss address. So did the next one and the next making me feel weird, with Horst's letter in my pocket. I went to pull it out and compare addresses but an open notebook next to a line of propped up watches caught my attention. The writing was tiny; dense letters, symbols, crossing outs and miniature pictures of watch faces. The first few pages listed clocks, their type and location including the British army base where I'd seen Wolenski, a POW camp called White Cross in St Columb Major, another in Par, Lady H's Trenogar Farm and my old school.

More watches were lying face down; their backs open like hospital patients whose gowns didn't quite meet behind them. It didn't stop me peeping into a particularly bulbous one: inside, tucked up neatly alongside the mechanism, but not interfering with it, was the tiniest piece of paper curled up like a sleeping mouse.

"What are you doing?"

"Oh my goodness! You frightened the life out of me!"

"You are trespassing!" If Wolenski had looked deflated the first time I came here, he certainly didn't now.

"I called out – no one answered," I said.

"Is that an excuse?" his grey eyes darkened.

"No – sorry – I'm looking for my watch."

"And so you trespass in my private quarters to search for it, yes?"

"No. Yes. I'm sorry. My watch is…" I stopped as he sighed in a way that said my watch was not a topic relevant to the situation I was in.

It was obvious I'd been snooping in his book. "Who sent you?" he said, slowly closing it.

"No one – I didn't mean to pry," I looked for exit routes – the only one was through him. "I just want my watch."

"How did you get it? Did you steal it?"

"No! I told you, it belonged to my great grandmother."

"That is impossible – these watches were made just five years ago, issued to the Luftwaffe only recently," the Luftwaffe? Was that why Horst had been interested in it? "Anyway, I no longer have it," he said dismissively.

"You what?" he was bluffing.

"It has been sent – who gave it to you?"

"Where – not to Switzerland?"

"That is the agreed procedure."

"Procedure? What are you talking about – it's my watch." His face was a blank mask, but mine wasn't. My ride home had gone. "I'm running out of time…"

"And I am running out of patience," he lied. He wasn't in a hurry. He knew he'd got me, so he let me go. He took a step back and indicated for me to scurry back under the counter.

"I need that watch. I can't believe you've… when's it coming back?"

"The watch is – " he stopped himself.

"Is what?" He betrayed the tiniest quizzical look before impassivity locked down again. "What is the watch, other than my watch, my great grandmother's?" I was trying not to cry.

"We will talk when you are ready."

"Get my watch back – then we can talk all you want," about what I had no idea but pretending I knew what I was doing seemed sensible. He nodded, implying it was a fair exchange and I left.

Back out in the street I felt sick. My head was spinning; I was weak, faint and collided with someone.

"I say are you – Louie! Whatever's wrong?" it was Shirley.

"You told me to look after it, every day you told me. I didn't listen – I was so arrogant!"

113

"What are you talking about?"

"I was trying to fix it, but it's gone – I don't know how I'll get back!"

"You're talking gibberish – and you're making a scene," I was crying. "Here," she guided me to a bench outside the cathedral.

"Shirley? Louie? – You alright old girl?" it was Ellie. "I saw you from – whatever's the matter?" They looked at me with frowns midway between concern and irritation.

"Why are you here?" I said, looking at Shirley who sat down next to me.

"Looking for my ID – I needed to sort some things out, but then I couldn't travel on the bus because I couldn't find my ID. One of the GIs gave me a lift. I saw the truck and remembered I'd left the damn thing under the dashboard. I was just walking over to get it when you crashed into me."

"I'll look – you stay with Louie," said Ellie.

"I'm sorry," I said, knowing Jake had Shirley's ID.

"For what? It doesn't have anything to do with those beastly stories you've been telling Ellie does it?"

"No – no. It's not like that, I – "

"I think it's pretty poor of you – Ellie has enough to worry about with her brothers away fighting, parents in London, working in appalling conditions – blast. It's not there," she said looking at Ellie who was walking back towards us, shrugging her shoulders with empty hands in the air.

"Sorry old girl – are you sure that's where you left it?" said Ellie.

"Absolutely – this is too bad. What am I going to do?" I looked at my feet.

"We're off to Trenogar," said Ellie. "Come with us. We can drop you back at your hostel after. Maybe you left it there?"

I remembered Horst's letter, "Sorry. But I…" I was up, waving my arms at the post office. Before either could say anything, I was across the square. Legs unsteady, mouth dry as sandpaper, I walked in.

Free of displays telling me when it was my turn, how to buy insurance or get foreign currency, it was dark, dusty and brown – but it was vibrant. A hive of busyness. People waiting to post a letter, parcel or have something official done to the pieces of paper and ration books they were holding. Be-

114

hind the counter and through a door, rows of women conjured thousands of letters that flew like playing cards into pigeonholes. Two uniformed women marched past the queue I'd joined, lifting up half the wooden counter and pushing open a door next to the sorting women. Slapping down their empty sacks, they exchanged them for full ones. A fat man with a greasy comb-over stepped forward and proffered a tied-up packet of papers; they both paused before one woman took the bundle.

Looking down at the papers, her body visibly slumped; she showed her colleague the top of the pile, and she sagged as well. Telegrams, I guessed, to a family they knew. Telegrams holding handfuls of crudely printed words, making real the darkest fears for anyone who has ever had to wave goodbye to a soldier.

They swung their heavy burdens back on their backs and into their post-office issue pouches, passing the queues, unseeing and unseen, except by me. The sounds of people chattering jarred in my ears now, the dull colours of their clothes too bright, lipstick disrespectful and laughter, just cruel. Didn't they know they had just been in the presence of words that spoke of death, loss and pain?

Horst's letter weighed heavily against the telegrams. "Next!" Everyone looked at me and I hid by stepping forward to take my place. The lady behind the counter, no security glass required, wore lipstick that sat awkwardly on pinched lips. Her black-pencilled eyebrows, more skilfully applied than Primrose's, disappeared into her hairline, waiting for me to make the first move. I tried out my strangulated voice asking for a stamp to Switzerland. She opened her drawer. She knew, she was pushing a button to alert the secret service and I'd be arrested.

"Thruppence." What? My blank face tried to say. "For the stamp. Thruppence!" Relief flushed through me, but so did common sense. I mumbled an apology, retreated backwards and stumbled outside. I should have thrown the letter away – but I stuffed it back into my pocket.

On the journey to Trenogar, huddled against the window, I tried to make myself as invisible as possible. My hand wrapped around my empty wrist feeling where the watch should be. Fear and loneliness gnawed at my insides. I'd held on to the belief that the watch was my Tardis to transport me back to when my great grandmother was old and irritating, not cool and intimidating. If I'd got the watch, or timepiece, working then maybe I could realign this piece of time, with its future piece of time…except, I didn't even have it anymore. I was trapped. I so wanted to be home, where the peaks and troughs of the day were measured by inconsequential events, like the Internet being cut off, not whether or not I'd found a way to avoid being killed in a few weeks.

Chapter EIGHTEEN

Primrose was in a flap, "I'm so glad you're here. The Min of Ag – they just turned up. We didn't know they was coming."

"Has she given them gin?" said Ellie like a doctor to a nurse.

"Yes, but – they seems awful official and I know m' Lady's not up to date with all the records and whatnots."

"Don't worry Primrose, we can help with the whatnots," said Shirley.

"The mulberry bush manoeuvre?" Shirley asked Lady H who'd flitted out to greet us. I didn't know what the whatnot they were talking about.

"Absolutely. They're totting up in the first barn now," she said her voice trailing off, distracted by a smart black car pulling up. "Excellent! Reinforcements." The not-quite retired Headmaster was using his stick to get out of the car.

"Cornelius – it's the Ministry monsters again. Would you be a dear?" Lady H said as she went to help him.

"Be delighted, Kitty" he took her hand and raised it to his lips.

"Join me indoors or outdoors with the troops?" she asked warmly.

"I think on the field," he said, turning to look at the three of us, clearly enjoying himself. I wished my Head-teacher were as encouraging.

"You are a dear. Now, when they move to the second barn, you team of darlings scoot the chooks out and into the third – if we're quick enough the numbers should tally. Primrose will keep their drinks topped up. Between us we should have them fuddled enough to tick all their wretched little boxes." I was beginning to get it, but chooks? I hated the blessed things. We'd had a few of the horrors at home: nasty little peckers. "Back to the fray; I'll give the signal."

"Same as last time?" said Shirley.

"Absolutely. Cardigan round shoulders, fix with one button at neck."

"Splendid. We'll watch from our post," said Ellie, our post being a garden shed.

"And we'll stand guard over there," said the Headmaster, pointing to another shed-like outhouse. "Shirley isn't it?"

"Yes, sir."

"Oh, Cornelius, please," he said.

"So," I said to Ellie when in position, "these Ministry people have counted the first lot of chickens, we're going to take those same chickens and, without them noticing, herd them across the yard behind the barn where they'll be counting the second batch of birds, to the third barn. Then they'll count them again, thinking they're new chickens."

"Exactly."

"Right. Why?"

"So, the Min of Ag can see for themselves that Lady H has as many chickens that her books say she has – that she hasn't been selling any off for a profit."

"Has she?"

"I couldn't possibly say," said Ellie.

"Lady H is lovely and everything– but isn't this a bit dodgy?" I asked.

"Black racketeering? Probably, and look I'll understand if you want to sit this one out. I don't think she is, really, I just think she is a bit dotty with the books; they're so wretchedly complicated I'm not surprised she gets in a muddle."

"No, no – I'll help" I said, thinking of the servicemen that benefited from her charm and a few worry-free hours on a Saturday evening.

"Hey! That's the signal; she's buttoning her cardigan. Look sharp!" stage whispered the Headmaster from the other side of the shed.

We schlepped across the muddy ground, keeping our heads down low. The ferocity of the noise inside the small barn was matched by the stench. Hundreds of chickens trying to out cluck each other, making it clear that whatever was bothering one was no where near as important as whatever was bothering its neighbour. If I had to live in such stinky conditions, I'd be clucking too.

"Whatever is the matter with them?"

"They hates being in here in the daylight," said Primrose, who'd appeared from nowhere, the scent of her heavily powdered face and faintly alcoholic breath mixing uneasily with the smell of chickens. "These have been counted and they've started next door, so we best get a move on." Shirley opened the back door and started to shoo out a coop full.

It was no problem getting them out; getting them to where they should go was a different matter. We wanted them around the back. They wanted to go around the front, where the food was, in full view of the inspectors. Chickens only ever look at the ground and they're greedy, eating whatever's in their way, recycling even their own waste. So, throwing down a trail of seed was a tasty distraction that got them moving in the right direction, just not quickly enough for Primrose. She let out a second coop before disappearing back to the refreshments.

Chickens were everywhere. And so were we. Even the Headmaster was dishevelled. We finally got most of them to where they should be, but five out-dodged us. Ellie and I swooped in, picking up two each, practically kicking the fifth like a football towards a goal. As we closed the small back barn door, the inspectors came in the front and we thought we were home dry. As it turned out the chickens were, but I wasn't. Ellie, Shirley and myself were sat behind the barn catching our breath when the door opened and a small, haughty-looking man came out.

"I was unaware that Lady Hempstead had the assistance of the Land Army," he said. We all jumped to our feet.

"How do you do sir, Ellie Shimlief, I'm with the hostel at Chycoose sir, working with the Dorcas at Higher Farm. I'm afraid you've rather caught us out – we've just delivered the milk and were enjoying a crafty break in the sun," she handed over her ID.

"Indeed. And you?" he said looking at Shirley.

"Eloise Shircliff, sir. At the Devoran hostel, also working with the Dorcas." This was awkward. I looked at Ellie who was looking at Shirley – she obviously hadn't known her official name was Eloise and she certainly didn't know we shared the same surname.

"ID?"

"Ah – well, I'm afraid I've mislaid mine, sir."

"Mislaid? That is indeed careless, and may I say illegal. I'm sure you know this area has now been declared an exclusion zone. You will not be allowed to move about freely unless you are registered as an inhabitant and have an identity card."

"You?"

"Oh – I'm just an evacuee. From London. I don't have ID. I mean, I did, but I got shot, well not actually shot, just shot at – when I arrived – in a ditch, then I ran, and. Well. I lost everything. Sir."

"Does this tale of woe have a main character?"

"I'm sorry?"

"Your name, child!"

"Louie, sir."

"Louie what?" What could I say? Ellie was looking at me.

"Actually, old man, Bradstock, isn't it?" said a voice from behind us, "I don't wish to be impertinent," it was the Headmaster. "But an ID card clearly states here, on the back, that one only has to produce one's ID card upon demand to a police officer in uniform or a member of Her Majesty's Armed Forces in uniform on duty. You sir, are wearing no such uniform." He then extended his hand and gave the man one of his broad smiles. "I believe you're one of my ex-pupils?"

"Ah Bradstock!" The barn door had flung open and an older man with mottled cheeks and a large nose that was pretty close to purple stepped through. Lady H was a short step behind and together they looked as if they were taking in a breath of air at a cocktail party. Primrose, who was omnipresent that day, followed with a tray of drinks tinkling in her unsteady hands.

"May I serve refreshments?" asked Primrose.

"I think not, madam," said the one we now knew was Bradstock, hovering between outrage and humiliation.

"Everything seems to be ship-shape and tidy with these very fine birds," said Lady H's drinking partner. "Lady H had been regaling me with the most marvellous tales of India – it transpires we were there at the same time. Appallingly bad luck our people didn't cross over, what! I say – are you all right old man? You look like you have a poker up your arsenal! Give this man a drink!" Bradstock eyed his inebriated colleague with unveiled disgust.

"Girls – thank you so much for your help in delivering the milk. Louie, will you be helping us out again this Saturday?"

"Only if she has her papers in order, Lady Hempstead. She must report to the regional office before the end of the week, with her birth certificate, or whatever you have verifying who you say you are, so that a replacement may be processed."

"Oh, don't be silly man – I can verify who she is. She's Louie and she's marvellous," said Lady H. "

"And the same goes for you too, young lady," he said, cutting across the gushing aristocrat to look at Shirley. "I may not be wearing a uniform," he said avoiding looking his old Headmaster in the eye, "but I am part of Her Majesty's inspection team for the Ministry of Agriculture and as such I am endowed with particular powers that you would be unwise to force me to invoke." This he said with particular relish. "We take a very dim few of carelessness – carelessness costs lives! Before Friday." He then turned to the man who was smiling benignly at Lady H. "Sir, we need to go – I think we should pay a visit to Higher Farm."

"Bradstock – the words cart, leading and horse spring to mind. If you'll excuse me Lady H, I must attend to my duties, but it has been a pleasure. Until the next time." He took her hand, looking as if he might kiss it, but sighed instead, put his hat on and bowed. Bradstock offered no such regrets at leaving.

Chapter NINETEEN

"What a prig!" said Shirley in the truck, having extricated ourselves from the ladies' enthusiastic thanks. "Now, where is that wretched ID?" her voice was muffled as her head was hidden in the depths of the truck's dashboard. Ellie looked at me, as if to say, well?

"Ooh, that was a mistake," Shirley raised her head, looking green. I'd seen that look many times on Emily's face; she couldn't get beyond the South Circular in the car without heaving.

"Pull over Ellie," I said quickly. We banked on a verge and Shirley had barely clambered out before retching. I followed and did what I never did for Emily. I held her hair back and stroked her shoulders, until the contents of her stomach were emptied.

"Let's get you back to the hostel old girl. You're not up to working to-day," said Ellie leaning out of the truck. Shirley was looking a little better but smelling like the worst kind of cheese. Just before we climbed back on board, she turned to me say thank you, her beautiful green eyes looking into mine for the first time.

"Sure you're okay, Eloise?"

"Only Mallory calls me that," she hesitated, as if she'd seen something there. "That's so strange."

"What?" I willed her to make a connection.

"You – you just reminded me of him. I knew you were going to say my name." I mumbled déjà vu, instead of family likeness.

"Yes, that must be it."

"Come on girls, the milk's curdling in this heat!" shouted Ellie. She pulled away slowly, but in no way smoothly. It wasn't far to drop off my great grandmother and I watched her get smaller in the wing mirror. Ellie was looking ahead, her Jewish profile set to determined as she cradled the wide width of the steering wheel to navigate the beast around, but mainly over, the potholes in the road. I knew an explanation would be required but didn't know where to start; Ellie did.

"Why do you and Shirley have the same name?" Coincidence wouldn't really cut it, but would the truth? Why hadn't I been quicker on my feet and lied about my real name at the beginning? But how was I to know I'd run into my great grandmother? Ellie had stopped the truck. "Well?" I opened my mouth unsure of what would come out, but instead there was an almighty bang, an explosion, coming from the beach. I knew even before the reverberations had stopped what had happened.

"Wilfred. And Roddy."

"What? I'm sorry, but what?" snapped Ellie. "Are they your names too? And where the hell did that explosion come from?"

"Mines, on the beach. Wilfred and Roddy. I wasn't quick enough. I wasn't smart enough. I haven't saved them. Those poor little boys!" I was rigid as noises went off around me and people began running. Ellie was talking but I don't know what she was saying. There was wailing. The sound of a bell; Wilfred's mum in the street, wrapping the same housecoat tightly around herself; not holding on to her son's ear today. She started to run towards the beach. Mother's intuition – did she know? Did she know that moments ago her son and his friend had been blown up on the beach they shouldn't have been playing on. Why was I here? I couldn't even save two little boys, how was I going to save myself?

"That better old girl?" asked Ellie handing me a mug of tea as we sat on a woodpile back at the farm, having abandoned dispatching the milk. "I don't want to upset you again, but we need to talk about this name sharing business and Shirley's ID."

What did it matter now? I was going to be dead like those boys in a few weeks. It mattered to Shirley, a voice said. I had to make sure everything moved in the way it would have done if I weren't here – is that why they died? "What's the point of any of it?" I didn't realise I'd said that out loud.

"The point," said Ellie, "is that you've taken Shirley's ID, not just her card but her name as well – who are you?"

"Louie – my name is Louie," it sounded like someone else was speaking. "I didn't know it was hers; I thought her name was Shirley, we all did. I found the ID – she's always leaving it somewhere – and used it because I didn't have any."

"That story about getting shot at – was that all a lie?"

"No. It really happened. When I arrived at Higher Farm in the middle of the night, I had nothing, only the clothes I stood up in." Or, more accurately, fell down in.

"So, you used the name on the ID, not knowing it was Shirley's."

"Yes."

"So?" she looked at me expectantly, "what is your name?"

"I told you, it's Louie."

"Not Eloise Shircliff?" it's mad, but I didn't want to lose claim to my own name.

"It's complicated," I said.

"I just don't know what to make of you – what about that Tiger business? That's highly, highly classified. And these poor boys you say have been blown up – we don't even know if anyone was hurt yet."

"I do. It's Wilfred, and his friend, Roddy, an evacuee from Hornsey. Roddy's still fighting for his life, but he'll lose his battle in a few days."

"What are you – some sort of wretched soothsayer?" she didn't sound like Ellie anymore.

"I have a…thing. Not gift exactly, but, empathy, if you like," how could I explain without sounding crazy? "I didn't ask for it, it just happened one day that I knew more than the people around me. I'm struggling to manage it, sometimes I can and sometimes I mess up, like with your friend, Jake," I paused, but she let me go on. "I just don't get why I'm here. I thought the point of knowing that those boys would die would be that I could stop it from happening. But I couldn't – or didn't. Maybe I didn't try hard enough."

"What makes you so certain these boys have died, or will die?" Should I tell her I'd seen their graves, and mine too?

"It's so hard," I wanted to unburden myself and tell her everything – could I? She looked at me and softened, taking my hand in both of hers and waited. "I wish it wasn't the case, but I know with the same certainty that I knew about those boys, that your family is in great danger."

"Don't start that again – it's too awful!" she pulled her hands away.

"But the things that are going on over there, in Poland, Holland – "

"I can't listen to this."

"Ellie. Please. I couldn't change today. All I could do was warn her, his mother. That's all I can do for you. I can't stop anything. Change anything," tears were cascading down my face. "I'm powerless – how can I stop what's happening over there? That vicar talked about Esther, saying how she spoke up for the Jews, saved them. That she was made for such a time as this. I wasn't made for this time. I was – I was." I couldn't go on. But I wasn't crying for those boys, for their bodies smashed apart by the mine. I wasn't even crying for Ellie's family, probably facing the gas chamber. I was crying for me, and the fate I couldn't escape. I hated myself.

"What's all this then?" it was Mother.

"It's been a rough day," said Ellie. "There's been some sort of accident down by Church Cove and Louie's taken it rather badly."

"Alright young missy, best you come with me," she was using that dangerously soothing voice again. "I was afraid some'at like this might happen sooner or later. We'll just pop you upstairs and then think about calling that doctor."

"No!" Her voice was warm, but her words were a tossed bucket of icewater. "I'm alright. I don't need a doctor," I didn't want to be taken away, "Just give me a minute."

"Here," said Mother, handing me a muslin cloth that looked like the ones they wrapped around the cheese. Seriously? "It's all I got!" she said. I blew my nose. The cloth smelled rank.

"Come on Ellie," I said, "we've still got milk sitting in the back of the truck."

"You needn't worry about that, old girl," said Ellie.

"We can't just throw it away, can we Mother?" I said

"You not delivered it yet?" she visibly computed the situation: restrain loony and waste milk; risk releasing loony and sell milk.

"There's a war on, that right?" I said, taking the lead for her. "If you would," I threw away the un-drunk tea and handed her my beaker. "Apologise to George for us, we'll be late for milking. Maybe those lazy POWs could stay on a bit longer. Ellie?"

By the time we reached the villages, news had spread of the two little boys. People hoped the lad from London would pull through but wondered what was left here for him, since both his parents had been killed in the Blitz. Ellie looked at me with more fear than pity – if I was right about the boys, was I right about her family? But for me, a shell was hardening around my heart; it was thin, but it helped a little.

Chapter TWENTY

The early sun gave me the prompt I needed to stop tossing and turning but sitting down on the hard stool in the cold milking shed, waiting for everyone else to arrive, I began to regret the hasty exit from my bed. Picking up a jacket left lying on another stool, I huddled into it, hugging my arms in tightly. I thought of poor Roddy, fighting for his life without his mum beside him; Wilfred's mum, waking this morning maybe forgetting for a second, only to crash into that wall of pain again; Ellie and all the revelations I'd subjected her to; Shirley's ID, and the fact that Jake still had it. I pulled out Horst's letter that I was still carrying around, but the sound of bicycles being thrown against the shed and boots squelching in the slop made me quickly stuff it away.

"Gawd! Your hair! Don't you never brush it?" It was Queenie. Instinctively I put my hand to my hair. I'd forgotten how big it was getting without the benefit of a cut, conditioner or ceramic hair straighteners.

"Maybe you could show me how you do yours Queenie, it looks lush," I lied.

"Lush? What sort of word's that at this bleedin' awful hour?" said Blanche, hunched up against the cold morning light, squinting like a mole.

"Big night on the pale ale, Blanche?" I said.

"Where's Shirley?" squawked Queenie.

"Sick," said Blanche.

"Must be, to be with that darkie," said Queenie; "I don't know how she could, y'know. With him."

"I wouldn't say no," said Blanche.

"To what, old thing?" said Ellie who'd just walked, shaking off the rain.

"You wouldn't!" said Queenie like a pantomime dame.

"Shirley's bleedin' lucky," said Blanche.

"I don't think it's right," said Queenie, as if her opinion mattered.

"You talk a load of rubbish," I said.

"Keep that shut!" snapped Queenie.

"You're so full of it," I snapped back. "My skin, Mallory's, yours…it's no more relevant than the colour of your hair. Although, if I were you, I'd reconsider a re-dye. Yellow is so pre-war." If she replied I didn't hear as the cows herded in, hollering their objections to being wet and wedged into a cramped milking shed full of bickering land girls.

As the sun climbed higher, so did the temperature inside the milking shed. Putrid steam hovered above the drying cows and my stomach turned. How this process produced milk that didn't kill people was a mystery, but it gave me time to think about all the things I should have said to Queenie. We glared at each other as we both rummaged through the pile of jackets to find our own at the end of the shift.

"I think you've got Shirley's there, old girl," said Ellie as Queenie tried to squeeze into a jacket way too small for her.

"No. This is mine alright," said Queenie, pulling the buttons together under her ample breasts.

"Oh yeah," said Blanche pulling out the collar of the jacket. "This says Shirley in big black ink," but Queenie wasn't listening. She'd had her hands in the pockets trying to prove that it fitted her, and had just found the letter.

"What's this then? *My dearest Gisella* – who's bloody Gisella?" she said.

"Hey! That's not yours!" I shouted, lunging for it.

"No. Not yours neither," she said, holding it further away from my reach. *"I may be a prisoner of war but compared to what you must be going through it is like being on a holiday camp.* What? Cheeky git!"

"Let me see that!" Blanche snatched it, her eyes racing to catch up with the words on the page. "Sod, bleedin' bloody sod! Holiday camp? My mum gets blown up by them, my brothers God knows where fighting them, and this, this lazy basket gets to lounge around in a holiday camp!"

"It's not like that," I said, hearing the words differently now: holiday camp, holidays… seaside, Cornwall, Devon.

Queenie snatched back the letter and carried on reading: *I miss you terribly but I know that your safety is assured and Mother and Father are being looked after* – Aww, breaks your little heart. *Give them lots of extra cookies from me with their tea.* What's that supposed to mean?"

"Cookie is an Americanism for biscuit," said Ellie. An Americanism. The penny didn't drop so much as explode, shattering the fuzz in my head as Blanche read out the last sentence over Queenie's shoulder. I'd memorised the words: *I love you and will be thinking of you next month – I can hardly believe you will be five, my darling. I will think happy thoughts of the croissants on the beach we had to celebrate your last birthday; it seems the shortest time ago and remains a memory very close to my heart.*

He said five next month, June. The day D Day was scheduled, except it gets delayed for a day because of bad weather. Croissants on a beach: France. The secret Jake had searched all those bloated, smashed up bodies to safeguard. I'd almost posted a letter giving the game away: French beaches, June 5th, lots of Americans. Everyone was still speaking at once, Queenie was excitable, talking about 'her Hal', and Blanche was looking at me, expecting me to say something.

"Horst's one of them POWs. He's the one you've been mooning over," she said. Was it a question?

"So," said Queenie, not listening, "High and mighty Shirley's not only got a darkie on the run, she's knobbing a flamin' Jerry too!"

"You can be extremely vulgar. I'll take that." Ellie held out her hand. "Queenie?" She hesitated, reluctant to give up her treasure and the chance to make trouble for Shirley.

"No. This needs reporting. My Hal should know about it."

"Indeed. But you wear that uniform for a reason. You are part of the Women's Land Army and I am your superior officer. Hand over the letter and I will take the necessary action," said Ellie. Knowing she was beaten, Queenie shot me a withering scowl before giving it up.

"I'm still telling though," she said, flouncing out of the shed.

"The letter's mine," I said.

"It was in Shirley's jacket, old girl," said Ellie, almost apologetically.

"I borrowed it this morning. I was cold. Horst gave me the letter to post."

"You seem to have made a habit of borrowing things that belong to Shirley," said Ellie. "I need to take advice. Go in the house and get your breakfast." I was dismissed and felt humiliated. A naughty little girl who'd failed to cut it with the big girls.

Chapter TWENTY-ONE

After breakfast I muttered something about onions and hoeing and slipped out of the house, keeping close to the edges of the fields so I could duck into a hedge if a stray plane, land girl or POW were spotted. I needed time alone to take things apart and try to put them back together again, in such a way that I could work out how to get home, not get arrested, not die and save Ellie's family. Not necessarily in that order. Hopefully Ellie had asked Jake for Shirley's ID – adding falsifying ID to my growing list of misdemeanours, which currently included scaremongering, bragging about classified secrets, fraternising with and carrying a letter for a German POW and spookily predicting the death of two little boys. I'd made a great impression on life in 1944.

The air was a warm, melding all the scents into a honey smell and the sun had dried up all the rain. A spider dropped down from a branch like Action Man on a winch. He didn't look a bit like Incey Wincey. In a field full of buttercups I had a vivid snapshot of home: Ned holding the tiny flowers up to his chin to show us how much he liked butter; Sebastian saying it was a con as he hated butter but his chin still went yellow; Emily and me, bickering over the T-shirt with the faded Union Jack I'd lent her once and ever after she assumed was hers. I lay down in the yellowness, hoping to be enveloped in its softness and carried away to where I should be. Instead, the ground underneath was hard and uncomfortable. I released the breath I'd been holding and let the tears come.

I must have drifted off to sleep, as the next thing I heard was a bestial wail, old and tribal. A cow, but mooing at a pitch and intensity I'd never heard before. I scrambled up to the top of the field, hearing voices in the next. "Wrap it like this, and get a firm footin'," George was looping a thick rope around Shirley's midriff, the other end being tied around two stick legs poking out of the backend of a cow, who was panting heavily, eyes rolling wildly.

"No! Not so close, you'll – !" Too late, the beast kicked back and caught Shirley in her side. We both let out a yelp and I ran forward.

"Shirley! Are you alright?" I said, struggling to untie her.

"Louie?" She was ashen, clutching her tummy.

"You shouldn't be doing stuff like this," the wailing was even scarier close-up.

"Just winded."

"And," I was looking at Shirley's tummy, 'feels okay?" She looked alarmed. "I guessed," I said.

"D'you think it's…?"

"I'm sure the baby's fine," otherwise I wouldn't be there.

"We need to get this calf out," George shouted over to us. Its legs weren't moving. Taking the end of the rope that had been wrapped around Shirley, I looped it across my back and wrapped it around my wrists.

"Like this?" I asked.

"Right – stand well back and I'll hold her steady," he said. "Dig in hard then lean back into the rope, then pull, but steady mind." I pulled gently, terrified of wrenching something I shouldn't. "Harder!" I leaned my weight against the rope, like in a tug of war. The cow gave a low protracted groan. "No. No. This won't do," said George, moving in and rolling up his sleeve. "Slacken off." He rolled up his sleeve then shoved his whole arm up the cow's backside, pushing in the legs. He rummaged around, then: "Gotcha!" As his arm slid back out, his hand was cupping the tip of the calf's head. "Pull!"

"That's it, Louie," said Shirley from a safe distance. As I pulled on the rope subsumed into the cow, the head emerged, looking like a burglar with a pair of wet tights over its head. This wasn't like the films at school of babies being born; there was no hushed narration or nurse mopping up the mess, no sanitized sprays or wipes to mask the stench and no going back.

"At a girl," said George. "Put yer back into it!" I eased the rope through my arms, keeping the tension taut, then everything happened all at once. Tumbling out with a sickening rush of bloody fluids and no soft landing, the calf fell to the ground. A dead thing at the end of a rope.

"Well done old girl, splendid job!"

"But it's-" the mother began licking the lifeless calf and tears streamed down my filthy face.

"You did alright," said George, bending down to put his hand inside the dead thing's mouth and pull off the burglar disguise. It moved. The mother kept licking it, like a lollipop, then bit its way through the cord that joined them. It was gross, but amazing. In between licking, chewing and nudging, the dead calf showed itself to be very much not dead and within minutes tried to find its feet. I never really understood what that meant until then.

"Yay!" I clapped when he finally stood up, thrilled with the spectacle of new life. Shirley still had her arm round me; I wanted to say something but for once, I just stood there, enjoying the moment.

"Right then, best I go see if anymore cows is going to calf," said George wiping his filthy hands first on the grass, the sides of his trousers and then a handkerchief he pulled from his pocket. He took a cap out of another pocket, used it to wipe his sweaty forehead then rammed it on his head before walking down the hill. Shirley and I hung around, watching mother and calf get better acquainted.

"Does Mallory know?" I asked.

"How did you know? One of your weird I just know pronouncements?" she'd been talking to Ellie.

"I recognised the signs – vomiting? The protective way you touch your tummy, the land girls moaning about you ducking out early."

"Mallory knows – he wants to marry me."

"That's fantastic!" I said.

"I know, he's amazing, wonderful – in every way, but..." she was frowning, looking so much like Emily. Now I'd noticed the likeness, I don't know why it hadn't occurred to me straight away.

"What?"

"His CO. He's imposed a six-week waiting period – give us hot-heads time to cool off."

"Can he do that? Six weeks, that's..." that's way too late.

"He can and he has. It's a new power they've just been given – and he's loving every minute of it."

"Does he know you're – "

"No! Heavens no!" she was appalled. "This blasted missing ID card isn't helping."

"Oh – I thought Ellie might have – "

"Ellie?"

"Yes – she. I – "

"What do you mean?"

"Your ID. I'm really sorry Shirley. It was me, I used it. Mine got lost. Jake, Ellie's, you know, confiscated it."

"What? Do you know how difficult you've made things for Mallory and myself?" Yes. Yes, I did. I knew then that the reason Shirley became a single mother with a mixed-race baby was because I used her ID card, blabbed out of my big showy-off mouth and caused their marriage to be delayed to a time after D Day. Except Mallory wouldn't come back, Shirley would be disgraced and end up a sad old mental woman who smells and lives with her uptight, ungrateful, spoilt great granddaughter who hates her. Yep. I think that covered it.

"I'm so sorry."

"Well, Louie, you're resourceful. Get it back."

Chapter TWENTY-TWO

Shirley's words stayed on my heart and woke me early Saturday morning. Cycling to help Lady H with her charring, each rotating cog of the bicycle chain out-ran the cogs in my brain. My legs and feet took over, knowing where I was headed before the rest of me. The hill was as steep as it ever was, causing me to get off, push and acknowledge I'd detoured to my school. The Gothic façade bore down, making me uneasy. I'd found it so hard to fit in here, where everyone looked and sounded the same with no understanding that some of us were born with spoons in our mouths that came from Ikea. Propping the bicycle up against a wall I found a side-door and slid in.

It was very quiet. I thought that back then posh boys went to school on Saturday morning…maybe they didn't during the war…would he be here anyway? Classrooms empty of boys had the wooden desks I'd played with as a small child, and tried to make Mum sit behind while I was teacher. She'd been heavily pregnant with one of the boys and unable to crouch down, let alone squeeze in behind it, and I'd whined that she'd promised to play.

I walked down familiar corridors, darker, less shiny but more smelly. The sound of marching was coming from the Great Hall. Peering through the glass in the door, rows of young boys in blazers and ties were marching up and down, their unified stomping having a strange kind of rhythm, intense, persistent and ominous. A loud lone voice shouted above their noise and although it didn't sound like him, it was the man I'd come to see.

"Come on men, you'll have to be sharper than this if you're going to be in my army! We need to stay alert, vigilant, ready!" It didn't look like him either. He was wearing the sort of black gown my teachers pulled out of the bag for school photos; the walking stick that usually supported his stoop was being banged on the floor to keep the pace. I hesitated. A door opened and closed nearby and I turned to see the watchmaker scuttle down the corridor. What was he doing here? I was about to follow him when the door opened again. I made like Flat Stanley and peeled myself against the wall behind a trophy cabinet but the footsteps headed towards me.

"You do turn up in the oddest places," it was Lieutenant Johnny Hayward. "Are you hiding?" he stage-whispered.

"Waiting," I blushed, obviously.

"For?"

"The Headmaster, Cornelius. I don't know his surname. And you?" I said looking down the corridor to make it known I'd seen the watchmaker. "On duty or marking out time?"

"If those boys were marking out time they'd be marching on the spot – I hope you see me as more effective than that!"

"I keep seeing you, but effective…?" I shrugged my shoulders.

"Spend some time with me and you'll find out – this afternoon?"

"Sorry, working. At Lady Hempstead's after," I nodded to the door.

"I'll give you a lift."

"My bicycle."

"My truck. See you outside later," he said walking away as I pushed open the door.

Behind the boys hung a memorial listing former pupils and staff who fell in The Great War, unaware that Great would be downgraded to First. Only one pair of eyes dared to look in my direction, "Is that young Louie?"

"Sorry, Headmaster, yes. May I have a word, when you've…?"

"Hellebore!" A thin straggly boy nodded, stepped out of line and took the headmaster's position, growing in stature as he did so.

"By the left, quick march!" shouted the boy. The old man leant heavily on his stick and beckoned me to follow him.

"Well, young Louie, this is an unexpected but most welcome visit. My voice was going – haven't quite the force I used to."

"I don't know, sir, I was pretty scared!" I said.

"Cornelius, please, and you need have no fear of me. My bark, even at full strength, is worse than my bite will ever be. Here, please," he held open the door.

He led me back through the warren of corridors, his black robes flapping bat-like behind him. He was sprightly for an old man, as herding Lady H's illicit chickens had proved. "Does Lady H often rope you in to help with the counting?" I asked. He didn't stop but glanced over his shoulder, raising his arm and letting out a short snort of laughter.

"Kitty and I go way back, almost persuaded her to marry me once!" I wasn't expecting that.

"Too much of a bachelor at heart, she'd said. She was probably right. This place has been my wife – can't really see Lady H as the other woman, what?" I felt for him; that must be why he always seemed to be around whenever she needed him.

"Ah-ha! Here. We. Are." Each word punctuated with an action as he withdrew a huge bunch of keys from within the wings of his robe and picked out a large brass one to more or less insert in the lock. On the point of offering help, the key turned and the lock clunked home. "This isn't my official office," he said. "I keep that for parents, bureaucrats and pupils I want to frighten. This is my private space, strictly invitation only."

The room was small, cluttered, with masses of framed photos of schoolboys, former pupils probably, filling every space on the walls with more propped up on the floor, leaning against the wall, either discarded or waiting for their moment. Shelves of books captured what little enclaves they could, while one threadbare armchair and a small two-seater sofa, where I sat, occupied the middle ground, fighting off the encroaching memorabilia. Presiding over the room was a tall, jet-black cat with a fringed lampshade perched on its head. It was the most fantastically kitsch lamp I'd ever seen.

"Well, young Louie. How can I help?"

"How d'you know I need help?" I said trying to keep my voice light and nonchalant despite my heart beating louder than the marching boys' boots.

"Just by looking at you, my dear," he said as he pulled out a book that he'd sat on by mistake. "You're worried and uncertainty keeps washing over you like grey clouds on a spring day. You're very easy to read, I'm afraid!"

"And to play." He leant forward, concern and engagement in his old watery eyes, so different to the vacancy in Wheezy's.

"Why don't you tell me all about it." It was such a relief. I couldn't tell him everything, but I could tell him about Horst and how he had tricked me into almost sending a letter to Switzerland. "But what secrets could he possibly have known?" he asked.

"Being here, with all the American troops gathering, it's not hard to guess that something big's about to go off," I said.

"It's not unusual to have troops protecting the shores, it's where we're most vulnerable."

"Yes, but all those warning posters – Careless Talk Costs Lives, Loose Lips Sink Ships?" My lips had certainly been loose. "I agreed to send a letter for a POW to Switzerland – the same place that bonkers – " I stopped.

"Bonkers?"

"It doesn't matter, I'm bonkers. Bonkers for agreeing, for using Shirley's ID, for blurting out secrets about Operation Tiger to Ellie's boyfriend – he thinks I'm some sort of spy, but I'm not, and now she can't marry Mallory, they have to wait but it's too long, it'll be too late and it's all my fault." It was like freewheeling downhill on my bike – exhilarating but a bit scary.

"My dear child…." I looked up to see if he was laughing at me. "Does anyone else know about any of this?" He'd lent forwards in his chair.

"No. No-one," he sank back down again and tapped the knuckle of his thumb gently against his lips. "Well, apart from the people I blabbed to: Ellie, and Jake – Sergeant what's-he-called, Siegal I think.

"To re-cap…" he said as I let the bicycle glide to a halt. "This POW, Horst? He's used you to send a letter to Germany?"

"Switzerland – but I didn't send it."

"The man's a bounder and no mistake." Bounder. It sounded comical but I didn't feel like laughing. My generation would be more explicit, but his choice of word hurt me just the same. I didn't feel in my heart that Horst was bad, despite the writing on the wall being practically neon. Just hearing his name made me aware of how I breathe. My temperature rose and memories flooded from a place between joy and pain: the letter; the thrill of him standing so close in the rain, his warmth against my coldness; the humiliation of being used; the amazement that someone so gloriously beautiful wanted to be with me; the betrayal; our few kisses, his tenderness; his lies; the liquid balm that poured through my body whenever I was close to him. I stretched to remember how I felt then knew I didn't have to; I still felt it.

"You have this letter?"

"No. Ellie confiscated it."

"Can you remember the exact words?" I could but I wasn't sure about sharing them, even with this kind man.

"Something about lots of cookies and croissants," I said, "I can't really remember."

"Well," he snorted again, "if you had sent it, those diligent ladies at the post office would have picked it up. I received the most peculiar letter from my nephew in Brighton the other day – couldn't make head nor tail of it, so many holes, what! Now, this ID business."

"I was using Shirley's, but Jake took it away," I said.

"When you talked about Operation Lion."

"Tiger."

"How did you know about any of it?"

"Delivering milk gets me into all sorts of places where people forget I'm there," I improvised.

"So, what happened?"

"German E-boats. Attacked American ships on practice manoeuvres in Devon."

"Practicing for what?"

I couldn't say D Day, "Dunno – war?" I tried. "Hundreds drowned."

"So why don't we all know about this?"

"Classified – scared of damaging morale."

"So pointless, it could all be avoided."

"I don't see how – we have to defend ourselves, like you said to your boys. Be ready!"

"Knowing your enemy is the key, my dear," he said. There was no question in my mind, or the mind of six million Jews, about who the enemy was. "Now, if I'm not mistaken, you don't have an ID card either, if my recollections from our encounter with that officious little man from the War Ag are correct."

"Yes. I mean no. I lost it when I got shot at," was my official line but it sounded too fantastic now, like my dog ate my homework. "It wasn't that big a deal," I lied, remembering the terror of being machine-gunned. "It was the day I arrived, I dived into this ditch and my stuff got lost," marbles included.

"My dear girl, you sit before me so small and unassuming, apart from your hair," a little rude, "and tell me the most outrageous stories; risking life and limb, thwarted manoeuvres and consorting with POWs – all very cloak and dagger." He was right and I felt silly; all the faces in the frames seemed to be asking what did I think I was doing?

"Well, I can help you with an ID Card for you and the beautiful Shirley," he lifted the mood with a smile. "Will you be reciting poetry again this evening?"

"I'll be there, but only to help Primrose, not to recite poetry," I said, adding my smile to his as I rose from my seat. "No, don't get up," I said. "I'll see myself out – and thank you. I can't believe what a mess I've made of everything."

"On the contrary, my dear, you're doing rather well," he said as I left.

Chapter TWENTY-THREE

I wanted to find Horst. How had I got him so wrong? Why had he used me? Because we're at war. We're on different sides. I was an opportunity – gullible and soppy. I looked for my bike.

"Over here!" Johnny, I'd forgotten all about him. "You've got a face like thunder!"

"Yep, that's me, a regular weather-girl."

"I take it your meeting with the Headmaster wasn't helpful."

"Yeah – no, it was. He's going to help."

"But?"

"It's just... I'm, you know... usually stuff I do doesn't make a difference. I'm not saying I'm important or anything, but... since I got here... it's like I'm in this tiny shop full of valuable but really fragile things and I'm this clumsy giant and every time I move I knock something off. D'you know what I mean?"

"Not really. Louie you're the opposite of giant except... " He nodded towards the top of my head.

"Yeah, I know, big hair." I wanted to be cross, but I caught his expression and we both laughed. We lent against the side of his truck. My bike was already loaded in the back. "Seems you're giving me a lift then."

"If that's the only way to spend some time with you – what was your expression? Mark some time with you. Trenogar?" I hesitated. I wanted to see Horst but I didn't know where he'd be. "I can take you somewhere else – a picnic perhaps?" he said, beginning to pivot forward off the side of the truck.

"Why did you follow the watchmaker out of that room?" He slumped backwards.

"What watchmaker?"

"The one that came out of same room as you, half a minute earlier."

"Are you following me?" he said, his eyebrows which normally moved independently, bowed down to meet each other.

"Yeah – I'm your stalker."

"I'm flattered – but if you want to spend time with me, just ask.'

"I don't!"

"Well, if that's how you feel," he said pretending to look hurt and propelling himself away from the truck.

"No – I do, it's just that I wondered what you were doing with that creepy watchmaker – what he's doing here."

"I'm afraid I don't know any watchmakers, creepy or otherwise, but my guess is he's here to service the clocks? There are rather a lot of them in the school."

"Doesn't anybody round here wind up their own bloody clocks?"

"Meaning?"

"Him. Wolenski. He's everywhere!" Johnny's left eyebrow decided to go it alone. "The camps, in church doing card tricks with Hymn books. And he's got my watch, which he's packed off to Switzerland with heaps of other watches."

"And…?"

"Isn't it dodgy, sending stuff there? Why does he record all the settings?"

"Switzerland is significant in his line of work and, I don't know. So, spend the afternoon with me?"

"Don't you think it's odd? He could be sending out coded information!"

"Or he could just be doing his job and you have an over-active imagination – did you share this with the Headmaster?"

"No – I didn't want to sound completely barking. Would his packages get checked?"

"Everything does. It isn't often I get a free afternoon."

"Really? Letters as well?"

"Of course." He was groaning now. "Louie?"

"What about a letter from a POW?"

"POWs can't send letters," he said, a little bored. "Apart from a handful of words and then only through the Red Cross."

"I was asked to send a letter for a POW."

"A letter – for a POW." He wasn't bored anymore. "I think you'd better get in the truck and tell me what else you've been knocking over in that shop!"

We drove in silence for a few minutes, or at least as silent as you can be in a noisy truck sharing the road with military convoys. We turned onto the bumpy track that led to Trenogar. Just before we rounded the last bend, he pulled over under the shade of a tree and leant towards me. For a fleeting second I thought he was going to kiss me.

"So, the letter and the POW?" A kiss would have been better.

For the second time in as many hours I found myself repeating the story about Horst and the letter. It didn't sound any better on its second outing, especially as I expanded on the bit about stuffing it in Shirley's jacket and then Queenie finding it and reading it out to the land girls.

"Why Shirley's jacket – why not your own?"

"I didn't know it was Shirley's – I just wanted to hide it before anyone saw it."

"Why?"

"You know why."

"But you were going to send it."

"I didn't though – and I'm glad. When I read it again, or at least when I heard Queenie read it, I heard it with different ears. I realised he'd tricked me into sending a coded message."

"More codes? The watchmaker, the POW..." it didn't sound good. "Why did you take it?"

"I felt sorry for him, for his family. How hard not knowing, fearing the worst. I thought I was helping someone I cared about."

"The POW?"

"Yes. Horst. He's a bit like you," he guffawed his disagreement. "Younger maybe, but he didn't want to be at war any more than I imagine you did.

He went to university here, he didn't want to fight us. I don't know, I could imagine it – one day, in an instant, everything changes. All you want to do is go back to how things were, no matter how dull it was – it was better than being afraid, pretending all the time that this is the new normal. In a war, a different time, fighting, probably getting killed, maybe having to kill."

"Louie – he was reeling you in."

"No – yes. I know. I thought I felt something. Now I feel an idiot. Used. A stupid used idiot. I woke up to the fact that this isn't a gameshow. I'm really here, we really are at war and nothing is as it seems."

"No one thinks war is a game."

"No? One day, kids will.

"Boys playing soldiers."

"But if they really knew what it was like."

"Louie, that's why I put on this uniform – so they won't know what it's like." I had no heart to carry on, how could I tell him that in a few short years we'd be afraid to let kids go to the park, but leave the internet gate wide open? How could I tell him the word 'atrocity" would become a regular part of daily news bulletins or explain the brutality of child soldiers?

"And you wear it well, Johnny," I said instead.

"This letter," he said, part soldier, part Johnny. "Ellie's got it?"

"I told her it was my fault, it's nothing to do with Shirley."

"Can you tell me exactly what it said?"

"That the POW camp's like a holiday camp, cookies, croissants on a beach and his sister's fifth birthday next month."

"Why do you think his words are a problem?" Think, Louie, don't show-off.

"Well, holiday camp. He's saying he's somewhere people go on holiday. Cookies, American biscuits. Lots of cookies: lots of Americans. Croissants on the beach: French beaches.

"And you said something about next month?"

"He said it would be his sister's fifth birthday next month – June? He also said something about shortest time and close to my heart."

"Clever." I didn't know if he was referring to me, or Horst, but he wasn't saying it in a way that made me want to claim the compliment, "He said shortest time and being close to the heart?"

"I think so. Why?" I didn't get that bit.

"And the other land girls – Queenie, and was Blanche there too?"

"Yes. And Ellie. But they didn't make any connections – they couldn't get beyond the fact that he said he was in a holiday camp. Blanche lost her mother in an air raid, so… And Queenie was just happy as she thought she'd got Shirley in trouble."

"So, why have you made connections Louie?" he was fully soldier now.

"I haven't. Not really," I tried not to show I was lying. I held his gaze and didn't touch my head, or any other part of myself; I knew from watching a magician on TV that there were triggers that would give the game away. "I just knew it was a dumb thing to do. Sending a secret letter for a POW."

"Hmm. So, you didn't actually send it?"

"No – thankfully."

"Interesting," he was miles away.

"Look, thanks for the lift. I just need to get my bike." I got out of the truck while he stayed at the drivers seat. It was only when I'd clambered into the back and had almost lifted it out that he got out to help.

"Sorry Louie. Here, let me," Johnny again.

"I can manage," I wanted to get away before the soldier came back.

"You're cross," he said.

"Yes. But not with you."

"This chap. Horst. How did you get involved with him?"

"He sometimes works at Higher Farm. But we met at sea, his plane almost crashed into me."

"The pilot taken on Church Cove a few weeks back? Damn strange, no one's claimed shooting him down. And what were you doing there? That beach is off limits – two lads got blown up there earlier this week y'know."

"Yes," I said. "I do know."

"Louie, damn-it, you really are a mystery. And that shouldn't be a good thing in times like these, but you…Look I have to cancel our plans for this afternoon."

145

"We didn't have any – my plan has always been to go there," I said waving my arm in the direction of Trenogar.

"And my plan was always to persuade you otherwise," he said. "Alas, duty now calls." I felt irritated, not just because he assumed I would ditch my plans and go with him, but that he'd stopped trying to persuade me.

Chapter TWENTY-FOUR

Later that night I found out why Johnny cancelled 'our plans'. His new plans included getting better acquainted with the German Luftwaffe pilot who'd persuaded a young English maiden that sending a letter giving away the best kept secret of World War Two, would be an act of kindness.

He'd rounded up a posse of heavyweight soldiers and, armed with righteousness, indignation and strong fists, Horst had been made to make himself available for questioning. Apparently, the English contingent got there just before the Americans – Queenie had wasted no time in passing on to her Lieutenant Hal Johnson the Third the fantastic information she'd singlehandedly wrestled out of her land girl colleagues about the illicit letter. Both sides postured, throwing down gauntlets stuffed with official proclamations about the right to throw the first punch.

All of this Blanche told me at the party. She'd heard it from Lieutenant Charleston – Ira – who'd made my bottom his business ever since catching me peeing in the hedges.

"So, it's because of the letter," I said.

"Course it's cos of that bleedin' letter. Bloody hell Louie, what was you thinkin'? They're all rattled – Ira says they're in a right old two and eight, tripping over themselves to get at him. Keep your head down girl, I reckon they'll come for you."

Sitting outside on a bench I clasped my knees to my chest, shaking despite the warm and balmy evening air, feeling about nine years old knowing I was in the biggest trouble. We were beside one of the huge Georgian windows looking out across the garden dug over for vegetables. The party inside was in full swing – the partygoers thinking that this might be their last. It was Saturday, May 27th 1944. Next weekend would be a lock-down, lock-in preparation time for D Day – assuming I hadn't altered the whole course of world history.

The double summertime meant the sun hadn't gone down despite the hour, but the light was beginning to dim, which meant I'd have to organise the blackouts. Looking through the crisscrossed glass, I watched the abandonment of the dancing; they looked so happy. Lost in the music, excitement and thrill of being together – I could see Shirley, head to head with Mallory, and Blanche who'd left me to join Ira. Queenie was alone, helping herself to meat paste canapés, looking smug and not just because she was next to a food source. I searched for Ellie, finding her looking my way, peering through the window, but not seeing me. We got caught in that moment before the light changes – the sinking sunlight bouncing on the glass, making it hard to see inside or out. My own reflection became intertwined with hers. A sign I failed to heed. I waved and saw the recognition in her body language. Then it was time. I made to leave but Ellie was rushing outside to meet me.

"I – I don't know how you knew, but – " she could hardly speak; tears filled her eyes. "Grandma and Aunt Ruthie are missing. The children. Turned up on Mummy and Daddy's doorstep…. in the most appalling state. Strangers…smuggled them on a boat to Liverpool. The youngest boy hasn't spoken a word and Sarah…just sobs. The Nazis took Ruth and Grandma but these people hid the children – my uncle was taken months before…the rest were holed up in the attic. Oh Louie. It's so hideous – I can't believe what's happening." She was trembling with tears streaming down her face.

"I'm so sorry Ellie, so very sorry." We held each other very tightly and wept; Ellie for the fate she feared, me for the fate I knew they'd met. We stayed like that for a long while until we were disturbed by the sound of a heavy curtain being dragged across the window behind us, blacking out the last glimpse of the party.

Walking through the back door, Ellie turned to me, "Louie, you have to be careful! Jake – he's taken it further. That business about that mission

– the one you knew about. I don't know what's going on, but everyone's on red alert – something awfully big is about to happen I'm sure, maybe we're going to invade, I don't know. Everyone's talking about it – all leave's been cancelled. You know they've taken your friend Horst?"

"Blanche said. But Johnny got to him first, so that's okay… he's one of the good guys."

"Louie – if Horst's been giving away secrets then…" she said slowly.

"What?"

"You know what they do to POWs caught spying?"

"That's barbaric! Not without a trial. Not without proof, evidence? Not just because of a letter?" Not because of me. I felt faint.

"Louie – we're at war, he – he's on the other side and been caught spying!"

"And I helped him." It was Ellie's turn to support me. "I have to see him – to sort this out!"

We were standing at the threshold of the hallway. Primrose was standing aside as a collection of military men, not in the party mood, marched in. Two officers wearing white hard hats, white gun holsters and armbands emblazoned with the letters MP flanked Queenie's Hal. Taking surprisingly long strides for a short man, he quickly covered the distance to the doorway where we stood, and I stiffened in anticipation. But he didn't even look at me; he marched on to the drawing room as the music fizzled out. I heard the headmaster's clear authoritative tones, "I say, old man, I thought we'd established this is British territory, so British rules and good manners apply – there is no colour bar here!" We walked in to see Mallory and Shirley stood just behind him.

"Step aside, sir," said one of the flunkies.

"You will not take this man – he's a valued guest in my home and has done nothing wrong!" It was Lady H. "I shall be reporting this to Sir Richard."

"You do that ma'am – I'd like it known by as many big shots as possible that Lieutenant Johnson, that's Johnson with an h, was responsible for arresting a traitor. A hush fell over the room. "This your ID?"

"Where the devil…Yes, yes it is," said Shirley.

"So, can you confirm that you are Miss Eloise Shircliff?" he said.

"Yes," she said.

"Arrest her."

"Whoa – Shirley? What d'you want with Shirley?" said Mallory, towering above the pocket-sized Lieutenant.

"It's no business of yours, corporal, but if you want to stand in the way of my orders it would give me very great pleasure to arrest you as well."

"Mallory – it's OK, darling. There's just been a mistake," said Shirley. "Can I ask why you're making this dreadful scene?"

"I think these good people should know just who they're dancing with ma'am."

"And who exactly would that be?"

Sergeant Hal Johnson the Third was obviously enjoying himself. He flicked open his note pad, pretending to read something he'd obviously rehearsed: "A traitor. Someone who sought to help a POW to transmit vital war secrets and disclose highly classified information about military manoeuvres. Step this way, ma'am."

"But it was me who helped Horst, not Shirley!" Everyone looked at me. "I'm Eloise Shircliff!"

Lieutenant Hal Johnson the Third sighed, "Is anyone else here called Eloise Shircliff?" he said, looking around the room. "No? Is this your ID?" he said, holding out Shirley's ID to her again.

"Yes, but…" said Shirley.

"D'you have ID to prove who you say you are?" He said to me.

"No, but…" I looked at the Headmaster, willing him to come to my rescue, but he surreptitiously put a finger to his lips.

"Officers – take her away," he said, as if he'd been waiting all his life to say words like that. I caught sight of Queenie looking more shaken than satisfied as they marched Shirley away. I went to follow but Ellie yanked me back.

"I can't let them take her!" I hissed.

A pair of hands clapped quickly and Lady H's voice trilled shakily: "This is a party people! Music please! Primrose – these gentlemen are holding empty glasses!" A collective breath was exhaled and the room buzzed.

"I don't understand," said Mallory. "What POW? What classified information? Shirley don't know nothing!"

"I'm so sorry. It's a mistake, like she said – it's me they want." I looked for the Headmaster. "Ira – d'you know where they're taking Shirley?"

"Well, I'm guessing Falmouth – there's a holding cell in Swan-vale." Swan-vale. Swanvale. I knew that name and felt panic, why?

"What the bleedin' hell's going on?" said Blanche. "Why's Shirley calling herself you? And it weren't her what was given that letter, it was you."

"I know – I know." I said.

"Do something then – Shirley's not well, she's – "

"I know that too, Blanche," I said.

"Jake's passed on the ID to the Americans since it was their operation – and someone must have told Hal that the letter was found in Shirley's jacket pocket," said Ellie, knowing full well who. "What a mess."

"Too bleedin' right it's a mess. Why's Shirley's saying she's you?"

"She's not – she is Eloise Shircliff," I said.

"She's soddin' Shirley!"

"Shirley's a nick-name," said Mallory. "On account of her curly hair – Shirley Temple? Her name is Eloise – that's what it says on her ID, 'cept she'd lost it."

"I had it. I was using it," I said.

"But why, Louie? You can't imagine the trouble you've caused," said my great grandfather.

"I know – I'm so sorry…"

"Sorry? Sorry? D'you know what you've bleedin' done?" her anger making Blanche whiter than ever. "They can't get married!"

"I know," I said.

"You knows a lot don't you!" said Queenie, seizing the chance to deflect from herself.

"And you, shut it! What d'you bleedin' shop Shirley for?"

"The letter was in her pocket," said Queenie.

151

"Stupid interfering old cow," said Blanche. Everyone was talking over everyone else. I could easily slip away and began edging outwards.

"Where d'you think you're bleedin' going?" she wasn't going to let go. "I want answers – why use Shirl's ID, where's yours and what's your bleedin' name?"

"My name is Louie. I don't have ID; I lost it. I found Shirley's – I didn't know it was hers," I lied. "I thought it was just a random ID card that someone else had lost. Like you – I thought Shirley was called Shirley."

"Why didn't you get another one?"

"I didn't know how. My birth certificate and stuff was with my parents… none of it's there anymore," or rather yet.

"Look – we're all a bit fraught, said Ellie. "And this isn't helping Shirley. Mallory, Ira, any ideas? Louie and I will see Jake, Sergeant Siegal, in the morning – it all started with him."

"No, it started with her," said Queenie. "Shouldn't she be arrested? She said it was her what done it," said Queenie but no one was listening.

"I'll take Louie home and make sure Mother keeps an eye on her," said Ellie. "Where could she go anyway? I think we've all established she doesn't have any ID."

Chapter TWENTY-FIVE

My bicycle was lifted onto the back of a truck for the second time that day. I sank into the sounds of the engine clattering and gears grinding as we drove away; we didn't say a word to each other. Fires were lit across the water on floating mocked up boats for the looky-likey Falmouth to confuse would-be bombers. And that's when Swanvale started to mean more than a panicky feeling. The film Miss Probert had shown: the air attack on the D Day fuel stores; the huge firewalls; hijacking the streams to slide down the valley towards homes, communities and holding cells.

"Ellie, we have to get Shirley out!" I shouted above the engine.

"We will."

"That place they're holding her. It's going to be bombed!" I was finding it hard to breath.

"When was it? The 30th I think – when's that?"

"What? What are you talking about?"

"When's the 30th?" I was having a full-on panic attack.

"Tuesday, look – "

"We have to get her out before then!" This wasn't meant to happen. "Stop the truck!" I lunged towards Ellie.

"Louie!" Ellie pushed me away, swerved and banked the truck up a verge. We both shot forwards and I bashed my head on the dashboard. The engine had stopped but I could hear the mechanisms still whirring, powering down and then all was quiet except for the sounds of us breathing. I looked across at Ellie, gripping the steering wheel as well as her self-control, as she rounded on me.

"Are you trying to kill us both?"

"I'm sorry – I don't know what to do – I've messed up so badly."

"I'm at a loss Louie – you tell me appalling stories about my family, that become real. You know the names of two little boys that get blown up before anyone else does. And now you tell me that where Shirley's been taken will be bombed – on Tuesday!" She threw her hands heavenwards.

"Yes," I said, stopping myself from adding I know.

"Well?"

"My watch. I – "

"Your watch? Your watch? The world is crashing around you and you talk about your watch?"

"I don't know where to begin Ellie," I said hoping she'd stop shouting if I spoke quietly; I'd reached a crossroads. "I'm guessing you know about Shirley, that she's…"

"Pregnant, yes."

"What if I were to tell you the child she is carrying will be my grand-father?"

"I'd say you'd finally lost your mind and that Mother should have packed you off to hospital when she had the chance."

"I know it the maddest thing ever, and it's taken me a long while to get my head around it – not that I have, really. I know so much because my history teacher, she's obsessed with World War Two; we did a whole lesson on Operation Tiger because she was born in Slapton Sands, and I'd read about it on a plaque when I was on holiday there. But it had happened almost eighty years before."

"Or you're a spy with the most outlandish imagination and gall for thinking I'd believe such a ridiculous story."

"But I'm not. I knew those boys would die because I saw their graves. I saw them the same afternoon I saw my own, except I was alive and fifteen years old looking at the date of my own death, eighty years earlier."

"Poppy-cock!" If she wasn't so angry and I wasn't so stressed out I would have laughed.

"I'd had a row with my mum, I was angry. We'd moved here from London; I hated it. My dog. It was in trouble. I went to rescue him. In the water, there was this mist. That tin foil fell from the sky then wham! This plane almost slams into me. I think I'm drowning then Horst – the POW – pulls me out of the water, hurls me onto his wreckage and paddles to the shore. I didn't know what was going on. I thought it was a game. A reality TV show. I didn't think for a moment that in one afternoon I slipped back through time to wartime Britain, just before…" I couldn't finish.

"Before what?"

"The thing. The thing that all the troops are here for." Ellie eased herself away from the steering wheel and began to slow handclap.

"Bravo! That's the most preposterous story I've ever heard!"

"My name is Eloise Shircliff – I was named after Shirley. She's my great grandmother.'

"Oh give it up!"

"Ellie – why would I lie? Shirley's old in my timeline. I'm horrid to her because of it. She gave me a watch, the watch, maybe a watch that Mallory gave her. I think that's the link."

"Shirley doesn't have a watch – she never knows what the time is."

"But she will, she gives it to me."

"Why in heavens name should she want to give anything to you?"

"Because I'm her great granddaughter!"

"If I hadn't promised to keep you in my sights, I'd ask you get the hell out of out of my truck!" She was shouting again. "How dare you make mischief out of what's happening to my family. You honestly expect me to believe that you're some sort of, what? Time-traveller from an HG Wells novel?"

"No, well, yes. I know it's mad. It's mad for me."

"So. Who wins the war then?" she stuck out her chin in a challenge.

"I can't say – I – I shouldn't tell you anything that happens in the future."

"Oh, course not – that would upset the time travellers code of conduct. But it's perfectly fine to just pop up into our lives from when – from the next century was it? And just, just rummage around – get your so-called great grandma accused of something she didn't do. Oh, and let's not forget poor great grandpa – who can't marry his beloved because you played fast and lose with the past!"

"You think I don't know that? Everything I've done – it's been terrible. I don't know how to behave in 1944 – I'm not even born yet – or my parents, sister, brothers. I live at Higher Farm – but it's not a farm anymore, it's a holiday complex. I'd never been near a cow, pig or farming tool in my life before I got here.

"That school on the hill – it's the school I'll go to, but next century. Supermarkets stand where the military camps are, housing estates where your hostel is. I've never done rationing, IDs or gas masks – I spend my time on my phone, laptop. Then, one day I'm moaning about my dull little life, the next I'm washed up on the shores of Wartime Cornwall!"

"I haven't a clue what you're saying. I don't know what a super market or lap top is – except I know that none of us came equipped for war; we didn't choose it."

"I know, I know, it's just – this is your time. You were born into this time – I wasn't!"

"So you say."

"Look, whether you believe me isn't important – I hate lying and couldn't do it anymore, not to you. I thought telling you might help. Shirley isn't just in trouble – her life is in danger. And if she's in danger then so am I, and my family. She isn't meant to die. I am."

"What?"

"Like I said, I've seen my grave. Next to Wilfred and Roddy's. The day I checked out – in the graveyard at Church Cove. It was dated June 5th 1944."

"I don't know what's worse – believing your far-fetched tale, or believing you're a traitorous spy, cruelly mad or just mean and queer!"

"The watch is key to this, I'm sure."

"How?"

"It is Shirley's watch, she'll give it, she gave it, to me on my fifteenth birthday. She lives with us, in my real time, except she's old, really old and irritating. At least, I thought she was, because I didn't know she was Shirley – I didn't know she was anybody. We call her Wheezy, I guess because some toddler couldn't say Eloise, calling her Wheeze, which became Wheezy. I'm vile to her, but for some reason she's always kind to me, always makes sure I have my, her, watch on. Then I'm wearing it on the day I end up here."

"Like I said, Shirley doesn't have a watch. If you're right, she won't ever have one now to give to you when she's…old."

"I hadn't thought of that – maybe my task is to get the watch and give it to her?"

"You make it sound like a quest."

"I don't know why I'm here Ellie. Sometimes I think in some way I'm meant to follow Esther, like in the Bible, when she stepped up and saved all the Jews. But I can't do that – I can't turn the whole tide of history. Honestly, I wish I'd just swum back – or got properly shot by that plane. I can't seem to move without hurting someone – that whole letter business, getting Shirley into trouble…"

"I still think it's all gobbledygook, and I'm not sure why getting the watch is significant."

"Thanks Ellie."

"I haven't said I believe you."

"No, but you've stopped shouting."

"Not wishing to seem cold-hearted old thing, but if you're not going to die until next month, what's stopping you being bolder?"

"What d'you mean?"

"Well, go and get your watch back and let's sort this out."

"I can't, he said he's sent it away. And it's late. The shop will be shut."

"Do you believe him?"

"No. I don't know."

"Why don't we go and find out?"

"But – "

"Time waits for no man, or woman. Time you stepped up Louie."

Chapter TWENTY-SIX

Parking by the quay, we walked through darkened streets to the back of the cathedral, past muffled sounds and muted music played behind closed, blacked out doors and windows. Wolenski's shop was shut up. There was no way in without breaking in. Ellie leant against the wall, trying to weigh up how far I'd go to prove my fanciful story or maybe wishing she hadn't encouraged me to 'step up'. Either way, it was late, much cooler and I felt guilty as she struggled to get warmth from the thin cardigan she was wearing over her dress. Had we really spent time at a party on this surreal evening? In my rush to unburden myself, I'd forgotten about Ellie's own pain and everything she must be thinking about her family. I wanted to reach out to her.

"Ellie – I."

"Try round the back," she said. A very narrow alley ran in a dogleg beside the shop, scarily dark because the moonlight couldn't reach it. We shuffled forwards, clinging to the wall to guide us as it bent around to where the back of the shop was. "Over you go," she said, cupping her hands to give me a leg up. I looked up nervously; what was I hoping for? A back door or window left ajar with my watch conveniently lying on the side? I held onto her shoulders and levered myself up, straddling the wall.

"You coming?" I whispered down, dropping over my cardigan like a rope, pleased when she grabbed it. From up there we saw into the courtyard behind the shop, spiky darts of light from worn out blackouts piercing the blackness. We cut across the neighbour's yard, squeezing through a gap in the wooden fence.

"There's someone inside," I hissed. Closer, there were no blackouts, just badly painted glass to hide his day as well as night-time activities. The scratched-out holes in the paintwork from which light shot out also let us look in. We weren't looking in on the back of the workshop as I'd hoped, but a small kitchen. From there an open door showed Wolenski talking to someone unseen. An arm reached across and clapped him on the back; the watchmaker looked almost bashful.

"Is that him?" whispered Ellie.

"He's with someone," I said, as the door opened and he walked towards the sink by the window we were peering through. We pulled back against wall. It sounded like they were making tea.

"She's got the measure of you, old man." I knew that voice.

"She only thinks she has," said Wolenski.

"I was impressed nevertheless – wouldn't make a bad recruit. She knew what was in that letter."

"Has it gone?"

"Sent it myself – made sure it won't get held up again."

"That was close."

"Too close – how did she know what it meant? And she knew alright – terrible liar. Maybe not the ideal recruit."

"She is too fixated on this curiosity. Standard issue, so can barely be a year old – yet it looks about a hundred!"

"Can I see?" My heart stopped and I peered back through my hole to get a better look. Wolenski handed my watch to Johnny-I-don't-know-any-watchmakers. Johnny having a cup of tea with his old chum Wolenski.

"I see what you mean – may I?"

"Take it – I thought it was one of ours but there's nothing there – its value appears only to be sentimental."

"Maybe I can win some favour with it," he said, pocketing my watch in his uniform. I stepped backwards, knocking over a watering can. "Someone's there!"

"Go!" I said unnecessarily. We hauled ourselves over the wall as they tried to kick open the mercifully stiff back door. Skin on my knees was torn open by the broken brickwork and I yelped in pain as we fell heavily onto the alleyway, but relieved to escape the light that flooded the garden behind us. Shimmying along the side of the wall again, we were grateful this time to cling to the darkness before breaking free out of the alleyway, before becoming invisible in the crowds that had spilled onto the streets after last orders.

I tried to explain to Ellie when we were back in the truck what it all meant, but I wasn't sure myself. I felt shaken. I'd liked Johnny. Trusted him. But from what he'd said, he'd sent Horst's letter. How could he? He'd deliberately given away key facts about D Day – how could that be right? I thought I'd made the right choice by not posting it – except Shirley was now in mortal danger because I hadn't destroyed it. And he had my watch! That was a good thing. It was within my reach. He'd said he'd use it to win some favour. Well, use away, Johnny boy.

It was so late by the time we rounded the corner to Higher Farm. Ellie agreed to drop me at the foot of the lane; I wasn't about to do a runner – where would I go? And I didn't want the engine's noise to wake anybody, so I traced my steps up to Higher Farm in the darkness, like on that very first night. I heard their voices long before the dimly lit doorway came into sight, so slid unseen into the dairy to listen.

"What a to do!" said Mother.

"We've had the Yanks, the Home-guard, your lot – even the War Ag's been knocking on this door! " said George.

"What makes them think he'll come here? He dangerous? I've got the little ones to think of," worry tightening her voice.

"He's probably out of the country by now, can't think he'd risk being captured again." Not him again. His smoothness, crafted to induce calmness, made me cringe.

"What he want with her anyways Johnny?" she said.

"He's sweet on her, I reckon – dirty little Jerry bastard!"

"George! There's never no call for that sort of language!"

"She's a good girl, hard worker and no mistake," said George. "But what's she been doin' with a POW?" They were talking about Horst!

"Seems like he preyed on her good nature and managed to get her into all sorts of trouble," said Johnny. Just like you.

160

"She's not – ?"

"No Mother, not that sort of trouble!" he almost laughed.

"Enough to keep us out of our beds!" said George.

"She's in demand – everyone, from a commanding officer of a US ma-rine deployment department down to me, wants to talk to her," And what do you want with me Johnny? Afraid I might tell your grubby little secret?

"Like we said – ain't seen hide nor hair of her since breakfast," said Mother. "How much trouble she got herself in?"

"Nothing that can't be sorted out with a few sensible conversations. Trouble is, no one's in a mood to talk sensibly," said Johnny.

"Don't we know it – that War Ag bugger said he'd a mind to downgrade us – and you know what that will mean," said George.

"He's just bullying you – they wouldn't try to take away your farm!" said Johnny.

"It's happening though, my handsome. They down-graded Hexham Farm overnight, took away half the land – and that poor guy from up coun-try, ended up in a shoot-out when he wouldn't give up his land, God rest his soul," said George.

"No even the most nit-picky inspector could fault what you two have done here."

"That's very nice of you to say so Johnny – but that nasty little man wasn't of a mind to be fair. His cage was rattled and no mistake," said Moth-er. It must be that spiteful man that gave me such a hard time after the chickens, for not having my ID. "So, what's all the rest of them in a bother about? They's like dogs on heat – is it the advance?"

"Mother – you know he can't tell you nothing,' said George.

"What? Not after all them hot dinners I cooked him?" she said.

"Well, sometimes the gravy was a little under seasoned!" said Johnny, sounding like he was smiling.

"Cheeky beggar! Waste of black-market meat if the RAF's top soldier won't tell us what cares about him most what's going on," she said.

"You're a pair," said George.

How could they be so taken in by him? Less than an hour ago he was buddying up to a spying, conniving watchmaker. But why was he here? He must have seen me legging it over Wolenski's wall. Horst had escaped. How? And if everyone was looking for me, did that mean they knew Shirley was innocent? Was she free?

Chapter TWENTY-SEVEN

I retreated back into the darkness to wait for the sound of Johnny's engine to crank up so I could creep back into the house, and my bed. I was so tired. I slumped down against a wall to wait when I jumped at the sound of a rustle behind me, then a hand covered my mouth. I struggled and tried to cry for help but the pressure increased against my mouth and I was grabbed around my waist. I kicked out to twist away, but the grip tightened like a vice, forcing whatever air was left in my lungs into a useless space between them and my sealed mouth.

A truck door clunked, an engine turned over and I heard, "Ruhig, es ist mir gerade!" blacking out, not hearing it repeated in English, 'Quiet, it's just me!'

When I came to, I was on the floor, being cradled in a soldier's lap who was looking down at me. I scrambled to sit upright. "Horst? How? What are you doing here?" Backlit, I couldn't see his face.

"Ssh…I'm sorry, I did not mean to hurt you," he was pulling back a stray clump of hair from my face. "I do not have long, but I had to see you before I left."

It was electrifying to be this close to him; to feel his hand stroke my face and I instinctively put mine over his. He placed his other in the curve of my back to draw me to him then gently kissed me. There was nowhere then that I wanted to be but there, in his arms, feeling him pressed against me. I relaxed into him and gave myself over to the warmth that radiated from deep within me as we kissed each other. His touch was feather-light and as I began to respond with more enthusiasm, I felt him flinch. Mortified I pulled back and saw, as the moonlight filled in his silhouette, bruising and deep cuts lashed across his face.

"Did Johnny do this?"

"Johnny?"

"Tall, blonde, very British."

"I know him – yes, and no. It could have been worse."

"They found out about the letter," because I told him, I didn't add.

"I know," he said lightly.

"I'm so sorry," I said this time very gently touching his face in the places they'd missed.

"I am the one to be sorry," he took my hand and held it to his mouth to kiss, before leaning towards me and kissing my lips again.

"This feels like a dream – I thought they were going to – how – why are you here?"

"To truly say sorry – for getting you involved."

"You used me," I tried to recall my hurt.

"I had to, I – "

"Is that why you got close to me?"

"No. At first maybe. But I had no choice, I had to give them a sign that I was doing what they wanted – they hold a gun to my family's head," his body was heavy with pain, not pitiful but angry pain. "Always I am watched, and they wait, but they don't wait long. With my mother being English, they don't need an excuse. I had to give them something significant – if I can be valuable to them, there is a chance that – " he was searching my face as I searched his.

"Horst," I could hardly say the words. "I didn't send it. I couldn't do it. But he did – you've told them everything. Now everything will change. So many thousands, millions, more will die." I couldn't bear to look into his eyes and see something different. But he pulled me close and held me tightly, stroked my hair and whispered quietly.

"All is not lost, my liebling."

"All is lost. The guy that did this to you? He's sent the letter, I heard him tell his crony. I didn't destroy it, it was found and now someone dear to me has been arrested because of it and will probably get killed, and the letter is on its way, giving away details of the biggest, most important wartime operation ever – thanks to me!"

"Louie – it was just a letter to my little sister."

"It's coded and you know it.

"How closely did you read it?"

"Not close enough – even I didn't get it at first."

"Even you – what do you mean?"

I was done with telling the truth. "Call it intuition."

"Who are you working for?"

"No one, I just worked it out. It wasn't that hard – you and that Johnny have given everything away. Where, where from, when."

"No. I only gave them what they already think they know."

"But they shouldn't know anything. I thought it was a huge secret – I thought that was the point."

"It is, but there are secrets within secrets. Mis-directions, wrong sign-posts."

"But you practically gave them an itinerary!"

"Nothing is ever as it seems, Louie, even that which seems to be right in front of our eyes. War is a treacherous business that makes liars of us all." Poppycock, as Ellie would have said. "Please. I am treading a dangerous path and it is not over yet, but I have something to give you before I go."

"Not another letter?"

"No," he smiled so beautifully, despite the bruising. "It is something to replace what you lost and hopefully lift those shadows from your face." He pushed up his sleeve and took off his watch. Dropping it into my hand I felt the achingly familiar weight of it.

"My watch – it was your watch. She gave me mine, yours!" He looked bemused but I knew I'd never feel a connection like this again. I'd slipped back through time, just for this moment, to receive this gift. We were meant to have come together for this moment.

"Thank you," I reached up to him to carefully, delicately, and with a rush of love in my heart, kissed him tenderly.

"It is only standard issue for Luftwaffe pilots, but I had to keep it from the guards. They confiscate them but we all know they sell them on," he said. "Look, I have made sure you will always know it is yours and it is from me," he turned the watch over, pulled out the large winder that I knew so well, slid his fingernail behind and popped open the back as I'd never been able to do.

He held it up to a shaft of moonlight and I saw on the inside of the back plate, the scratched-out letters H and L in curvy, curly writing, intertwined. He handed it back to me and I closed my eyes and held it tightly, more scared than hopeful that this would be the trigger to propel me back to my own timeline. It wasn't.

"I have to leave before it's light," he said looking at me. "I am truly sorry for making trouble for you, but not for knowing you. You fill a place in me that was missing, does that sound strange?"

"It – it feels so right to have known you too," I said, desperately sad but happy too. "Despite everything sensible that says we shouldn't have been together."

"When this is over, I will come back to pick up my studies and we can be together, in a time when we don't have to hide, when the sun always shines!"

"Yes," I lied, "and live happily ever after!" My heart was breaking. Even if he did come back, he would never find me. I would either be dead or not around until he was as old as Wheezy.

"Had I the heavens' embroidered cloths," he began.

"You remembered!" I said.

"Enwrought with golden and silver light,
The blue and the dim and the dark cloths
Of night and light and the half light,
I would spread the cloths under your feet:
But I, being poor, have only my dreams;
I have spread my dreams under your feet:
Tread softly because you tread on my dreams."

I joined in for the last line because I could dream too, couldn't I? We held each other for a long while. Horst laid down next me, cradling me, caressing me so that we found each other in the closeness. I didn't want to fall asleep, to never again see those beautiful eyes, to know how it felt when they were looking only at me. But I did. When I woke it was cold; warm arms no longer held me.

Had it been a dream? I squeezed my eyes tighter and willed myself back to the warmth where we were together, the place where his touch and his words wrapped me in the softest blanket. I wrapped my hand around my wrist and felt my watch, his watch, and curled into a tight ball to hold in all the pain and joy of loving someone.

Chapter TWENTY-EIGHT

"Ah, you're awake. You've slept through church my dear, not just the morning service but almost into Evensong as well. I'm quite sure God won't mind, just this once."

"Headmaster," I said, "thank you." I hadn't known where else to go, I couldn't stay at the farm with everyone looking for me, putting the Dorcas' in a dilemma. The land girls didn't trust me, Shirley was possibly still imprisoned, and Ellie really needed a break from me. Besides which, I needed a break from her. I felt embarrassed about all my revelations, the grim outcome of my ominous predictions and the fact that I had spent the night with the enemy.

"Look my dear, if it was up to me, I'd say stay here for as long you like – but this is a boys' school and it's a bit awkward, having a pretty girl here and all that. I could contact Johnny, Lieutenant Hayward, or Lady H – I'm sure either of them will be able to sort you out with a bed. Gather that bounder you were talking about is on the run."

"Yes," I expected tears, but I was empty, hollow, against which a headache thumped from my temples.

"I can't go to Lady H and I don't want anything to do with Johnny, not after last night," I said.

"Whatever do you mean?"

"He was with him – chatting away like best mates. Said he didn't know any watchmakers. He's so in on it."

"In on what?"

"Spying. That watchmaker's definitely a spy. He sent the letter!"

"The watchmaker?"

"Johnny – the letter I was telling you about. He sent it – sorry, I know you're fond of him – he was one of your boys, wasn't he?"

"My dear, you're making very little sense – watchmaker?"

"My watch – he was supposed to be mending it. I went to his workshop – there were loads of them, set at different times. He kept notes. Packed them off to Switzerland – where that letter went – so I thought maybe, he was, like, you know, a spy. Sending secrets, in code, in the way he set the time. In the back of one – I swear, there was like, a tiny bit of rolled up paper. Anyway, Johnny said he didn't know him, but I saw them together, late last night at his workshop."

"How curious. So, he was with Wolenski…" he said.

"I thought you didn't know him," I said rubbing my temples; my head was really hurting, maybe from when I bashed it against the dashboard in Ellie's truck.

"You got it back!" he said.

"What?" He'd seen Horst's watch when I raised my hands to my head. "No – well, yes, sort of," I said looking at it. "He gave it to me."

"Wolenski?"

"No – how come…?" I felt uneasy. The ground was shifting.

"Look," he interrupted me. "Stay. You're in no fit state to go anywhere." His eyes that I'd found engaging now looked watchful, guarded. Seeing but not allowing themselves to be seen. "I can sort you out with a dorm – or the sanatorium, nobody's using it at the moment."

"Sanatorium – that means medical centre, right? Not a place for loons like me!" Those creases I'd thought were laughter lines didn't lift with his smile, his face now seemed weighted down by them. Maybe it was the lack of natural light. I realised there were no windows, and began to feel trapped, hidden away from the main school. He'd said it was his private, not official, office. Would anyone know it was here? "I'm fine. I'll make my way to the hostel – it's not far from here."

169

"I won't hear of it. Make yourself at home, I'll see about some food," he sprang up from his chair, no stick required, and the door clunked behind him. Had he locked it? I got up too quickly, making me dizzy and aggravating the headache. The handle was stiff but it wasn't locked and I felt silly as I sank back into the chair. The pictures of schoolboys on the walls looked back at me mockingly. There seemed to be more on the walls and less on the floor. I must have drifted off again as whispering voices filtered into my consciousness.

"…No – no, she's been sleeping."

"Can we take the risk, Sir?"

"Don't worry Hellebore, my radar's up."

"I thought he would have had it under control by now, what if – "

"No – impossible. We've come too far. Besides, most boys have shifted. Those that haven't are too scared not to stand shoulder to shoulder when the day comes." What were they talking about? "Get the door will you," I closed my eyes again.

"Grub's up!" He said with a tray in his hands, stick hooked over one wrist. "Tea, and a Spam sandwich. Sunday, I'm afraid. Ration's a bit stretched," I sat up.

"What day's coming?"

"You really are a most observant young lady," he said handing me the plate with the sandwich.

"I thought we all had to be, in times like these," I said trying not to look as if I was talking with my mouth full. I was hungry though, even if the Spam tasted like a slimy mash-up of butcher's leftovers.

"Have some tea," he said, pushing the cup towards me. "There's sugar in it." Whether it was the way he said it, or the fact he wanted me to drink it, I just knew I shouldn't. I smiled and put down the sandwich; suddenly I didn't feel hungry either.

"I ought to be going – I've imposed on your hospitality too long. Thank you, for the food, and the bed."

"You haven't touched your tea – sit down my dear. I insist."

"Do people always do as you say? What about those boys you were just

170

talking about – why are they too scared not to stand shoulder to shoulder? Do they get left on the floor?" I said looking at the frames not yet hung.

"He alone, who owns the youth, gains the future, my dear. Do you know who said that?" I didn't, but I think I could guess – short guy with an ugly moustache and grim knack of getting sane people to do insane depraved things. "The boys' training is coming to fruition. We shall not be caught wanting when the day comes."

"That day being…?"

"When the Fuhrer comes, of course," he was smiling as if what he was saying was perfectly obvious not completely absurd.

"You mean you'll be ready to fight him."

"You know I don't, your modicum of intelligence has already worked it out." I hoped that wasn't true, I hoped that what was in my head was a wild misunderstanding of everything that was unfolding. "Your instinct about the watchmaker is impressive, he underestimated you."

He spoke in an off-hand way, not revelatory, his coolness chilling. "Rest assured, I won't make that mistake. Curious that he was talking to Hayward, who sent the letter giving away crucial information. Thank you for alerting me," he never once moderated his tone, got angry or sounded like a villain from Scooby Doo caught out in a devious plan by those darn kids. It was his calmness and control that was most scary. "I thought about recruiting Johnny in the early days. Too blinkered, or so I thought then. Drink your tea."

"No – it's too hot."

"It would be better for you if you did."

"Hitler's not coming, you know," I said.

"Don't let compliments about cleverness go to your head. He is coming. We're preparing the way spectacularly. The skies will be ablaze, and the preposterously ambitious plans of an advance stopped in their tracks."

"Yeah, right," I said.

"The troops are like those chickens, packed so tightly, looking intently out towards the water, they've taken their eyes off what's coming overhead," he was so arrogant. "In a few days they will not only be headless, but powerless."

"Because the fuel depot at Swanvale will be bombed – you think they won't have enough 'power' for their plans?" I said, waiting for the impact of what I'd said to permeate his haughty superciliousness. He wasn't going to give me that satisfaction.

"You know child, a little knowledge is a dangerous thing, it makes you think you have influence. Drink the tea." He moved closer.

"No – you drink it," I said and threw it at his face, then ran to the door. The handle was still stiff and I couldn't get it open.

"Oh my dear, you really should learn to do as you're told." I turned to see him wiping his face with a handkerchief in one hand, holding a pistol in another.

"If you shoot me, you won't know who told me about the depot," and my number's not up, as Ellie had said, for at least another week. Although, staring down the barrel of his gun, I was less convinced. Maybe he'd shoot me but it would take a week for me to die, like poor Roddy.

"I don't need to know," he said raising the gun and taking a step closer.

"Not even if it was someone you care about, really care about" I lied, thinking of Lady H and that poster that looked like her, listening in to all the military secrets over the cocktails she got everyone drunk with.

"You're bluffing," he said.

"You think it's a coincidence that I was recruited to work at Trenogar? Where better to become informed? I thought you said you two were close – yet you didn't know?" I tried not to look at the gun. If I made it sound like I was in on a master plan, maybe a plan would come to me. "They're on to you. You said Johnny was in your sights – maybe you're in his." Although why send that letter? I tried a different tack. "How could you, an English-man, betray everyone?"

"An Englishman!" it was the first time he sounded angry. "You say it as if it should mean something to me! A new world, a new order is coming, and I will be part of that – not part of a small island with small people and even smaller ambition.

"There's nothing small about upholding freedom."

"Freedom? Where was the freedom in the German oppression after the last war? From that, a great power has risen – a power that has galvanised, brought true freedom, possibilities and hope for the future."

"Tell that to the six million innocent Jewish people Hitler is annihilating in the name of 'freedom' – flash the word 'hope' in front of their children. Talk to them about 'possibilities' as they're dying in his death camps."

"What is there to mourn? The Jews are neither innocent nor undeserving."

"I was so wrong about you, just being here makes me feel grubby, like I've walked into the heart of darkness."

"How deliciously dramatic – but I like your reference to Conrad. I am a bit like Marlow, waiting for the tide to turn."

"I wasn't making a literary comparison."

"Oh, I know, my dear, your ignorance is a match for your knowledge – which makes you dangerous. Who told you about the oil depot plans?" The pain across my cheek didn't register until I tried to regain my balance. He'd used the gun as a truncheon to slam across my face, but his action was as relaxed as if he'd swatted a fly. "Who?"

It was the nightmare of my childhood, trying to strike back but not being able to connect, like punching through water. But I was awake and could take control, this wasn't supposed to happen, remember? Not yet anyway, I kept telling myself. If I kept my head low, drew all my strength together… but I wasn't quick enough and buckled under the slam of his stick across my spine.

Anger, adrenaline and a weird kind of arrogance that I should have the upper hand surged through me and I flipped my head back sharply, bashing it into his chin. I twisted and kneed him as hard as I could, like my dad had told me to if I ever got in trouble. He was preparing me for a mugger not an elderly headmaster, but the outcome was the same. He crumpled and for a second the gun loosened in his grip. I kicked again, this time aiming for the gun. It fell to the floor and we both grabbed for it, but I was quicker.

It was heavier than I'd imagined. My hands shook as I pointed it at him. Was I really doing this? I came here for sanctuary and end up pulling a gun on an old man. There was pain in my body I couldn't give in to it, although

173

the bleariness in my left eye and metallic taste in my mouth told me he'd made a mess of my face, filling me with the outrage I needed. I held the gun more tightly.

"Throw me your keys," I said, and he fumbled in his pocket. "And drop the old man routine." He threw them on the floor. "Sit in your chair," I ordered.

"If I refuse, will you shoot me?"

"Yes. I'd aim for your thigh," I was a big fan of CSI and imagining I was in a TV show was the only way I could get through this. "There's a big vein there that if I shot it you could bleed to death. But I'm nervous and my aim won't be so good so I'd probably miss and shoot higher, which wouldn't be fatal but pretty unpleasant all the same." I was shaking, my mouth was bone-dry but the rush was exhilarating. "Give me your keys." I watched him carefully as he pulled them out from his jacket pocket, "Slowly." He looked pathetic. I took the keys, unable to reconcile the cold-hearted thug who'd just beaten me, with the kind man who'd stood up for my great grandfather. "Why did you try to help Mallory? Inclusivity isn't part of the glorious plan."

"Who would suspect the perfect Englishman of ever being anything other than he appears. Go tell your far-fetched little tale about the respectable hard-working headmaster from the school at the top of the hill. Who will believe your word against mine?" I'd found the key and was struggling to open the door while still keeping the gun on him.

"I can't stop the depot being bombed," the key wouldn't turn. "But it won't stop what comes next," I quickly glanced at the door. "Sit back down!" I shouted, as he made to get out of his chair.

"You won't shoot – you haven't got the courage," he was standing now, and he was right. I wasn't going to shoot him. He was walking towards me. Bloody door! My hand was shaking, my finger on the trigger. I didn't take my eyes off him – I remembered what Dad had said when we'd found ourselves in a field of long horned cows. Look directly at them; that will be enough to scare them and make them back away. It wasn't working. I pulled the trigger.

The noise was incredible. "I said sit down!" The shot had gone very wide – I hate to say it, but I'd hit the cool cat with the lampshade hat into oblivion. I was really shaking now, but it seemed to be enough to stall the Headmaster and I felt the key turn. I grabbed the handle and backed into the open door, still pointing the gun at him.

"You won't get far," he said before I slammed the door shut, quickly locking it behind me.

Footsteps were running towards the sound of the gunshot. I'd barely made it around the corner before I was confronted by a bunch of boarders. They looked younger and less scary out of uniform than when they'd been put through their drill paces. They stopped a few feet away, uncertain what to do with the mad looking female with blood on her face.

"We heard a – you're hurt, where's the – ?" It was Hellebore, I recognised him from the drill.

"In here," I said, attempting to open the locked door of a classroom. The gun tucked under my armpit, I fumbled with the keys.

"Those are the Head's," said a scrawny, spotty boy with that sticky rhythm of a voice not quite broken.

"And so is this," I said waving the gun at them. They all backed away.

"I say old girl – I think you'd better be careful with that. Maybe you should sit down before you fall down," it was a rounder, softer looking boy who spoke.

"Which one opens the door?" I felt hot, cold and clammy, all at the same time. The door to the Head's not so secret office rattled from around the corner.

"Hellebore? Get me out of here!" They all looked beyond me then back at the gun, their indecision palpable. I helped them along by firing a shot above their heads; plaster came tumbling down, but it had the desired effect. No one moved.

"You," I said pointing the gun at the soft looking boy, "Open this." I was trying out the headmaster's technique of keeping my voice even. He did as he was told but I felt bad as he had a kind face.

"Inside. All of you. Now!"

"Don't listen to her boys!" the spotty one again.

"Really?" I said randomly pointing the gun, knowing I looked deranged. They obliged.

"Sit down at a desk – not you," I said to Hellebore. "Now pull out your slates, or whatever it is you use in this century, and something to write with." Again, they all did so; holding a gun was definitely the way forward for teachers.

"Now. Write these lines until you can't write anymore: 'I will not make my mother ashamed by listening to the twisted headmaster and betraying my countrymen.' You. Come with me," I said to Hellebore. When outside, I asked him if he could drive.

"Sort of."

"Good, let's nick a car and you can drive me to the land girl's hostel."

Chapter TWENTY-NINE

"What the bleedin' hell state's you in?" said Blanche.

"Louie!" Ellie's hand shot to her mouth.

"I'll explain – he needs to be secured somewhere," I said waving the gun towards Hellebore. Everyone staggered back. I was bloodied, bruised, wearing a filthy dress and wielding a pistol. "Here," I gave the gun to Blanche. "Keep it well away from him – he thinks it's for turning on his own." Helebore had the grace to look sheepish. "Besides, not sure I can trust myself if Queenie's around – is she?"

"No. Not seen since Shirley – "

"Is she – ?" I began.

"Dunno why, everyone knows it was you what done it," said Blanche.

"Jake's spoken to the Americans but because you blew the gaff on their operation, they have jurisdiction," said Ellie.

"But didn't he tell them they'd got the wrong person?"

"Yes, says they're all out looking for you."

"So why don't they let Shirley go?"

"Processing, he said. Sunday. Blasted paperwork."

"Ira says Hal was sweet on Shirley and got the hump when she weren't interested, going for a coloured geezer instead. He reckons he's keeping her there so's it looks bad for her and delays them getting married."

"Can he do that?' I asked, knowing he easily could. "We have to get her out – that place will be bombed the day after tomorrow!"

"You're not going anywhere," said Ellie looking at the mash-up that used to be my face. "I didn't mean for you to think yourself invincible."

"I didn't go looking for this, it's a long story, but Hellebore will be able to help."

"What d'you mean the place will be bombed?" said Blanche.

"Ask him. It's part of their grand plan to cripple the troops and stop the – "

"You've got to be kiddin' – this skinny little runt's got a grand plan?" she said, pushing him with the heel of her hand into a tiny little room off to the side. "You can slum it here – not so plush as what you're used to."

The room was tiny, four bunk beds, nose to tail, and no windows. The hostel was a thin wooden shell filled with life's basic requirements: somewhere to sleep, eat and wash. One room was a sitting room, that is, land girls I didn't know were sitting in it. Discarded knitting, books and cups were on a table, postcards took the place of pictures and dresses hung off whatever they could.

I was guided into another bedroom, laid down on a bottom bunk and gently attended to. I closed my eyes as a cold compress was laid across my forehead and I welcomed the coolness, feeling and hearing the land girls working away on me, loosening my clothes, using warm rags to gently rub down my battered body.

"Yowch!" I'd forgotten that one, as someone tended to the knee I'd ripped open scrambling over Wolenski's back wall.

"You know Johnny's been here today," said Ellie. "He was frantic, asking after you."

"Better him than that bleedin' Nazi you been with!"

"Blanche!"

"It's OK. I deserve it."

"Did you say anything?" I asked.

"No, course not old thing. Not after seeing him with that spy fellow," said Ellie.

"I don't know," I said, taking the compress off and trying to sit up. "I've a lot to tell you, but I'm not sure Johnny's what he seems. Or maybe he is what he seems, just not what I thought he might be."

"You've lost me," said Blanche.

"The Headmaster said he'd had Johnny in his sights," I said.

"For what?" asked Ellie.

"Headmaster Cornelius Barnabas isn't the kind-hearted old duffer we thought he was. He's a treacherous scheming bastard that's been setting up his own secret army of schoolboys – he seriously thinks Hitler's the good guy and has been brainwashing his boys to be ready to welcome him with open arms if he invades."

"Please tell me that doesn't happen," said Ellie grabbing my arm.

"No. Not in the history books I've read."

"How would she know?" asked Blanche.

"It's a sort of gift…"

"Like a fortune-teller? Read us me palm!"

"Barnabas? I can't believe it. D'you you think Johnny was on to him?" said Ellie.

"What? Don't change the bleedin' subject."

"Maybe. But why send Horst's letter?"

"What about that watchmaker?" asked Ellie.

"Don't know," I said.

"You're a rubbish fortune teller," said Blanche.

"I'm sure he knew Horst, that there was some sort of connection. Horst said their watches get confiscated – the soldiers probably sell them on to Wolenski. Maybe the POWs, knowing this will happen, put coded messages in their watches for Wolenski to decipher. Maybe he gathers all the intelligence then transmits it to whoever picks up the packages he sends to Switzerland."

"That's a lot of maybes," said Ellie.

"I know, but it fits with why Wolenski was given access to all these places – the soldiers were making money from him. He wasn't winding up the clocks, he was trading with them."

"So, what was going on last night? What was Johnny doing with a spy – if he is a spy – they seemed pretty tight to me," said Ellie.

"What if he's been working with Wolenski to send false information? To misdirect the Germans?"

"They'd soon realise, wouldn't they?"

"If the information was completely inaccurate, yes. But if Johnny's working with him, he could distort the information so it's almost right, but actually useless. And sometimes they'd send real information, so the Germans would learn to rely on the source until wham! A big whopper to misdirect a whole operation," I sat back on the hard pillows behind me. "But again – the letter blows all that apart. It tells the Germans everything about what's coming up – there was nothing in it to misdirect anyone."

"I don't see it – the letter just talked about biscuits, croissants and holiday camps," said Ellie.

"It was coded – it said a lot more than that," I said.

"And maybe you've had one too many bangs on the head!" said Blanche.

"Louie, she's right. You look a fright. I think you should try to sleep now," said Ellie.

"But what about Shirley? We have to get her out of there."

"Shirley's not in danger tonight. In the morning we can find out exactly where she is and try to come up with a plan. In the meantime, sleep – what do we do with soldier boy?"

"Keep him locked up – we could take him to Jake," I yawned heavily. I tried to say, it would make more sense for Johnny to have him. But it got lost in another yawn. I didn't need any more persuading to keep my eyes closed.

The sun was hot behind the blackouts and I knew I'd slept late, even though my perception was I hadn't slept at all. I painfully eased myself out of the hard bed. With a total absence of cows and farmyard noise, it was very quiet. Monday morning. The land girls would have left for work long ago – they would be at Higher Farm now. I had an unexpected yearning for Mother, to feel safe with her big sausage arms around me.

My grim reflection more than matched its back-story. Would I ever look like me again? One eye, closed, swollen and multi-coloured; the gash on my right cheek, raw, ugly and recalling the shock of his gun butt slamming into it. How had I got him so wrong?

There was a note –

Please rest! On milk deliveries, will try to get to you sometime later today.
Taking gun and (14 year-old!) soldier boy to HG.
Ex.

Fourteen? Perfect age to mess with his brain. H G? Who was that? There wasn't much I could do here, except worry about getting Shirley away from Swanvale. She wouldn't be held at the actual fuel depot, but anywhere near it was at risk.

Clean kit had been left on the bed next to mine, with another note saying Wear me. I got dressed feeling a little bit pleased to look like a proper land girl – with corduroy trousers, shirt and the green jumper that wasn't anything like the Pets at Home uniform that I'd first thought it was. I felt proud, then fake, then pleased to be wearing something clean. I held the enamel badge – gold coloured with a sheaf of wheat in the middle and red crown on the top. I didn't have the right to wear that so I tucked it into my pocket. A headscarf bound and restrained my hair, and a breakaway tendril helped to camouflage my black eye.

The date was the 29th May 1944. Tomorrow the depot would be bombed and a week later Cornwall's deep pockets would be turned out of all troops for D Day, and I would meet my grisly fate. The Disney-like scene outside made it hard to believe what lay ahead: birds played chase in the sunlight and rabbits bobbed free of farmers in the fields. With the beautiful creeks as a backdrop, it couldn't be a more idyllic, peaceful snapshot of Cornwall. But my body jarred with the harmonious landscape; so many parts of me hurt, and some I just couldn't nurse. Trying out my feelings for Horst, I settled on wondering where he was then strayed into how it felt to be so close to him. But before long, I was back with the Headmaster.

He'd be freed from his office by now. Would he be on the run? Or would he come after me? The sylvan scene darkened and my breathing became difficult as I saw hiding places, dark bushes and wide tree trunks that would easily camouflage him, waiting to take his shot. I ran back inside, pulling tight the door then falling over myself to shut every other door and window to the outside. Sliding down against a wall, I clasped my knees tightly and felt as I did when I first began to accept that, somehow, I'd slipped back in time: I was frightened, vulnerable and way out of my depth.

Chapter THIRTY

I didn't hear the truck until it scraped across the gravel outside, a hand-brake yanked and a door slammed, maybe two in unison, then someone banged on the hostel door.

"Miss Shircliff?" I curled myself tighter as the door was banged again. "Miss Eloise Shircliff? Are you in there?" The voice was old and Scottish. "Go round the back, I'll check the windows." Footsteps crunched across the stones, then the sense of someone just above me cupping his face to get a better view inside. I shrank against the wall below.

"We know you're in there, lassie." A Miss Ellie Shimlief came and told us all about it this morning." Who was this man? "We have a lot of questions that we need to ask you. Your wee friend said you're in a bad way – we'd like to help," he said. "My name's Captain Abernathy, from the Home Guard, and that sound you can hear from the back of the hostel will be Sergeant Vivian. He'll no doubt break his way in to you in a few minutes – t'would be better for you if you let us in," the Home Guard. Granddad Josh had the box set of Dad's Army the Christmas before he died. Old guys playing at being soldiers in the parish hall and Granddad crying with laughter in his armchair, even though he knew every joke that was coming.

I stood up and saw the silhouette of the Scotsman through the door's frosted glass panel, wearing an over-sized peak cap. I imagined him with a huge grey moustache and a brass-topped cane tucked under his arm. As I reached the latch, I squealed as a voice behind me said, "Sensible girl." He leant forwards and opened the door, sandwiching me between two old soldiers in thick green uniforms, not a moustache between them.

"She wasn't wrong when she said you needed help – how did this happen lassie?"

"Hellebore – have you got him in custody?"

"The young lad? Did he do this to you?" said Sergeant Vivian.

"No, the Headmaster."

"Barnabas? Aye, he said you'd say that," said the Scottish one.

"Hellebore said that?" I asked.

"Come with us lassie, we need to get to the bottom of this," his voice was so warm and calming and he looked so concerned for me I didn't feel I had a choice. Their offices weren't that dissimilar to how I'd imagined, a requisitioned primary school on the outskirts of Falmouth. I'd thought they would have taken me in the other direction, but at least this way I was closer to Shirley.

The room I was led to had a tall ceiling with exposed rafters; a single strand of bunting dangled forlornly from one of them, waiting for someone to notice and pin it to the other side. There was a wooden table, couple of chairs, huge high window and a hatch in the wall, out of which came a cup of tea handed to Captain Abernathy. He gave it to me.

"There's no sugar to sweeten it," he said.

"That's OK, it's hot, warm and I'm guessing not poisoned," he raised his eyebrows. "Don't suppose you have anything to eat?" I was starving. I hadn't eaten since the bite of greasy Spam sandwich at school.

"Mrs. Treworlan? Do we have any of that malt-loaf left over? And how about some Spam sandwiches? This wee lassie needs feeding up." He winked at me and beckoned me to sit down.

"Should I send for the doctor?"

"No, no, I'm fine," I lied.

"You're getting quite a name for yerself lassie – by all accounts you've been dallying with a POW and giving away classified American war secrets."

"No, well, yes, but I need to talk to you about Headmaster Barnabas and his secret army."

"Ah, thank you Mrs Treworlan," he said as a hand came through the hatch holding a delicate china plate, a huge doorstop of a sandwich with the same pink slimy meat of yesterday and a thin square of dark brown cake. "Go ahead – eat!"

I didn't hesitate. The sandwich tasted better than yesterday's but still weird, the grease in the Spam sliding on my teeth and my jaw aching from the bruises, but I didn't care, I was so hungry. I paused only to sip the hot tea and felt one of those yelps of air from eating too quickly jump up my windpipe. Captain Abernathy pretended not to notice.

"So, a secret army, eh? Tell me what you know."

I told him how the old man had attacked and threatened to shoot me, how I'd locked him in his office and taken Hellebore hostage to drive me to the land girl's hostel.

"I see…the trouble I have – is it Eloise or Louie?"

"Louie."

"The trouble I have, Louie, is we're talking about Headmaster Cornelius Barnabas, who's been head of the boys school for at least as long as I've been in Cornwall and that's a few decades, am I right?"

"Yes, I know it sounds far-fetched," I said.

"Sergeant Vivian?" He shouted, but not loudly, backwards through the hatch. "Bring him in." The door opened and the Headmaster appeared. He was hobbling on his stick, wearing his tweeds and an expression of compassion and trustworthiness. I jumped up from my seat.

"Why is he here?" I shouted, positioning myself next to Captain Abernathy.

"Louie, my child – are you alright? What a dreadful state you are in!" he sounded genuinely shocked. "Drummond," he said to Captain Abernathy, "let me take her to our school nurse, the child has been through the most frightful ordeal."

"Aye. Mrs Dorcas says the same. She said the lassie was prone to hysterics on account of her history, poor wee thing."

"I'm not mad, and I'm going anywhere with that monster! Haven't you been listening? He did this to me. He's brainwashing those boys – ask them, ask Hellebore! He was going to shoot me because I wouldn't tell him what I knew!"

"And what do you know, young lady?" asked Sergeant Vivian.

"He knows Wolenski the watchmaker, who's a spy. I think they're working together. And I know that he's part of a plan to blow up the fuel depot in Swanvale." The Headmaster said nothing. He didn't need to. His look to the two Home Guards said it all – see what I mean?

"These are serious allegations Lassie," said Captain Abernathy. "It's kind of you to offer to take her Cornelius, but I think we'll keep her in our accommodation for the time being – she's a handful and no mistake."

"Indeed Drummond, but where will you put her? Every barracks, Nissan hut, even garden shed is full to bursting with infantrymen of every nationality – I can assure you we'd take great care of her," said the Headmaster.

"I'm not going anywhere with that man," I said, slowly and deliberately. "You can lock me up wherever you like, so long as it's away from him!"

"The only place she can go, sir, is Swanvale – 'cept according to the young lady here, he's planning for it to be blown up!" said Sergeant Vivian, like he was saying a line in a pantomime.

"D'you know what? Even knowing it'll be torched, I'd still rather take my chances there than with him." I said.

"Sergeant, find a driver to take the Headmaster back to school then take the wee lassie here over to Swanvale – mind out for stray bombs on the way, though!" To me he added, "I think we'd better have you where we can keep an eye on you until this is all sorted out – perhaps for your sake, if not for ours."

Anything was preferable to being put at the disposal of the Headmaster and it sounded like I was headed for the same 'accommodation' that Shirley was enjoying, although they must have let her out by now. I couldn't tell if the Headmaster was pleased or not – either way I was doomed, which must have been a result. The Captain had obviously been taken in, who wouldn't be? Headmaster Cornelius Barnabas was as familiar and established in his community as Christmas trees at Christmas.

Chapter THIRTY-ONE

I'd seen it loads of times on TV dramas, the moment when people go to prison for the first time. The solemn footsteps walking through long corridors with door after barred door being slammed behind them. Keys turning and bolts bolted in industrial sized locks. Cameras zooming in on prison bars as the new captives fade and surrender themselves to the depths of the cold embrace of incarceration.

Well, it wasn't like that where they took me. It was a glorified tin hut, a bigger version of the pigpens where I'd mutilated those poor piglets. I was escorted down a corridor that stretched the length of the hut, past rows of narrow single doors, all closed, to a door that wasn't. The short fat man that Sergeant Vivian had handed me over to stood outside and grunted towards the door, bolting it behind me. It was minuscule, a hard looking bed, similar to the ones at the hostel, taking up half the space. There was a window, too small and high up to be useful, and a pot too gross to imagine having to pee in.

I sat down heavily, then wished I hadn't, everything hurt. I put my hands in my lap, lay down on my side and fell asleep. It was amazing how quickly that happened in 1944; I used to have to plug into music or watch a re-run of something before sleep would come. The door opened and the fat man was back with a tray of food.

"Is anyone else here?" I asked and he looked briefly around the room, "Funny. Not. Are there any other prisoners?" I said.

"This isn't a prison."

"Excellent. I'll be off then," I said and began to stand up.

"You are however to remain here until – "

"What? Until it gets blown up?"

"Eat your lunch and be grateful that everyone's too pre-occupied with war business to bother with the ramblings of a land girl."

"I'm not a land girl. Can you just tell me if Shirley's here – Eloise Shircliff?"

"They said you was Eloise Shircliff – and that you might need a doctor, you've been hurt, maybe your – "

"I'm fine. Thank you for my lunch." I wanted him to go but winced when the bolt shot home again. I heard the squeaky trolley wheels; pause, bolt drawn back, another door opened then bolt returned home again. The sequence was repeated three times; I don't know how many doors he'd stopped at before he got to mine as I'd been sleeping but my guess was there weren't many other inmates.

"Shirley?" I called out. No reply. "Shirley? Is there anyone there?"

"Having a séance?" someone growled.

"Louie?"

"Shirley! You okay?"

"Not really – if you're here…why am I?"

"I don't know – it makes no sense. How are you feeling?"

"Scared. Have you seen Mallory?"

"Not since Saturday night. A lot's happened since then."

"Not for me," said Shirley.

"Keep it down," said a different voice. "Some of us were enjoying the peace and quiet."

"And some of us weren't, " said the growler. "Keep talking lovely ladies!" I instantly wanted to clam up, but we needed to get out of there.

"Have you seen a doctor or anyone?"

"No. No one. Only the rotund fellow for food and to, you know, sort out ablutions. I haven't seen daylight – my room has no windows and I haven't been outside."

"What? But you haven't done anything wrong!"

"Ha! We've all tried that one!" said the growler. We dropped our voices as low as we could, and I tried to persuade Shirley to get some rest. I couldn't tell her we were about to be bombed but if we were going to get through this, she was going to have to dig deep. We both were.

The moon was up when I woke again, shinning on the supper that must had arrived hours ago – grey potatoes, unidentifiable meat and a covering of starchy brown gravy that had grown a skin. As I attempted to rustle up an appetite, ripples broke across the surface of the gravy and the floor vibrated beneath my feet.

An air raid siren whined, the first I'd heard, but it had barely got to first gear before an almighty explosion, then another, then a series of blasts that changed my perception of war in Cornwall forever. They sounded nothing like the explosions I'd seen on news footage of war in Afghanistan or Iraq; those were muted and happening to someone else. These were loud, deep and shattering. Outside were the sounds of fear and panic: people shouting, heavy vehicles being mobilised on the ground and the unrelenting drone of unseen aircraft above.

"Shirley!" I shouted.

"Those are bombs!"

"Help!" people cried out, banging their doors.

"There's no one here at night!" Shirley sounded as terrified as I was. I tried the door, which was as pointless as I knew it would be.

"Don't worry, I'll find a way!"

"Your name Houdini?" The macho growler didn't sound so macho now.

"Help! Help us!" The shouting and banging ramping up the horrifying collision of sounds. I kept telling myself there had to be a way out; it wasn't my time. Except, the only escape was through a window too high to reach and probably too small to climb through. I shifted the bed onto its end, propping it against the wall, then scrambled onto it. I could just about reach the window but only with my fingertips; I didn't have enough leverage to break it. The only tools to hand were my pee pot, no longer empty, and the food tray. Climbing back down, I grabbed the tray then, back on the bed, tried to bash it against the window. But it was flimsy and I couldn't get high enough to take an effective swing. I tried again with the pee pot –

after emptying it on the floor – swinging it back then hurling it as hard as I could against the window, ignoring the splatters that showered me as the pot swung past. It shattered, but so did the glass in the window and I fell to the ground, narrowly missing my pee puddle.

Bang! Another explosion shook and lit up my room, close enough to feel the pressure waves and hear the flames and crashing of burning debris, sounding spitefully like thunderous applause. "Shirley?" I shouted. "I'm getting out, but I'll be back for you."

"I'm frightened Louie!"

"It's okay – everything will be alright, I promise," I said, giving myself the boost I needed to pull myself up to the small window and, using the tray to smash out the rest of the broken glass, squeeze myself through the narrow space. Being a land girl, even a pretend one, in 1944 had definitely had a shrinking effect on my bottom.

It was chaos outside. Surreal. Like stepping into the old film footage I'd seen at school, except it wasn't black and white or silent. This was a roar of technicolour with surround sound, smell and fear. Less than twenty metres away, a hut identical to the one I'd escaped from had been hit. It was like someone had gone crazy with a giant tin opener and lethal shards of metal had been fired through the air. Some had pierced the ground, standing at awkward aggressive angles like abstract war sculptures, blazing light blistering off them. Others had been more deadly, beating people in the race for their lives.

Those sights will live with me forever; a man in agony, pinned to the ground by a spear of metal through his thigh; a woman, her limbs horribly contorted, lying like a ragdoll on the grass and a uniformed soldier, without a mark on him, lay face up with eyes wide and unblinking. I wanted to scream, run, hide – but I couldn't. Head down, I ran to the front of the hut and tried to open the main door, but it was impossible.

"Lassie, we have to clear the area!" it was Captain Abernathy. "I don't know how the devil you knew, but the fuel depot's been hit and we're directly in the path of the burning oil!"

"People are trapped in here!" I shouted. "We need keys!"

"I don't have any! I didne think the guards had left," he tried to open the door, then put his shoulder against it to ram it, but it wouldn't budge. A spark ignited behind us and suddenly a wall of heat hemmed us in. "We can't leave them!" I was screeching now. "They're bolted into their rooms; some have no windows to escape from."

"Lassie – we have to leave – we'll either get burnt by the aftermath of the bombing or swept away on a river of burning oil!" he shouted back over the din of vehicles, fires and collapsing buildings, the reflective glow from the flames on his face making it impossible for him to hide his own fear.

"I'm not leaving – not without Shirley. We need something to ram this!" Heavy smoke was making it hard to catch my breath when out of the chaos I saw an angel running towards me, a tall black angel who I knew would make everything alright.

"Mallory!" He was with Ira.

"Louie – where's Shirley? Whoa – what happened to your face honey?" I put my hand to my cheek.

"Trouble at school. It's Shirley – we can't get it open." I moved aside so Mallory could have a go.

"It must have swelled in the heat – she in there?"

"Can't get out. No window. All doors are locked and bolted," I shouted in between the pauses Mallory took from throwing himself against the un-yielding door.

"Let me try," said Ira taking over the battering.

"We have to leave – let me take the child away," said Captain Abernathy. "It'll not be long before that burning oil slides its way down here."

"Not without Shirley!"

"He's right – there's no sense us all ending up like jerk chicken!" shouted Ira.

"Get me in there," I shouted, pointing up at a small side window. "I think that's the office; it might not be locked," I said.

"Honey, this building is burning from its back-side. I'm going in, " said Mallory. That wouldn't work – no one told me how Mallory died, I just knew that he did. I couldn't take the risk of Shirley losing him any earlier than she had to. Besides, I knew my number wasn't up yet – I was protected at least for another week.

"The window's too small. There's no time – let me. We have to get Shirley and your baby out!" His eyes widened, he didn't say anything but lifted up a shard of roof and hurled it at the high window. If it was hot, he didn't let on. The window smashed.

"Ira – help Louie onto my shoulders," in seconds I was lifted as if I weighed nothing at all and was using Mallory's shoulders to lever myself through the broken window. Headfirst made the downward journey the other side uncomfortable, but I was in, the fires outside giving enough light to show I was in the office where Sergeant Vivian had handed me over. The door was thankfully unlocked. "Shirley!" I shouted down the corridor before tucking my head into the crook of my elbow.

"I'll be Shirley!" shouted back gravel voice.

"Is there anyone else here?"

"Think everyone else found a back door," he said, smiling, as I released him. He looked nicer than he sounded.

"Not Shirley, her room doesn't have a window either," I said.

"Let's go get her then," he said, making it my turn to smile.

"Louie!" it was such a relief to hear her.

"Bang on your door!" the bang came from where the smoke was thicker, blacker and more acrid. Unbolting every door, we found a man slumped on his bed, groggy but semi-conscious.

"I'll take him, you get ..." the rest of it was lost in a barrage of coughing that was contagious; I started to cough, but it didn't clear anything and drawing breath only made it easier for toxic fumes to get into my throat.

The next door was Shirley's, "Thank God! You okay?"

"Louie! Your face!"

"Long story. Let's get you to Mallory." The way back was feet away, but the fire had curled itself around us and was travelling hungrily along over-head rafters. At any moment the roof could collapse. It's not your time, it's not your time. If I said it enough, maybe I would believe it. The two men had reached the door but getting it open was the wrong thing to wish for:

the air that swept in was the food the fire craved. One of us screamed, or maybe we both did.

"Louie – we can't do this!"

"We can – it's okay." I took her hand and looked into her eyes, seeing my own terror reflected back. "Stick with me; you'll be alright." I so wanted to believe that.

"That a promise?" It all happened so quickly there was no time to answer. I'd always imagined, like my brother Seb, that if I were ever truly in danger, there would be enough time to sidestep it. He always argued in the car about putting on his seatbelt, saying he'd be able to do it just before there was a crash. But when the roof collapsed in front of us, barring our way, there were no seatbelts to cling to. Mallory and Ira were shouting from the other side of the carnage, the fire was greedily reaching for us and the only thing we could do was side step. We launched into the room I'd escaped from earlier and slammed the door behind us. The bed was still propped up against the wall under the window.

"You go first! " she was coughing badly and I ignored the voice in my head that reminded me it wasn't fire that killed most people but smoke; it was pouring in under the door and the room was filling up. I had one arm pushing the back of my great grandmother and the other shoved up her backside – but I couldn't just propel her through the window, it was a long way down the other side and she was pregnant. Suddenly all the strength drained out of me and I called out weakly, "Please, someone, help!" At the point of giving in, Shirley was lifted from me.

"Come on Louie, your turn. Give me your hand!" I looked up to see Johnny peering down through the window, arm outstretched. I didn't hesitate and within seconds I was pulled through into the cordite fuelled night air. Shirley was being embraced my Mallory, coughing, but very much alive. "Well done Louie," said Johnny. It didn't feel well done; it felt like a mess.

"Aye, well done lassie," said Captain Abernathy. "I've got to ask, how does a wee slip of a lass like you get to know the fuel depot will be bombed, before it happens?"

"I wasn't lying earlier," I was looking at the Captain, nervous of looking

193

at Johnny. I didn't know where I stood with him, or, more accurately, where he stood.

"How did this happen?" said Johnny, lifting up my face.

"I ran into a bit of trouble."

"Guys," shouted Ira running towards us and out of breath. "We got to go, oil from the depot is heading downtown, it's like a volcano!"

"I'll take the lassies, come – away with me now!" said Captain Abernathy.

"Shirley needs help," I said. "Are there any medics on site?"

"We can get her to help – and you too. I'll take them, Captain," said Johnny.

"No – I'm not going yet. We need to stop this fire before it gets lower down the valley," I said.

"Honey – you done enough fire-fighting for one evening!" said Mallory.

"But I know how to make it stop, or at least slow it down," I said.

"I don't think so – grown men are struggling to steady hoses aimed at a firewall almost fifty-foot high," said Johnny.

"I've an idea. Random, but I've seen it work!"

"We gotta get Shirley out of here," said Mallory.

"I'm okay," said Shirley, coughing in a way that really wasn't.

"Can you drive a tractor?" I said looking at Mallory and Ira.

"Buddy," said Ira turning away from me and putting his arm on Mallory's shoulder. "How many guys can you round up to put their hands to the pump?"

"Thirty I guess, but they're as many minutes away, the fire – "

"Can either of you drive a tractor?" I was shouting now.

"Hey, baby-doll. Leave this to the men!" said Ira.

"Yes or no? Cos I don't think I can, but I'll try if that's what it takes."

"Sure," said Mallory.

"Yeah, but I don't – " said Ira

"If you load up those diggers with mud and drive them into the fire, or at least just ahead of it, you'll stifle the flames." I said.

"You trying to get us killed girl?" said Ira

"I know this will work," I said.

"Ira – she's a crazy lady but she has a point," said Mallory. "All that water they're pumping on the burning oil's just splashing it around. We need to find a way of starving it. It could work."

"Yeah – and we could get ourselves vaporised! You really gonna drive a gasoline fuelled tractor into fire?"

"I'll do it," said Johnny.

"Count me in," said Mallory.

"No Mallory," said Shirley. " I couldn't bear it – "

"Honey – if I do this and it works – who could refuse a hero marrying his sweetheart?" said Mallory.

"Let's saddle up, partner!" said the English wannabe cowboy. And cowboys they were, heading out to beat off the flaming posse, astride their mechanical beasts. Shirley and I held each other as we watched them scoop up earth, drive directly into the line of fire, dump their loads then reverse out to repeat the process time and time again. It looked terrifying and I was horrified at what I'd asked them to do – just because I'd seen someone do it on YouTube, didn't mean it would work now. The flames towered above them. Ira was right; it was insane to keep driving straight towards them with petrol-fuelled tractors. Shirley and I gripped each other more tightly.

"Now come on lassies – I have to get you to a hospital," said Captain Abernathy. "My wife will never forgive me if I let anything happen to two brave, wee land girls!"

Chapter THIRTY-TWO

I'd woken up in so many different places over the past few days it was no surprise to open my eyes that morning to unfamiliar surroundings. But it was a surprise to find Johnny sitting on the edge of my bed.

"Where's Shirley? She okay?" I said, checking I hadn't left a trail of dry dribble.

"Shirley's fine and so am I, thank you for asking – eyebrows a little singed but otherwise fighting fit." He looked tired and the bandage on his arm suggested more than his eyebrows got caught in the fires.

"Sorry. I'm in hospital?" I tried to run my fingers through my sooty hair, attempting to flatten the expanse of madness that must have created a wild halo around my head.

"Only as a precaution – Shirley wasn't the only one to overdose on smoke."

"Breathing hurts," I said. It really did hurt, like something heavy was sat on my chest stopping me from taking the full breath I needed.

"And so do a few limbs, ribs and your left eye I imagine. Want to tell me what's been going on?" he said.

"Mallory? He's okay?"

"Tip top – with Shirley now." I sank back onto the bed.

"And the fire?"

"We stopped our bit of the valley being decimated, but the bombing blasted the oil in different directions. I gather it's still burning in some parts, but that trick of yours is working. Pretty good for a baby doll!" he said, smiling.

"And how is Ira?" I said, trying to smile back.

"Haven't seen him, but he's the sort of chap who'll always be alright." He crossed his arms so that the bandage faced me. "So. Will you tell me now?"

"Is that a white flag or a poke at my conscience?" I said nodding towards his arm.

"It's a bandage. I want to know everything since dropping you off at Lady H's – you've got everyone from the Yanks to the Home Guard to the Ministry of Agriculture arguing over whether to lock you back up or give you a medal."

"Locking me up wasn't a good move but I don't deserve a medal," I said.

"We need to talk about the Headmaster."

"I tried talking about him after this happened," I said waving my hand in front of my face. "Got locked up and this happened." I waved vaguely in the direction of my chest and his arm. "I'd quite like to hear you do some talking instead."

"I'm an officer in His Majesty's service – I'm forbidden to talk."

"Ha! That's convenient," I began to cough. "Can you at least tell me if you've arrested him?"

"No."

"What – no you can't tell me or no you haven't?" I coughed again.

"Both."

"So, he's still up there – playing at being lord, headmaster and general to those deluded boys and you're okay with that?"

"No."

"To both?"

"Yes. No."

"You're not very good at this."

"He's still in post."

"What? Don't you know what he's been doing?" Breath eluded me and my cough racked up.

"Louie, stop talking. You need to rest."

"But – "

"But nothing. We can talk again when you're feeling better."

"No – I need to know."

"You need to rest. Let me do my job. Yes, I do know what's been going on up on the hill. Yes, I have been watching Barnabas for some time. Yes, he's still there because that's where I need him to be – where I can still see him. Now, enough!"

"I don't understand – how could you, after what he did to me, after…"I began coughing again.

"Now, now! Come on young lady," a nurse had rushed to my bedside and was rubbing my back while handing me a cloth to cough or be sick into, it could have gone either way. "I think you should leave my 'andsome."

"Louie – I'm so sorry."

"Off with you – shoo!" said the nurse. I couldn't really hear what he was saying. I wanted the pain in my chest to stop but I wanted to keep on coughing too, coughing until I was empty and raw. I was given water and closed my eyes. When I opened them again Johnny was gone.

People came and went throughout the day but I knew I could sleep. Shirley was safe, Mallory was with her and all was as well with the world that it could be – in a time I wasn't supposed to exist in. A day and a night passed, I think. Strange dreams blurred the line between sleep and awake. Ellie held my hand, while Blanche shouted at me for trying to get Ira to drive one of the tractors into the fire without putting his socks on. Queenie was bragging how her Hal was going to take her to America on the Titanic and I was trying to warn her it wasn't a good idea but couldn't get my words out because of the coughing. Hadn't she seen the film? I was trying to tell her to remember what happened to Jack. Then the Headmaster was sharing a drink with Primrose while Lady H danced with Horst in front of the grand staircase. I told myself I'd put in the wrong DVD and turned to Mother to get her to agree but Mum was there, crying because I wasn't asking her and why hadn't I put on the washing? Then Reg barked and I pulled on his lead but he was too strong and he dragged me towards the grave, the one with my name on except this time it wasn't blurred, it was crisp and newly carved but no one noticed, they were all at Lady H's drinking gin gimlets and eating Spam sandwiches.

"Louie! Louie!" I knew the voice.

"Em? Emily? Reg won't stop pulling on his lead!"

"Louie...it's me," I felt my hand being held and opened my eyes to find Ellie looking at me, her big brown eyes enormous in her tiny face, so full of concern. She was sat on a chair next to my bed, leaning towards me. "You have to wake up darling, Shirley gets married tomorrow!"

"Married? She's marrying Mallory?" This was different. In my world Shirley didn't make it to the altar.

"Who else, silly!"

"How?" I spluttered in between coughs.

"Special license, in church, having a do at Higher Farm – Mother's pulled out all the stops!"

"Tomorrow?"

"There's a war on you know!"

"That's such good news – so, Shirley's off the hook?"

"Rather. And Mallory's the man of the moment, together with the dashing Johnny. I gather you weren't exactly sitting back letting the men get on with it!"

"The Headmaster?"

"Haven't heard old thing – only that a load of boys have been evacuated there from Kent and the vicar's been drafted in to help."

"The vicar? Will he have time to marry Shirley?"

"Time can always be found for the important things," she said. "Think they needed someone on the inside ..." but I wasn't listening. Her throw away comment had struck a chord.

"Got to be better here than in Kent..." she went on. Was that how I got here? Time was found for me to do the important thing? Was that giving Shirley, Wheezy, the chance to be married and begin her journey with a mixed-race child through 1950s Britain with the credentials to access a war pension, respectability and hope? Or was it just because it gave me the chance to see the old, irritating inconvenience as a real person with just as much heart and zest for life as me?

"Even if they were being trained to swim in the opposite direction!" went on Ellie.

"Sorry?" I said, tuning in.

"The boys – better than being in Kent!"

"Absolutely. And Wolenski? Anything developed there while I've been sleeping?"

"No – I'd rather forgotten about all that, what with Johnny being such a hero."

"He was here," I said. "Johnny. When I woke up, yesterday I think. I seem to have done so much random sleeping in the past few days – what actually is the date?"

"Thursday, June 1st – 1944, in case you were wondering! And tomorrow is the day Shirley gets married!"

Chapter THIRTY-THREE

It became a day I'd never forget – not that I think I'd forget any day I spent in 1944 – the sun was shining, everyone was smiling and I was going to see my great grandmother marry her beloved. Mother had offered Higher Farm for Shirley to top and tail the wedding, but I was nervous about how she would react after all the drama I'd caused. She was standing in the doorway, almost as I first met her, except her hair was in curlers and she had flour on her fingers. Children clung to her skirts, but this time they were smiling at me. I walked towards her and she opened her arms and enveloped me in her warmth.

"Goodness gracious me child," she said to the top of my head. "You have been through it!" She raised my cheek and made a clucking sound. "Come on inside, there's a bride upstairs asking for you. She's in your room for now, but it's still yours if you want it."

"Thank you," I said as we bolted up the stairs. "Wow!" was the best I could manage when we walked into the bedroom.

"Ah! At last, thank goodness – help me with this will you?" said Shirley with both hands trying to fix a small hat to the side of her head. She wore a beautifully tailored suit in a pearl coloured satin that showed she had the most amazing figure; the neckline was scooped and sat proud of her shoulders and the pencil line skirt nipped in at her knees. The hat I was trying to help her with had a chiffon veil that fell to her chin. I don't think I had ever been that close to someone so beautiful.

"Lady H has been a darling! This was one of hers; Primrose has been working all night to make it fit," said Ellie. "Doesn't she look a delight?"

"Have you asked her?" said Shirley looking at Ellie.

"No, darling – that's your prerogative," said Ellie.

"Asked me what?" I said, beginning to feel nervous.

"Would you be my bridesmaid?"

"Me? But – "

"Oh, do say yes!"

But," I felt like Cinderella. I was wearing some sort of institutionalized outfit that the hospital had cobbled together for me – my dress-up as a land girl outfit hadn't fared too well in the fire. "What am I to wear?"

"We guessed your size," said Shirley. "Lady H opened up her wardrobe and from one her old ball dresses Primrose managed to cut up these – one for each of you!" I saw then the puff of creamy paleness on the end of the bed. Shirley held up a piece and a dress shaped itself from the flurry of chiffon, lace and silk.

"Primrose made these?" I was having a hard time picturing the elderly lady, sober, with a pair of sharp scissors, needle and thread working like one of the shoemaker's elves to produce such divinely delicate clothes.

"She used to be a couturier before the war," said Ellie. "She wasn't always Lady H's drinking partner!"

"So, you will?" Shirley was looking at me.

"Yes – of course! You couldn't begin to know what an honour it would be for me!"

"Louie – you saved my life for goodness sakes!"

"But if it weren't for me – "

"Stop! Not another word. Now – I have something old – Lady H gave me this beautiful pin for the hat, and something new," she said touching her tummy. "What I don't have is something borrowed."

"Here," I said. "Take this." I slipped off Horst's watch and handed it to my great grandmother, "Ellie says you never know what time it is so now you won't have an excuse to be late for your wedding."

"Your watch! Louie – you got it back!" said Ellie.

"Yes and no. Horst gave this to me before he left – look," I opened up the back now that I knew how and showed them our initials. "It's identical to the watch I gave to Wolenski to repair."

"Identical?" asked Ellie

"As in the same – except this one hasn't travelled, yet."

"So…now there are two?"

"I guess there always were, I just always assumed the watch my great grandmother gave me belonged to her – I didn't realise it was always mine."

"I haven't a clue what you two are talking about, but, watch or no watch, we will be late if you don't get dressed!" laughed Shirley. "Thank you for lending to me something that's obviously so special to you, Louie." It wasn't the most delicate wrist-wear and I'm sure it wasn't Shirley's first choice of wedding accessory, but she was very gracious, and I knew without a doubt I was supposed to do this. "I shall look after it and give it back to you after the wedding."

"Honeymoon is fine – you are going on one, aren't you?" Maybe Mallory wouldn't have to go to D Day now…

"Only for a night – and not far, just the Helford. Still lots of military but at least we will be somewhere different," she rubbed the watch gently like a magic lamp, and I wondered if I'd fade away like a picture in the sand when the tide comes in. The truth was, I didn't want to be washed away out of their lives, at least, not at that moment when all these good things were happening.

"Well? Shall we?" said Ellie, taking her puff of loveliness from the bed. Downstairs, everyone had left for the church, but a feast was laid out on the long kitchen table. The food was covered with cloths, but wildflowers filled every available space and delicate young ivy dangled down loosely from the sides and corners. Outside the sun welcomed us with a blinding beam of approval so that we shielded our eyes. Even the milk truck had been transformed by a sprinkling of wildflower fairy dust and holding the passenger door open was Johnny.

"Your carriage, m'ladies." It wasn't a day for mistrust and, besides, he looked amazing in full military uniform, medals and other shiny bits. I also loved my dress – it felt like being dressed in butterflies after all the corduroy, dungarees and scratchily heavy materials I'd got used to. The short trip to the church gave Shirley time to explain that Johnny was going to give her away as her parents lived in Suffolk and couldn't get down in time; it seemed he was everyone's new best friend. The wedding had to be today or after the big event that everyone was pretending not to talk about. So it was now or never, as the big event was D Day and the ending to never was disappointing.

The day became a montage of joy; as they left the church through an impromptu arch of land girls, Mallory's smile could not have been wider nor Shirley's eyes more sparkling. The sepia tones from when I first arrived had been banished and colour sang out in high definition. Everything felt renewed, hopeful and full of possibilities. If Shirley had got married and changed history without the sky caving in… couldn't I?

Back at Higher Farm, Mother was radiant. It was hard to reconcile this beaming woman with the curmudgeon who wanted to charge the land girls for their lunchtime milk; she took so much pleasure in giving and sharing the feast she'd prepared. People had donated their rations and there were a couple of oversized chickens that I felt sure I'd been chasing a week or so before at Trenogar Farm. Some exquisite slow cooked pork owed its sweetness to the swift knife action of a few grossed out land girls and its presence to the blind eyes of the neighbours. George's good humour was enhanced more by the fermented apples he'd been not so secretly nurturing in one of the sheds than joy in the nuptials, but it was true to say that no one could help being touched by the love that flowed from my great grandparents on that day.

Lady H and Primrose were there in full flutter, and so was Blanche – even Queenie made an appearance, but thankfully without her Hal. I no longer felt the need to reach for a gun or sharp implement when I saw her, so that was progress.

I took a moment to soak it all in – Johnny was dancing with Doreen and all the pieces that were missing from my puzzle didn't seem to matter. My watch hung off Shirley's wrist; would this be the time to ask Johnny for the other watch she'll give me in eighty years? What would happen if both watches, the same watch, were side by side? I went over to Doreen and asked if I could dance with her soldier.

Chapter THIRTY-FOUR

Dancing with Johnny was way more fun than I thought it would be. It was not as frenetic as the Americans' dancing, but he was much lighter on his feet than I expected. I hadn't a clue what to do but it didn't matter; in between taking my lead from him and copying everyone else, we managed to laugh our way through. A group of friends from Mallory's camp were playing a mixture of jazz and swing and offered me a trumpet as a dance came to an end. I insisted my performing days were over and gratefully accepted an escape when Johnny asked if I wanted to go outside.

We were laughing and trying to catch our breath at the same time, leaning against the back wall of the barn that would one day be my home. The pauses between our giggling lengthened with the shadows. The evening was warm, the sky held the promise of stars, but a deep humming below was distracting me. It wasn't crickets or birds but heavy machinery manoeuvring in the valley, the trees camouflaging the sight but not the sound. Johnny must have registered it too.

"Let's walk, shall we?" he said. He'd taken off his jacket and was holding it over his shoulder; with his free hand he took mine. Holding his hand was different to incidentally holding it while dancing and I became self-conscious and aware of how it felt to be this close to him. I glanced up at his profile and was unexpectedly intimidated; he looked cool, adult and out of my league. "Madame," he said with an exaggerated swoop of his arms, inviting me to sit down. He'd stopped by some felled trees and laid his jacket on the ground.

"Well thank you kind sir," I said, my calmness belying my thumping chest. He sat next to me. His face very close to mine. I felt exhilarated, I think, I wasn't sure. I definitely felt nervous. This was Johnny, everyone's hero and friend, albeit with secrets. I didn't feel relaxed with him anymore, I felt something else, but what? We were both in very different places: he was going off to war in a few days' time and he may never be with a girl again. I was a teenager who'd slipped through the back door of time to spend a handful of hours and receive a watch from a soul mate that I'd never see again.

"Since the moment you slapped butter on me, I've wanted you to myself," he said, making his move. "To lean forward," which he did, "stroke your hair," which he tried, "and kiss you."

"The last time I fell for a kiss, I almost ended up sending state secrets in the post," I said quickly, shrilly and in fact with a snort. I so wished I was cooler.

"I don't want anything from you Louie, I just want to be with you, while I can." That sounded good, and I really should have fallen for him, but it was Horst who held my heart. "But there's something we have to talk about."

"O-k-a-y," I said, stretching the word to sound nonchalant. "Wolenski?"

"Wolen…What? No – Horst." I pulled away, embarrassed, feeling I'd been caught doing something I shouldn't. "We were at university together," he went on. "Before the world went mad."

"I didn't know that."

"Neither did I, until I interviewed him," he said.

"Interrogated, you mean," I said without a hint of a snort. "I saw the bruises." His eyebrow lifted, giving away his irritation.

"Louie, he was a POW caught spying, he was lucky to get away with just bruises."

"He didn't look lucky," I said.

"You told Barnabas about the letter, in fact you shared your whole bag of ponderings, observations and suspicions with him. He knew, hoped probably, you'd tell me – good old Johnny Hayward. He'd be expecting me to react, do the right thing – which would be execute the spy by firing squad." I tried not to look shocked.

"You mean Horst?"

"That is generally the fate of someone like him," he said. "What message does it send to Barnabas and his cronies if we do nothing?" I realised he was expecting an answer.

"That Horst must be of value to you," I said.

"Hence the charade."

"I thought charades was something you acted out, not actually did – those bruises weren't painted on."

"We had to make it look convincing."

"Why's he of value and what does it matter what the Headmaster thinks?"

"Horst is…we'll get to that. The headmaster's a jewel in the German circuit – a respected totally embedded pillar of British society. Who would suspect him of anything deviant?" He paused and his voice softened. "Not even you." He stroked the side of my face with the back of his hand; the bruising didn't hurt so much anymore but I flinched nevertheless.

"You haven't arrested him."

"No. It suits us that he thinks he got away with it. I'm afraid you were locked away, ironically, to keep you safe and sound-less until the storm past."

"Except I was in the eye of it."

"Indeed – I am sorry you've been through so much. Abernathy said you knew the fuel depot would be hit – did Barnabas tell you?"

"Not exactly, but he knew alright – can we get back to Horst now?" I was anxious to find out that he was okay.

"Horst was our jewel in the German circuit. Turns out we were both approached by the same outfit at university – but he's been playing the long game."

"You mean he's been on our side all the time?"

"To everyone, including the Headmaster, he was here on a German ticket. But we paid the fare."

"But he crashed here, surely…?"

"It was a good cover, audacious certainly. But he was always on a round trip, here to get intel on Cornwall," he said. "We knew someone was coming, but we weren't sure who or how they'd arrive. It was a while before we knew the dashing crashed pilot was our man."

"So, you provided a belated welcoming slapping him around party?"

"It wasn't like that but if you bought it, old Mrs Suspicious, then there's hope the Headmaster did too. I can't stress enough how important it's been to hide Horst and the others' real mission."

"The others?"

"Don't expect me to give away all our secrets," he said. "I'm only talking to you about Horst out of fairness to him, and you."

"Ok, so if he was on a return ticket, as you say, his plans here were never long term."

He nodded, "His work here was almost done. He was becoming a liability – becoming known, which made what he had to do harder."

"So, you helped him pack for the journey home."

"Let's say we oversaw the luggage he sent on ahead," he said.

"But that's not true is it? You didn't just oversee it – you sent it yourself." I knew I had marched into dangerous territory, no matter how handsome Johnny looked or whose best friend he had become. "You talk about Horst giving away secrets, but you made sure they had everything!"

"How in – how did you know that? Yes. I sent the letter. If I hadn't Horst would have paid a high price – I owed him that much."

"But. But I couldn't send it, no matter how I felt for Horst – thousands of men will now die…the months, years even of planning – "

"I'd very much like to know how and why you think that, but we'll come to that later. The letter wasn't entirely accurate, but it was mostly – which is what we need. Everyone knows there will be an invasion, even the press is writing about it – so of course Jerry's expecting it. They just don't know when or where."

"But Horst as good as said it would be in June and on a beach in France!"

"Yes, but what beach? We want the Germans to be ready, to amass as many troops as possible – letting the Headmaster think he's safe is part of that."

"I don't understand – it couldn't have been clearer."

"Can you remember the last line?"

"He said it seemed as if his sister's birthday was the shortest time ago…a memory that was close to his heart." I was beginning to see. "Shortest time – shortest crossing! He was telling them the landings would be in Calais! Close to my heart – close to the heart of Germany! He was feeding the lie, making sure the big guns are ready at the right time, but on the wrong beach!"

"Well done – too well done – "

"If you two are such big mates – why didn't he get you to send it in the first place?"

"You've encountered his comrade, Heinrich?"

"The archetypal angry bulldog," I confirmed.

"Horst thought he was on to him; you presented the perfect opportunity to prove what a cold hearted committed Nazi Horst really was."

"Glad I was so obliging – how did Horst connect with Barnabas – through Wolenski?"

"I can't say," he said.

"You can't bail on me now!" He sighed and looked as if he wished he hadn't started any of this, but I couldn't stop now.

"We laid random threads, hoping they'd mesh. None of us was sure what we were knitting until you damn near got strangled by it."

"Part of the make do and mend campaign?" I said.

"Funny girl. The threads may have been randomly laid, but they were top quality."

"Wolenski's not a thread and he doesn't seem top quality to me, more a spiky knitting needle," I said.

"Wolenski – you always come back to him. I need to stay with Horst if I'm ever going to have a moment's peace with you before the night is out."

"Sorry."

"Horst was brave. He took huge risks, worked in the shadows – I have an enormous amount of respect for everything he did which makes it hard to be here with you, alone, knowing how he felt about you."

"You said was," I said as all the life within me plummeted to my feet.

"Louie, I'm just not sure…he's off the radar. We haven't picked up a single message from him." He took my hand and searched my face. I willed myself not to cry. "We let him 'escape' – as I said, he was all but done here. He was due to rendezvous with an exit team but it seems he made a detour," that would be to say goodbye to me. "We've heard nothing – we don't know if he made it, or, if he did, what happened when he landed in Germany." I looked at Johnny but wanted to see Horst, and he knew it.

"So, he's missing," I said, small comfort, but comfort nevertheless.

"There's more I'm afraid," said Johnny. Stars tiptoed into the sky behind him, keeping hushed and quiet so they wouldn't interrupt what he was saying.

"Please…don't tell me he's dead, not today…"

"No, no! I don't know – but there is something I have to ask," he looked so sad. He still held my hand massaging the back of it with his thumb, like he was drawing courage from the action. "Were you working with Horst?"

"What? Because of the letter?"

"That didn't help. It's more the fact that there are no records on you, anywhere – you just seemed to materialise the day that Horst did. You know an extraordinary amount of information you shouldn't, including a highly classified training mission that went badly wrong."

"Operation Tiger."

"You see? You shouldn't be putting those two words anywhere near each other. What do you know and how the hell do you know it?" He was close to shouting, but more out of frustration than anger. "Did Horst tell you? How did he know? Is it the latest victory propaganda to be pedalled?" He'd dropped my hands and was getting to his feet.

"Horst didn't tell me, nor any other German, spy or otherwise. And the secret hasn't gone viral."

"Viral?"

"No one knows, except those that should."

"And you," he said.

"And me. Look, what happened that night was tragic…all of those young men drowning, burnt, I can't think of a more terrifying way to die."

"So, how did you know? I barely know the details, just the faintest sketch that Jake – Sergeant Siegal – felt he could outline. He's a mess. God knows the stuff of his nightmares."

"He was on the recovery team, retrieving and searching every body to be sure the few men who knew about the planned invasion were accounted for," I said, resigned now to my fate.

"How in – ? How do you know that?" He was pacing around me now.

"If I told you, you wouldn't believe me," I said, my voice small.

"Try me – it can't be any worse than the smoke and mirrors we're trying to pull off," he said, frantically pushing his fingers through his own hair now, having given up all hope of caressing mine.

"You're doing great – was sending the schoolboys from Kent to the school here part of the plan?"

"Plan?"

"I know there are huge camps in Kent – well there would be if the invasion target is Calais – the boys would love to tell Barnabas that."

"Possibly."

"But the camps are as fake as the looky-likey Falmouth across the bay."

"How would you know that?"

"That watch, the one you took from Wolenski?"

"It was you outside!" he looked shattered.

"It was given to me by my great grandmother."

"This is... If I'd brought my gun to the wedding, I'd have pulled it on you by now – is there anything you haven't seen, any secret you don't know?"

"I don't know why I'm here."

"And I don't know who you are. Bloody hell – that time I met you in the graveyard, you were upset. You kept saying you weren't Esther – does she have something to do with this?"

"Esther's from the Bible. She saved thousands of Jews," I said.

"From the bad guy – Haman – so?"

"He's like Hitler – I was upset because I'm not Esther, I can't even save a handful of Jews. She was told she was made for such a time, a time to act

211

– what am I made for, why am I here? I haven't saved anybody, not Ellie's Jewish family, those boys on the beach – I sort of thought, maybe, getting Shirley married off was the reason, but that's not big enough. Not for all the effort – "

"Louie – you're not making any sense," his tone was softer now. "Oh Lord, come here," he extended his hand again to me and I took it. Pulling me towards him he wiped away the tears I didn't realise I had. "You said the watch was given to you by your great grandmother – what does that have to do with anything?"

"It was on my fifteenth birthday – Wheezy wore it on her wedding day before her fiancé, husband now, went off to fight and die for our country."

"In the Great War?"

"This one."

"The watch is very old Louie," he looked at me sadly.

"Do you have it?" I asked, half scared, half thrilled at the prospect.

"Yes – but not here," he said. "We should get back to the wedding."

"Can I just ask, was I right about Wolenski?"

"What d'you mean?"

"About him being a spy as well, sending messages using the watches confiscated from the POWs and sold to him by the guards – that was why he was everywhere. Picking up watches, not winding up clocks. Messages would be coded either in the time set of the faces or in the back of watches he sends to Switzerland."

"Why are you asking me – you've got it all worked out and anything I say you know already," we were walking back to the farmhouse. I could hear people laughing and tried to pull myself back into the happiness of the day. I could make out two figures walking towards us in the moonlight.

"Louie?" one of the figures called out, it was Shirley.

"Come on you two – this bride wants to go on honeymoon!" said the other, Ellie.

"Sorry, we're coming," I said. "Shirley, I don't want it back, but could I just show Johnny the watch I lent you?"

"Of course, darling!" she said slipping it easily off her tiny wrist. I opened it for the second time that day and held it in the moonlight.

"See here?" I said. "Horst scratched our initials here, just a few days ago. When you have a chance Johnny, open the watch you took from Wolenski – you'll find all the answers you need to your questions about who I am, where I'm from and why I know more than I should." I closed the watch and handed it back to Shirley. "Keep this safe. If, for whatever reason, I don't see you when you get back, hold on to it – you'll know when it's right to pass it on." A horn tooted.

"Mallory!" said Shirley torn between not wanting to interrupt her new friend talking nonsense and hurrying to her new husband.

"Let's get you in that jeep!" said Ellie, pulling Shirley away. Johnny and I started to follow but just before we got to the gathered crowd, he pulled me towards him.

"Louie – I…" he clasped my shoulders tightly and searched my face, but I couldn't read his. Then bent his head and kissed me so tenderly, so longingly, I thought my heart would break.

"She's throwing the bouquet!" Queenie and Blanche reached up for it but Blanche won and looked at Ira in the driver's seat of the getaway jeep. A roar went up from the guests, Blanche blushed and Ira revved the engine.

"Don't forget the watch – maybe even give it to a namesake one day," I said to Shirley.

"You're a funny little thing!" said Shirley before catching me in an embrace I didn't want to end. The engine revved again. I quickly reached across and grabbed Mallory's hand.

"Take care of each other; you're both very, very special to me." And they were gone, probably thinking I'd been at the gin and was overcome by the emotion of the day – how would they know they'd just said goodbye to their great granddaughter?

Chapter THIRTY-FIVE

The weather had closed in – last night it seemed like a cloud would never dare enter the pure clear skies, yet under the cover of night a storm had swept them in and now filthy weather whipped angrily around the farm. History said this would happen. D Day was meant to be tomorrow, June 5th, but the weather was so grim it was postponed a day. Had that call been made, or was everyone, like me, thinking they might be standing at the foot of their last full day on earth? I didn't want to die. Looking out at the storm I felt small, weak and afraid.

I was drenched just getting from the farmhouse to the milking parlour. The land girls were already there and so was George, looking even worse than I felt. The only stool available was next to Queenie. "Didn't see your Hal there last night," I said.

"Surprised you noticed who was there, apart from your blue-eyed boy," a ripple ran across my heart.

"Johnny's not mine," I said, realising it was with regret.

"That why you've got a face like a wet weekend?" said Blanche.

"We've had a falling out as well," said Queenie.

"I'm sorry, I know how much you liked him," I said.

"Yeah well, this war – makes us hold on to things we wouldn't have picked up in a shop sale," she said.

"Why go for him in the first place?"

"He showed interest in me – so," she shrugged. "Didn't think I'd get another chance."

"Queenie, you just need to believe in yourself! This morning, without your make-up and your hair not so, you know, 'done', you look lovely, soft-er."

"Fat liar!" She directed a teat at me and squirted my boots with the cow's milk, but she was laughing and blushing at the same time.

"Nice. Pay a girl a compliment!" I laughed too.

"Keep it down girls!" said George.

"Too much of the special apple juice, eh?" said Blanche.

"You can talk – wasn't sure you'd be here this early," said Ellie.

"Haven't been to bleedin' bed yet, that's why!"

"Dirty stop out!" said Queenie.

"It weren't dirty – it was lovely," said Blanche. "Ira was lovely. Said I'm his girl, for proper."

"Chop! Chop! Girls – it'll be standing room only in church so if we want to get a last glimpse at our military friends ,we need to get a move on!"

The parlour was wet, the cows stank, the job was filthy, but I was happy enough. Enough to want to live. I had friends who cared about me and knew how I fitted in here: I didn't know what was ahead but for now all I wanted was to be alive and present.

Before I knew it, I was standing outside the church again, this time allowing myself to look over into the graveyard. I saw two fresh graves in the place I'd seen them decades from now. The two friends had been laid side by side.

"I'm sorry boys – I really thought I could have made a difference for you."

"Louie – we should go in," it was Ellie. "Are those the boys from the beach?" I nodded. "You mustn't feel badly old thing – you said you saw the graves in, you know, your time. You can't change what has already happened."

"But I did – in a way. Shirley isn't married in my time – she's a lonely old woman who talks about tinned ham and her watch. She'd had a hard life, bringing up a mixed race child on her own – the way ahead gets even narrower than it is now, for a good few years anyway. She did a great job – my grandfather, her son Joshua, was a good man. But with no war pension, no piece of paper to say she was married, life was a struggle – by the time she comes into my life her light has gone and I only saw the worn out shell. I didn't cherish Shirley, I didn't take the time to hear her stories. I didn't even know she played the piano…!"

"But she's married now – you did that."

"Yes. And I really hope that does make a difference for her."

"So…Mallory. He doesn't…?" she couldn't say the words.

"Not many do Ellie," I said as gently as I could. "But what they're about to do will make a difference. It's going to be hideous, but it will end the war."

Church was a sombre place that day. The placard over the door said it was a "Shelter from the Storm," like it would say in my day. And inside was peaceful; it did feel like a shelter, but like all shelters, it wasn't permanent. The atmosphere was heavy with fear; soldiers looked ahead or into their hands, seeing only tomorrow and weighing that one day against all their yesterdays. They thought of loved ones, wives, children, parents, siblings, their final letters written, their goodbyes on their way to being delivered.

"And the Lord…goes before thee; He will be with thee, He will not fail thee, neither forsake thee: fear not…" the vicar's words penetrated my sorrow. Fear not, how easy to say, how difficult to believe. I looked around at all the young stoic faces, holding it together with bravery and dignity. Their courage humbled me and every time I thought about what may lay ahead for me, I thought of them.

I'd like to say my last full day was full of poignant memories but it passed in a rainy haze. No one ventured out; I sat with Doreen inside by the window, watching the weather wrap itself, tighter and tighter, around the farmhouse and we helped George run around with buckets to catch the rain as it found it way in. Mother and me combed the children's hair for nits, seeing who could find the biggest one. No one came to the door; no one knew this was my last day, no last special supper – just the wedding left-overs. And then it was Monday morning.

Chapter THIRTY-SIX

I knew the day would end badly for me, I just didn't know what time it would end. Ellie and I were on the milk round; everyone was on tenterhooks. There was only a thin military presence, yet the county seemed pregnant with it. We had butter and cheese on the truck, which usually created a frisson of excitement, but that day people barely noticed. They just wanted to talk.

"So, what's going on in the camps? Been there today?" said Mrs Barnicoat, pushing her way to the front of the queue.

"Wait your turn please, Mrs Pascoe was here first," I said.

"Thank you my dear. I don't think we should be talking about the camps – loose tongues and all that. You don't know who's listening in, do you?"

"Quite right, Mrs P – do you know you're getting your milk from a genuine fire-fighting heroine?" said Ellie. "If it wasn't for Louie here, they'd have lost half the valley at Swanvale."

"I heard they did," said Mrs Jago, who was second in line.

"Well, the other half then," said Ellie.

"I heard they was all leaving," said Mrs Barnicoat, bobbing up at the head of the queue again.

"Well, they're bound to leave some time, else what's the point of them being here? Don't reckon it's 'cos Hitler's got Cornwall in his sights!" said Mrs Jago.

"Shame when they goes, I've got used to having all those lovely young men on my doorstep!"

"Mrs Barnicoat – and you with your husband out fighting for king and country!" said Mrs Pascoe.

"He's not fighting – he works in the kitchens!" You wouldn't need to try too hard if you were a spy trying to get information on what was going on locally. Stand still long enough with a pitcher of milk in hand and you'll find out all there is to know. We drove the milk truck into the British Camp. I still didn't have any ID but it wasn't a problem on the gate.

"It's because they all know what you did, old thing!" explained Ellie. "Bit of a local hero!"

"Does that mean Jake won't try to arrest me if he sees me?"

"I doubt it – I don't think Jake's up to doing very much at all at the moment. I'm not sure he'll be heading out with his team; he's been taken off duty for the time being."

"Poor guy," I said and meant it. I felt guilty; blundering in like I did couldn't have helped him come to terms with the aftermath of Operation Tiger. I was glad for him, though, that he would miss the trauma of D Day – I'm not sure he would survive the shock of reliving the horror of the dead or dying bodies in the water. This time he wouldn't be retrieving them but clambering over them to get to the shore, or using them as shields to protect himself from the enemy fire.

We took the milk to the canteen, but it had the feeling of the last day of term, without the excitement. Everything was being taken down, packed away; it was just the very basics left to feed those with an appetite. I really hoped I'd see Johnny – I even had butter. I thought I saw him walk across the yard in the distance as we climbed back on the truck, but if it was Johnny, he didn't see me. The soldier was in control, focused and lost to me.

Our last stop of the day was Trenogar. I felt cheered at the thought of seeing Lady H and Primrose and tried to let the anticipation lift my spirits – I'd made it through to lunchtime, who knew if I couldn't cheat my fate? What I failed to even consider was that the fate was never mine to cheat.

The roads were quiet, so we pulled over before we got to Trenogar to have our lunch. The wedding had released Mother from all past stinginess and she had given us both great doorstep sandwiches. They were filled with jam and egg-like custard. I smiled as I bit into the delicious starchy sweetness and relished the thrill of eating so many carbs in one mouthful – no low-carb-diet this side of the millennium. Mindful of George's fuel ration, Ellie turned off the engine and we watched the rain lash across the windscreen. Our breath and the mizzle outside obscured all visibility, making the cabin intimate but slightly creepy, so we couldn't see beyond the glass.

"Have you had any more news of your family?" I asked, tentatively.

"Not really. Daddy's been making inquiries but it's impossible to get anything useful from anyone. The children have been opening up a bit more, but what's inside them isn't good. Mummy's torn between encouraging them to let it out – you know how we Jewish families like to talk – and just leaving them to heal in their own time."

"I heard children communicate better using crayons, pictures and stuff. Probably best to do both; be there when they want to talk, but not push them."

"Did you hear that here or, you know, there?"

"There. It must be very weird for you," I said.

"Not as weird as it is for you – I have to admit I go from thinking it's quite a rational occurrence, I mean who can understand the enormity of time, the universe, God even? To thinking it's a load of codswallop and you're pulling my leg."

"That's exactly how I feel, if it helps. I wish I'd got my watch back from Johnny."

"You mean this one?" To my amazement she pulled it out from her dungarees.

"Where? How? When did Johnny...?"

"After church yesterday. You'd gone already. He drove up as people were leaving, he was looking for you but he couldn't stop. He gave it to me – I've been waiting for the right time to give it back to you – I wasn't sure what would happen when I did."

"Did he look inside?"

"If he did, he didn't say," said Ellie. "Go on, open it!"

"I'm trying," I said, pulling out the winder and running my fingernail along the thin line where it should open.

"What if – ?"

"Nothing will happen – I had this theory it might, if I'd got the two watches together, but I couldn't take the risk of Shirley not having the watch. You know, so she could give it to me, after I'm born. It's all so weird!" The back flipped open. Debris, salt and decades of wrist crud fell away; Wolenski might have looked at it but he hadn't cleaned it out. I had so wanted Johnny to see the two etched initials I was looking at; they were exactly as they were in the watch he saw at Shirley's wedding.

"Louie! I don't know what to say," said Ellie, looking at me with a mixture of fear and awe. I felt shaken – it was properly true. I really had slipped back to 1944, making what lay ahead for me properly true too.

We were in a state of shock as we drove into the grounds of Trenogar. Ellie had so many questions, but I couldn't trust myself to speak – I was tempted to tell her to put her money on any company in the future that had an apple icon – but mostly I wanted to hide. The confidence, bravery and sheer bloody-mindedness I had in the fire had gone, I didn't have that certainty anymore that it wasn't time. Now it was, and it would happen today.

A smart black car was parked outside and as we walked past the front doorsteps heading for the scullery entrance, a bicycle was propped up against the wall. Something felt wrong, and as we walked into the hallway, I realised why. Heads bent together, deep in conversation, near the open door of the grandfather clock was Lady H and Wolenski.

"Lady H?" I said, thinking what the – ? Wolenski turned away to bury his head in the clock mechanism.

"Ah!" she said. The harsh greyness of the day made her look older, more painted, and I breathed in her heavy scent and face powder as she began to greet us with butterfly kisses. "My goodness me, Louie – your face!" I'd almost forgotten about my bruising, but as she grabbed my chin to get a better look, I felt the pain of them again.

"I trusted the wrong person," I said, thinking maybe I'd made the same mistake again.

"Clock trouble?" asked Ellie nervously, quickly looking at me and trying without saying anything to find out if the man with his head in the clock was who she thought he was. He stood up and I pushed Wheezy's watch further up my jumper out of his sight.

"Found anything?" boomed a voice from behind. I couldn't believe what was happening, we'd walked into a viper's nest. Walking down the stairs was Headmaster Cornelius Barnabas.

Chapter THIRTY-SEVEN

I stood closer to Ellie. What had I got us into?

"Ah ha!" said Wolenski. "The cause of your trouble!" Was this it? Someone was going to pull a gun, but which one? I tried to keep all three of them in my sights when, from inside the clock's cupboard, Wolenski slowly withdrew not a gun, but a glass, half full. "Perhaps Primrose put it there for safekeeping, yes?" He said and actually smiled at Lady H, completely transforming his face.

"Oh Mariusz!" said Lady H. "Let's keep this amongst ourselves." Mariusz?

"The infamous land girl," he said, looking at me.

"Louie's our brightest bravest star!" gushed Lady H.

"Indeed," said Headmaster Barnabas. "I do wish you had let me take care of you that night, then you would never have faced such perilous danger." He sounded absurdly sincere.

"But then who would have saved all those people?" interrupted Lady H. "No, I am sure Louie was made for such a time!" she said warmly, taking both of my hands in hers and saving me from another wrong turn.

"Thank you," I said. "Your words…you have no idea what they mean to me," I was looking into her eyes, so relieved to see only good things. Could she be right? Was I really like Esther and made for such a time as this?

"Dearest Kitty, isn't it time for drinks?" said Barnabas.

"Splendid idea."

"No, no!" I said. "Not for us, thank you. Besides, I had a cup of tea recently that really didn't agree with me."

"What a bore! Things are so dry around here now that all the troops are leaving – Oh! I really shouldn't say that should I?" said Lady H.

"I don't think it's too much of a secret that our boys are moving out imminently," said the headmaster.

"Our boys!" I said. "Curious choice of words for you, sir." I couldn't help myself. His eyes flashed with anger.

"Louie? Time's ticking," said Ellie.

"Allow me to walk you out," it was Wolenski, I'd forgotten about him.

As we walked to the truck he turned to Ellie, checking over his shoulder that we weren't being followed, "I am sorry to ask, but have you received any news of your family?"

"Nothing that's good, I'm afraid, but how did you…?"

"We share a Rabbi, although we have not met with him together," he said. "Rabbi Cohen?"

"Yes, he came down from London last week," said Ellie.

"He asked me to keep an eye on you. I am sorry that I have not done so very well. He told me of your family's plight – it is very hard, yes?"

"Yes, it is very hard – Louie didn't say that you were Jewish," she said.

"I perhaps intimidated your friend, yes? Often people hear my accent and think I am German – which also has its uses." I looked guiltily at my feet. "I fled Poland after the loss of my own family," he said. "They, the Germans, rounded us up one day – we were marched to the woods where we had to dig a large pit and then…" His eyes that I'd found so threatening were filled with sadness. "I am ashamed to say I played dead, my sons were less fortunate. I do not know why God spared only me, and some days it is hard to be grateful."

"Mr Wolenski, I am so very sorry for your loss," said Ellie. "The evil being unleashed on our people – it is beyond human comprehension."

"I do not mean to frighten you – I pray to God that your family will fare better," he said as he clasped both her hands with his.

"Shalom," said Ellie.

"Shalom, my dear," he said before saying the same to me. I didn't know how to respond. "It means peace, completeness," he said.

"But how can you find peace after all you've been through?" I said.

"Not on my own. No. It is a peace that only God can bring; He completes me, even on those dark days when I feel very far from complete. But if we cannot find peace within ourselves how can we bring peace to others? Your watch?" he said, spotting it. "Did Lieutenant Hayward?"

"Yes, yes, thank you," I said.

"I am sorry I did not make it work again – I wasn't sure of its provenance and so apologise if I was less than helpful. Drop by anytime and I shall have another look – I have plenty of spares that I'm sure can be put to good use. It is a very curious piece. It should be new but has been so filled with time in its short life, it is worn out, yes?"

"Yes – that's a good way of describing it. Thank you. And sorry. Sorry I was so, you know," I said.

"You are very inquisitive, which is a dangerous quality in times such as these."

"Louie," said Ellie. "We have to go!" She was looking back at the house worried Barnabas would make a move.

"Would you like a lift?" I said, opening the truck door in unison with the heavens.

"No, thank you. I like to ride my bike, even in this rain," he said, raising his eyes skyward. "It gives me time to think and see bigger than a clock face!" I slammed the door and waited for Ellie to start the engine.

"You okay?" I asked.

"Bit unnerved." The rain fell hard on the roof of the truck and the windscreen began to steam over again. "Seeing the headmaster and then Mr – I had no idea. I only get to see Rabbi Cohen every six weeks or so, but he came last week and it was good to talk with him. It was kind of him to mention me to Mr Wolenski."

"I'm glad you've got someone else here who understands," I said. "I feel such an idiot – I'm always banging on about being non-judgemental, not making assumptions based on the colour of anyone's skin and there was me, judging that poor man because he has a foreign accent!"

"Come on girl, what's the matter with you?" She was talking to the truck. Nothing happened when she turned the ignition.

"Maybe the rain has dampened the spark plugs?"

"What on earth are spark plugs?"

"I've no idea, but my dad was always blaming them when our car didn't start!"

Ellie laughed: "I'm not sure they've been invented yet, my friend from the future! Don't know what's up with her – sometimes she's slow to get going but she always wakes up in the end." There was a tap at my steamy window and we both squealed and jumped.

"Want some help?" I cleared a hole in the window to see Headmaster Barnabas face leering in with his jacket over his head.

"No, we're good," I said, go away.

"It's not starting," he said.

"She will," said Ellie.

"Let's take a look under the bonnet."

"Is there a problem here?" it was Wolenski again, who also had his jacket over his head. We heard them talking through the window, the rain muffling their voices.

"Reckon they've run out of diesel, old chap," said Barnabas.

"Impossible," said Ellie to me. "George topped her up only yesterday."

"Let us take a look," said Wolenski before disappearing under the now open bonnet. Ellie and I got out of the truck and huddled with the men under the steel canopy; rain cascaded down our backs as we peered into the open mouth of the truck's engine.

"I wish Blanche was here, she always knows how to fix it," said Ellie.

"The tank is empty, perhaps you knocked it on the track here – I cannot easily see as the ground is wet, but I can smell the fuel," said Wolenski.

"Damn bad luck," said Barnabas, unconvincingly.

"No worries, we can walk, can't we Ellie?" I said

"In this torrent?" cried Barnabas. "Stuff and nonsense; I've got my motor – I'll drop you off and George can come out and have a look."

"Wouldn't dream of putting you out," said Ellie.

"Decided to keep us company after all?" said Lady H, from the dryness

225

of the doorway.

"Truck trouble, Kitty, but not to worry I'm giving the girls a lift," shouted back Barnabas.

"No, you're not," I hissed.

"Cornelius, you are a treasure – well come along girls, don't look a gift horse in the mouth and all that!" We just stood there, soaked to our skin. There was nothing we could do.

"Why don't you come too?" I said to Wolenski, trying to keep my voice light but hoping he'd read the desperation in my eyes.

"My bicycle is my trusted, and only, form of transport – I cannot leave it behind, and it will not fit in this car," he said.

"I'll have to find a way back to pick up the truck – I could pick up your bicycle then," said Ellie.

"I think that will make things far too complicated for Mr Wolenski – come on girls. Get in!" shouted Barnabas above the rain, clearly not wanting to add the watchmaker to his party. The rain was pounding, Lady H was standing at the door and I had this stupid sense of obligation that I shouldn't make a fuss.

"Girls! Get in!" said the Headmaster, an edge now to his voice.

"No." I stepped closer to him to make sure he could hear me above the storm, "I'm still wearing the bruises from our last encounter – you've engineered this, probably sabotaged the truck."

"Get in the car, now!" he said so that only I could hear and see the gun concealed in his coat. So this is how it ends. "I won't spare your filthy Jewish friends if you don't." I opened the car door.

"Louie?" said Ellie, as if to say what do you think you're doing? I shook my head, my fear saying everything as in a flash she was round the other side and about to get in too. "Mr Wolenski, please?" she pleaded.

"You are right. It is too wet to cycle."

Soaking, cold and fearful, Ellie and I squelched into the back of Barnabas's car; I never imagined I would have felt so relieved to have had Mr Wolenski close by, sat next to the Headmaster at the front. None of us were safe, and I felt bad that Ellie was now also in danger, but there was a certain comfort in numbers. He was driving very fast but there was little traffic on the roads, apart from the odd military vehicle. I imagined them nipping out for last minute supplies while everyone waited for the weather to clear.

"So, Mr Wolenski," said the Headmaster. "I've heard your name a lot in recent weeks, rather too much for someone supposed to be keeping a low profile and getting on with his assigned work, don't you think?"

"I have no complaints about deliveries, on the contrary, people have been very pleased with what I have sent over."

"Well, that rather depends on what people we are talking about, doesn't it? Young Louie here has been extremely helpful keeping me up to date with who you have been spending time with – I wouldn't have thought Lieutenant Hayward was a chap that someone in your position would get close to, would you?" He was speaking in that same measured tone he used with me. Before he tried to kill me.

"You know what they say, keep your friends close but keep your enemies closer," said Wolenski and my heart stopped.

"No doubt you told your sad little tale you told these impressionable young girls about your tragic past," said Barnabas cold sarcasm. "Did they buy it?" No! This couldn't be happening. Please don't say I'd been wrong about Wolenski too, the pendulum had been exhausting, swinging from cantankerous watchmaker, to spy, to schemer with a double-crossing Johnny, all the way over to tragic escapee from Poland. Ellie and I held our breath and each other's hands, but Wolenski was silent. "Oh, I know all about it," went on the Headmaster. "As soon as the young lady raised the alarm my interest was piqued. Pretty cowardly, hiding beneath the bodies of your sons. Shame on you. Fortunately, I can finish off what my comrades started," he said, pulling out the gun.

"NO!" I screamed and rammed myself against his seat, pushing forward the old man's head so that he slammed into the steering wheel. The gun went off and the windscreen shattered. The car swerved crazily and Wolenski tried to take the wheel, as we must have veered onto the other side of the road.

"Look out!" screamed Ellie. It happened in seconds but felt like forever,

227

just like they say. But my little brother Sebastian was wrong; there was still no time to buckle a seat belt, even if there were one in this old car. The impact was bone jarring and the shock of metal ramming into metal unforgiving. I was thrown free-fall inside the car, which rolled over and over and but was being propelled forward and down. And then there was water. It engulfed us. We had fallen into the river running at top speed because of all the rain and were sinking fast.

"Ellie!" I screamed.

"Louie, I'm –" but her words were drowned as the river claimed us and pulled us into its depths. It was murky and dark and without seat belts I floated but was disorientated. I searched hopelessly for where I thought the door handle or window wind would be in the old car, finding the hardness of the glass. I tried to bash against it. It wouldn't give and I was back in that dream again where I tried to strike out, but something slowed me down and prevented my hand from delivering the force I wanted. My lungs were bursting, I'd been here before. I knew what it was to drown, but I hadn't said goodbye. I wanted to see Mum so badly, and Dad. And Wheezy. I wanted to say sorry. Too late. The wait was over. Finally. I felt almost relieved. It was dark, no longer cold and not exactly unpleasant.

Suddenly, I was being pulled. Horst? Then I was free of the car, saw the light above me and kicked my legs like mad until I burst through the surface, gasping for air. "Ellie! Thank you!" We'd both grabbed onto an over-hanging branch, feeling the current pulling us back to the centre.

"We need more help," she shouted above the sound of the raging river. "People are trapped in there!" she hollered to men on the bridge we'd just careered off from. Some were pulling off their jackets and some were diving in already.

"I'm going to try and get Wolenski out!"

"No, it's too dangerous" I started to say but she was gone. Men were everywhere, wading in and diving from bridge. Everyone was shouting, issuing instructions, people thrashing about and then, all of a sudden, nothing. Just the unbroken surface of the fast-moving river. It was taking too long.

"Oh no you don't Baby-doll!" My arm had been grabbed and I was being pulled to the shore.

"Ira! Ellie – and Wolenski! They're still in the water!" Stuff the Headmaster. Vehicles were stopping, car doors slamming. "Please – the water's so fast!" Within seconds Ira had joined the others under the water, just as Wolenski was pulled out. People ran towards him and helped to drag him out. He was coughing and spluttering but there was blood.

There was further commotion in the water – Ellie? Another man emerged dragging a bundle in the crook of his arm. But it was the wrong bundle.

"Where's Ellie?" I screamed at him.

"I need help!" the man shouted. I froze. He was wasting time, cut the bastard adrift. I just stood there while others rushed past me and reached for the heavy lump; two men took an elbow each and dragged him onto the bank then rolled the sodden pile over. He looked dead.

"I've got her!" it was Ira; Ellie was in his arms.

"Ellie!" I waded in and helped him to bring her to shore. We laid her gently down on the bank; riverweeds covered her face. Men crowded around, I looked up at them all staring down – "Do something!" I screamed.

"Louie, honey, she's…" said Ira.

"NO!" I'd seen people do it countless times on TV shows and cursed myself that I hadn't done it at school when I had the chance. I started to pump her chest – one one thousand two one thousand three one thousand – then I tipped her head back so that her mouth opened, pinched her nose and covered her mouth with mine to try to give her the kiss of life.

"Baby-doll, what in God's name you doing?" CPR probably hadn't been invented yet, but I kept going anyway.

"Louie," I recognised the voice. "Let the medic help." I was pulled away and a man lent down and rolled her on her side. A blanket was wrapped around my shoulders, then a pair of arms. I looked up and saw Johnny. "She's gone," he said.

"NO!" I howled. Everything fell away, the world stopped. Ellie was lifeless on the ground, but unlike that calf, there was nothing anyone could do to make her live. The circle widened and I knelt down next to my beautiful brave friend. She looked asleep. She was cold. I took off my blanket and laid it over her, tucking it under her chin and lifting her head onto my lap. "I'm so sorry, Ellie," I said, pulling back the wet strands of hair that had fallen over her face. My tears mixed with the rain that pounded down and I wanted to be washed away with it. I wanted everything to disappear. For this pain to go, this over whelming pain of loss and anger at the bitter irony of this gentle soul risking everything for the wretch who'd caused this.

"You know the lassie?" I looked up to see Abernathy.

"It's Ellie," I mumbled

"It says here on her ID 'Eloise Shimlief? Would that be right?" I glanced at the name and saw my mistake. Let time erode the M, saltwater distort the E, add a spooky sea fog, a dash of irritating sisterly drama and a huge dose of self-pity and there it is.

ELOISE SHIMLIEF : ELOISE SHIRCLIFF

An easy mistake on a worn-out grave in eighty-years' time.

Chapter THIRTY-EIGHT

Crouched in a tight ball in the back of a military truck, the rain crashed down on the canvas roof above my head, reminding me of camping but without the warm, smug feeling of being somewhere safe and dry. My body shook and shivered but I wasn't cold. Two stretchers were carried past. One had a blanket covering the body. Ellie? Wolenski? The other carried the Headmaster. He was alive. How could that be possible? How could that be fair?

I heard the stretchers being slid onto the back of a truck and doors slamming. If that was Ellie, they had better not be putting them together. She couldn't travel with that piece of –

"Where d'you think you're going?" it was Johnny.

"Ellie – she needs me," I said. "I let her down – I didn't realise it was her and not me – all this time. I should have been prepared. Not let her come in the car. He said he would kill them."

"Who – Barnabas?"

"And now he has – it should have been me. What is the point of any of this if I can't save anybody? Not Ellie, those boys, not even Wolenski!"

"Wolenski isn't dead. Look. He is cut and bloodied but it's not as bad as it looks, they say. Come." He took my hand and we went to the back of another truck where Wolenski was being bandaged. There was a lot of blood, but he was very much alive.

"Thank you, my child, you saved my life."

"No. It was Ellie. She saved your life and probably that monster's too."

"He will not see the light of day again," he said angrily.

"I don't think he ever did," I said. "He won't make it– he didn't look good," I said.

"He won't be given the pleasure of slipping away," said Johnny, with a brief nod to Wolenski. "He'll be brought to justice to answer for his crimes."

"In this world, or the next," replied Wolenski. "Louie. I am so sorry for your loss, for our loss. May I take this?" He was holding my limp wrist with the watch hanging off it. What did it matter? What did anything matter? I slipped it off and let him take it from me.

"I have the time now and I certainly have the intention of helping a friend. I will make this work again, he said, sliding it in his pocket. "It will be done by this evening, but how can I get it to you, my bike, even if I could ride it…"

"I'll pick it up from you," said Johnny. "I'll leave it at the entrance of my barracks for you Louie – I think we both owe you that."

"Did you look inside it?" I asked him

"I don't understand what it means. It is identical to the new watch you gave Shirley."

"It is the same watch, just older."

"Louie," said Johnny pulling me away from Wolenski. "You will always be a mystery to me," he gently raised my head to hold my gaze in his. "I have to go, I shouldn't have been here anyway."

"I know," I sighed. "Bad weather. But tomorrow you'll be gone. All of you." He looked as if might say something but settled instead on a simple slow nod of his head.

"Abernathy will take you back to the farm." I put my hand out and stroked the side of his face; he took it and pressed it to his lips. "The next time you see the stars, think of me and think of Horst – there's a poem, by Laurence Binyon. The last verse goes like this:

As the stars that shall be bright when we are dust,
Moving in marches upon the heavenly plain;
As the stars that are starry in the time of our darkness,
To the end, to the end, they remain."

And then he was gone too.

I don't know how news like that travels without mobile phones, but somehow it had. Blanche and Queenie were at the farm by the time I got there. Mother was waiting at the back door and stood there with wide, open arms to hold me. She'd lit a fire and the bathtub had been dragged in front of it. Blanche was filling it up with hot water from the range and Doreen had been out in the rain to collect some soggy wildflowers that she was busy pulling apart to put in my bath, as I'd done for her. Little was said. George was banished from the room and the girls helped me to get undressed and into the warm bath. I didn't feel embarrassed. I didn't feel anything.

People spoke in hushed tones, some practicalities were discussed about whether Ellie's body would go back to London, but I knew she would be buried here. The sadness of the evening enveloped our group and we pressed in hard to each other. The grief of losing Ellie was severe but we all knew there was more to come; Shirley wasn't there, she was saying goodbye to her husband. Blanche would have to say goodbye to her boyfriend and Queenie to all the possibilities of thousands of Americans in Cornwall.

It was the noise that woke me. At first I thought it was a thunderstorm but then I knew it was the planes taking off and flying overhead on their way to D Day. I got up immediately but quietly; Doreen had crept into my bed in the night and was curled up like a kitten. I softly kissed her sleepy head and crept downstairs. Mother was up as well and heard me as I turned the key in the backdoor lock.

"Where you off to?" she said.

"I just want to see it," I said. "The planes and everything. And my watch has been left for me at the British barracks – I want to make sure it's there before they pack everything away – I'll be back to help you with the breakfast." I then rushed over to her and gave her a kiss, something I'd never done. "Love you!" I said and left before we both became embarrassed.

I took the bicycle and pedalled like mad down the hill. It wasn't quite light, but I could see smoke drifting up into the sky from the camp. No one was at the sentry-post, so I pushed the little door and inside on a shelf behind it I found what I was looking for. A small brown paper parcel, very like the hundreds I'd seen in his workshop, with the words, For Louie, from your friend, Mariusz W.

I opened it and found my watch. Wheezy's watch. It was working! Despite everything, I was pleased and said a silent thank you.

Walking on into the camp there were three or four huge bonfires. Men were throwing everything on to them – whatever was to hand and had been left. Letters, photographs, odd bits of clothing, tables, chairs. It was like every trace of the soldiers was being erased. I wanted them to stop; it was so disrespectful.

"What are you doing?" I screamed. But they couldn't hear me. The noise from above was oppressive and intense as plane after plane droned over, scattering their radar defying silver ribbons as they did so. The smoke rose to capture them, and they danced in the heat and vapour. My vision blurred as the smoke stung and my eyes watered.

It was underway, storming the beaches of Normandy, code-named Gold, Utah, Omaha and Sword. Thousands would have already fallen but still less than if the deception hadn't been successful. I thought of Hitler, asleep in his bed. I knew that his guards were too afraid to wake him. I thought of the Germans waiting arrogantly in Calais and Caen and Norway, while all the while the Allies were fighting and dying side by side to liberate Europe from the least likely point of attack, Normandy.

I threw back my head and opened my arms wide, looking up to God and became engulfed in the enormity of it all. The sense of time marching on relentlessly. I surrendered to the shower of silver, thunderous noise and thick, engulfing smoke.

Chapter THIRTY-NINE

"Louie!" She was calling me back. "Louie." My face was being licked. The tongue was long, wet and stank. "Are you alright?" I opened one eye to blistering, blinding sunshine and lifted my elbow to block it out. A dog loomed into view, grinning and dripping slobber on me. It was Reg.

I sat up. I was on the beach. My beach. Emily was crouched next to me.

"Emily," I breathed. "Emily, Emily," in and out, as if saying her name was filling my lungs with oxygen.

"Louie – you gave me such a fright! I couldn't find you in the mist. It was so thick – I've been searching for ages and then when it finally cleared, you were here, lying on the beach – I thought you'd drowned."

I sat up and threw my arms around my sister. I held her so tightly she fell over and we both crumpled on the beach, but I wasn't going to let her go. Reg started barking and jumping all over us and I threw my arms around him too.

Walking through the gates was weird but exciting, everything looked fresh, the same but different. I could see where things had been changed, renovated, removed. I looked towards the farmhouse and thought of Mother then Mum came out into the yard.

"They arrived early, as I expected. Feel better now?" she said.

"Oh Mum," I couldn't say anymore. I ran to her and gave her the biggest hug. "I'm sorry," I sort of said into her shoulder.

"Hey! It's okay love, I know things have been hard – I'm sorry I lost it with you," she said.

"I love you Mum, so much," I could feel the exchange between her and Emily.

"I think she's had a near death experience," said Emily, half joking.

"What?" said Mum, she pulled my chin up and looked at me, worry and love in her eyes. "Is that bruising on your face?"

"I found her on the beach – I'm not sure what happened, abducted by aliens and had a personality transplant I think."

"I'm fine – where's Wheezy?" I said, ignoring them but smiling.

"Er, inside, probably in her chair where she always is – you didn't lose her watch did you?" said Mum anxiously. I looked down and instinctively clasped my wrist; it was still there. Lifting it to my ear I knew it was still working. I ran inside to find Shirley.

She was where they said she'd be. Alone with her thoughts on the worn-out armchair she favoured.

"Wheezy?" I said. "Shirley?" There was a slight flicker, but not the beaming smile of recognition and reconciliation that I'd hoped for. "It's me, Louie. I came back Shirley, I brought your watch home safely." She grabbed my wrist and turned it to see the watch better. Satisfied she dropped it again and drifted off to wherever her mind had taken her.

I wanted to cry. "Shirley, it's me. Louie – I was with you when you got married, to Mallory. Shirley?"

"You alright love?"

"Dad!" I stood up and ran to him. "Whoa! Mum said you were a bit emotional – what's happened?" I'd thrown my arms around his waist and breathed in the dad-ness of him, a mixture of smells from the sheds he'd been rummaging around in, the Bolognese he'd probably made for supper and the jumper he should have put in the wash a week ago. He rubbed the top of my head, like he used to do when I was younger and let him.

"Why are you hugging her? She made Mummy cry!" it was Sebastian.

"Yeah – she shouted at Mummy," said Ned.

"I'm sorry, boys. I'm sorry for being so horrid," I bent down and opened my arms to them both. They stood still staring at their mad sister. This was different, they thought. "Come here," I tried. They walked tentatively towards me, then looked at each other and smirked and I scooped them both

236

up in my arms and buried my head in theirs, telling myself it didn't matter if they had nits. I thought of Doreen and wondered if Christmas ever came for her and she went home to Hull and her family.

"Dad, is Sheridan at the farmhouse at the moment? They've got a piano, haven't they?"

"A bit random darling but yes and yes. Why?" he asked.

"I thought Shirley might like to play it."

"Shirley?"

"Wheezy, sorry," I said.

"I dunno – I forgot she used to play the piano," he said. "Do you want to play the piano Wheezy?" he said in a voice that was slow, loud and annoying.

"I'll take her," I said.

"You? Sorry, did I hear you say you'd take her?" He pretended to shake his head and check if his ears were working. The boys giggled.

"Yes. Come along Wheezy – upsy daisy," I said and gently hooked my arm through her elbow and lifted her from her chair. "We're going for a little walk – not far."

She wasn't too pleased with being moved but once we were outside, she didn't seem to mind too much. I was glad to have her to myself, even though I knew it was completely at odds with what everyone was used to.

"I've been on a journey Shirley. Your watch took me to meet you when you were a land girl; I met Ellie," my heart jolted. "And Blanche and Queenie. And I met your husband, the lovely Mallory." I looked at her, but she didn't seem to register anything I was saying. I took a deep breath as I stood on the steps of the farmhouse and knocked on the door.

"Hi! Louie isn't it?" said Sheridan, dressed in the way city people think people dress in the country – brogues, overly bright mustard cords, plaid shirt, V-neck sweater and Downtown Abbey-like jacket.

"Yes, hi. This is my great grandmother, Shirley, except we call her Wheezy even though her name is Eloise. Sorry, I was wondering, would you mind very much if we came in? Shirley loved to play the piano, but I don't think she's had the chance to play for a very long time."

"Of course! Please," he said standing back to let us in, although he didn't really have much choice as I was almost over his threshold. "Marcus? Some of the family from the barns are here." Marcus appeared with a tea towel.

"Hello – how lovely. We love visitors. Tea?"

"Yes, yes thank you. That would be lovely," I said, realising I was parched not having had anything to drink for almost eighty years.

"Here it is," said Sheridan, taking us into what would have been Mother's posh parlour, a room I only went in once when Shirley got married. A highly polished baby grand sat in the corner. I steered Wheezy to it and helped her to sit down. She was so old, so frail and confused; I wanted to cry. Where was Shirley? Why do we have to get old?

Sheridan pulled back the lid and Wheezy sighed ever so slightly. She slowly lifted her fingers and stroked the keys very lightly. Then she put them back in her lap again.

"Why don't you play something Shirley?" I tried.

"I can't play."

"I've heard you, many times. At Trenogar?" I said. "At Lady H's parties – with Mallory? Blanche, Queenie?"

"Gin gimlets!" she said.

"Afraid not, but there's tea?" It was Sheridan laden with a large tray with a huge teapot and an oversized lemon drizzle cake.

"Thank you," I said. "Oh my goodness, that looks amazing! Cake – real cake! May I?" I couldn't wait for an answer, holding a huge slice to my lips and inhaling the sweet citrus smell as my mouth salivated. I bit into it. It was so light in my mouth but full of sweet, moist flavour that touched on every part of my tongue.

"Sugar? Milk?"

"Yes please, lots of both," I said. He handed me the steaming cup and I sipped it quickly, scorching my lips but I didn't care. Hot, sweet, nectar.

"Wow! You were hungry – and thirsty. More cake?" said Marcus who'd sat beside me on the sofa.

"Oh yes, yes please – it's divine."

"Well it's our business – Celtic Cakes?"

"But you're not Cornish!"

"No, but the people who make them are!" said Sheridan.

"That's –" cheating, I was going to say, but the piano was being played "Shirley?" I went over to her. Her eyes were closed, and she was playing Clare de Lune.

"It's beautiful," I whispered.

"Louie?"

"Yes, it's me."

"You left – we missed you after Ellie…."

"I came home Shirley, but only just."

"Johnny said you probably had."

"Johnny? He came back?"

"A long time after. He came looking for you and wanted to see my watch again – I showed him your initials. Yours and Horst's. He said they were the same. He said he knew where you'd gone. I didn't understand until later, much later." She stopped playing the piano. "Mallory. Is he here too?"

"No, my darling, I'm sorry."

"He never came back, you know."

"I know Shirley, but he loved you very much."

"He did. He did. And I loved him too. Is there cake?"

Later, in my old room, lying on my bed trying not to count the rivets on the beam above my head, I took off Wheezy's watch and opened it up. This time it looked different. Wolenski must have replaced a few parts to make it work, but there was something else. Behind the bigger of the two small cogs there was a small rolled up piece of paper. With my tweezers I carefully pulled it out and unrolled it. In the tiniest of writing I read:

'For Louie, your own secret message: Shalom. MW.'

Afterword

I was inspired to write Namesake after moving to Cornwall from London and finding out about the part it played in D Day. A lot of the information I have used in the story is factual, based on research and articles from newspapers of the day, with names and dates changed. There was indeed a fire at Swanvale just before D Day, and it was put out by men driving tractors into it to drench with water.

I met and interviewed land girls, including a lovely, larger than life lady called Tiny, who called me Mother. I also found two graves in a churchyard beside the sea in Gunwalloe, of Ronald and Harry, both aged 12, who sadly did die after stepping on a hidden mine on the beach.

Lady H was inspired by a wonderful morning spent with Major Hibbert, a decorated war hero, at Trebah, who was disappointed I didn't share a large gin and tonic with him at 10.00am (something I've always regretted). He told me wonderful stories of his sister in Hampshire, the parties she held for young soldiers, injured during the war, and the flowers she smuggled up to London in a hearse.

Acknowledgements

Thank you to my family, especially Elsie, who suffered endless readings and revisions, and Millie who helped get the front cover over the finish line.

And thank you to the Kates in my life, Kate James and Kate Neal. Both have helped me in so many ways, practically and emotionally, encouraging me never to give up.